Killer Kisses

✳

A Short Story Anthology

By

Sharon Buchbinder

ALL RIGHTS RESERVED

Cover Art provided by Wicked Muse Productions

COPYRIGHT © 2012, Sharon Buchbinder

Sharon Buchbinder, Romance Author

PO BOX 15005

Pikesville, MD 21282

Visit me at **www.sharonbuchbinder.com**

Table of Contents

~*~

DEDICATION

To my husband, Dale, who fills my life with love and romance.

A Kiss on the Cheek: Hurricane Jason

~✳~

✴

TWO HOURS AFTER LAUREL Canyon arrived in Punta Gorda, Florida, she stood at the window of her hotel room and gaped. *Was it really raining sideways? And was that a flying lawn chair?* She stepped over to the little battered nightstand and the lights went out. *The phone, surely that must be working!* She lifted the receiver. No dial tone.

Panic bubbled up in her chest, and the room began to twirl. *Deep breaths. Stay calm.* The weather service had predicted only a tropical storm, not a hurricane.

Pounding on the door startled her. "Everybody out! Time to evacuate!"

Her heart rate kicked up, and she threw the door open. A heavy-set, gray-haired man in a hotel uniform raced down the hallway, and banged on the next door.

She called after him. "Where am I supposed to go?" A Baltimore girl, Laurel had never seen a storm quite like this.

He stopped and turned to face her. Red from exertion, sweat poured into his eyes. He pulled out a limp handkerchief and mopped his brow. "Go to the lobby. The hotel bus will take you to the storm shelter."

"But—"

"They've upgraded the storm to a hurricane. Category four. We're too close to the Peace River. Grab your purse, anything important, and get downstairs."

~*~

The shelter, really a converted high school gym, was jammed with people. Children wailed, a dog yipped incessantly in its carrier, and an elderly woman called for someone named Carol.

Laurel had thought it déclassé when she'd had to stay in that cheap motel; clearly she had grossly underestimated how bad her business trip would be. She sighed. All she had to do was snap a few photos of a cheating husband holding hands and kissing his latest bimbo, and she would have been gone. But no. *Mother Nature really is a bitch.*

An old man with alligator skin leaned against her, and shared his beery breath. "You gonna eat that?"

Laurel clutched her purse, attempted to move sideways on the metal bleacher, and found she was wedged against the cinderblock wall. She glanced down at the limp ham and cheese sandwich. At the sight of his dirty finger touching the bread, her appetite fled. Wordlessly, she handed the food over.

He gave her a gap-toothed smile, stood, tipped his dirty sailor's cap, and said, "Thanks." A burst of laughter came from a short distance away. He swaggered over to a group of men and waved the sandwich as if it were a trophy. A pot-bellied man in an aloha shirt handed him a twenty-dollar bill.

A wager. She hissed in annoyance, shook her head, and unzipped her small rolling suitcase. *Where is that hand sanitizer?*

A shadow fell across her open bag. "Someone sitting here?" A deep-voice asked.

Great. Another jerk. She didn't even look up. "No, and I'd like it to stay that way."

The man sat down beside her, jouncing the bench. She clutched the suitcase, grateful for the padded case protecting her camera. "Hey! I said no!" She turned to stare down the interloper and found herself falling into his big coffee brown eyes.

He swept a shock of dark brown hair away from his face with a large hand. Heat rushed across her chest and up her neck.

Her breath caught in her throat.

"You sure about that? There's half a dozen more of those old shrimpers eyeing you like today's catch. I thought I'd sit here and fend them off." He smiled and his eyes crinkled with little laugh lines.

Mouth suddenly parched, she licked her lips, and said, "As long as you don't have a bet to see if you can get food or something else off me, you can stay."

"Good." He waved at the shrimpers.

Boos and hisses erupted from them.

He turned back to her. "You know why they're so interested in you?"

She put a finger to her chin in a thoughtful pose. "I think I hear a line coming. Is it my corn-silk blonde hair? My lapis lazuli eyes? Or my long, long legs?"

"All true. But the real reason is this…" He leaned in close to her ear, and his breath sent frissons of excitement racing in circles around her neck. "Your blouse is unbuttoned and they can see your lace bra."

She looked down, gasped, and clutched at her gaping blouse.

"Thought you'd like to know."

As she fumbled to close her blouse, more angry shouts came from the fishermen.

He shouted back. "Go sleep it off!" He shook his head and turned back to Laurel. "This time of day, they're usually in a bar in Matlacha having a beer after a hard night of shrimping. The storm is interfering with their drinking."

"They're not the only ones who had other plans for the day." Laurel shook her head and pulled her camera out of the padded bag. Still intact. She held it up and looked around the gym with the view-finder. And stopped. *Sleazoid hubby is here! In the flesh! With the bozo-haired bimbo!*

He leaned back and stretched his long legs. "So, what were you supposed to be doing today?"

"Research." *They're not touching. Just sipping water and looking angry. That won't hold up in court.* She put the camera down and gazed into his delicious eyes. She had a sudden intense craving for a latte. "And you?"

"I'm supposed to be doing a favor for a friend today, but I left my camera at home. Think I could borrow yours?"

She frowned and shook her head. Silky strands of hair slipped out of her pony tail and tickled her neck. "This is business."

He moved closer to her and spoke in a low voice. "So's mine."

Uncomfortably aware of his spicy aftershave, she scooted up against the wall. "I don't even know you."

He put his hand out. "Jason Spode."

She took his callused hand and a flash of heat rushed up her arm to her face. She felt as if she was melting. "Laurel Canyon."

He held her hand just a tad too long. And smiled, a long, lazy grin with bright white teeth, along with dimples.

Oh no. It's all over now. I'm a sucker for a man with dimples.

Jason chuckled. "Is that an address or an alias?"

Annoyed, she pulled back. "Look who's talking, my-last-name is-bone-china-man. Is that *your* real name? Or an alias?"

"Point taken." The damn dimples again. He spoke so softly she had to lean her head closer to him to hear over the echoes in the gym. "Look, I'm trying to do a job for an out of town company. And it involves taking photos of, shall we say, a naughty girl."

Reminded of her mission, Laurel scanned the room for the sleazoid husband. *Where the hell is he? It's not like he could leave.* Camera strap around her neck, she stood on the bouncing bleacher for a better look, teetered, and fell into Jason's lap.

Laurel turned her head to apologize and smacked his nose with her head. "Oh, my God! I'm so sorry! Are you okay?"

He put his arms around her and pulled her tight. "My nose hurts. It needs a kiss to make it better."

She pushed him away and slid off his lap. "No more fuel for your fishing buddies!"

"So." He took a deep breath and shook his head. "About your camera?"

Her hands shook as she handed him the camera. "What do you need to capture?"

He looked across the room, lifted the camera to his eye and said, "Them."

She glanced in the direction of where he pointed the camera and practically fell over.

Sleazoid hubby and his red-headed babe were lip locked, practically doing the horizontal mambo under the bleachers on the opposite side of the gym.

"What? No, they're mine!" She lunged at the camera, he pulled back, and they both tumbled to the hardwood floor.

Jason leaped to his feet, reached out and helped her stand. "Are you hurt?"

"I'm fine." She snatched at the strap. "Give me my camera. I have to catch that guy in the act with his bimbo."

Jason pulled her closer and said in a low voice, "You're making a scene! They're going to get spooked. We're both after the same thing: You get the guy. I get the gal."

A flash of understanding shot through Laurel and she laughed. "It's a deal. But you have to do what I tell you to do."

He nodded. "Agreed. Give me copies of the photos and I'll do whatever you want. "

Her gaze on the groping duo, Laurel grabbed his hands and swung him around with his back to the couple. "Now, hug me hard, like you mean it."

He complied by pulling her so tight to him that she could feel the buttons on his jeans. He whispered, sending shivers down her spine. "Are they still at it?"

Laurel gulped, looked over his shoulder, and nodded. "Yup."

Holding her close, he stroked her back, hummed a golden oldie, and rocked back and forth in a slow dance. His caresses almost made her forget what she was supposed to be doing.

She shook her head, raised the camera and snapped off a series of shots of the wayward couple engaged in a very public display of affection. "Gotcha!"

"Yes, you do," Jason said. He lowered his head, slanted his soft mouth across hers, and slid his tongue between her lips. Her knees went weak, and she responded with equal measure. The voices of the crowd faded to a dull roar, and Laurel felt as if she was falling.

In the distance, the shrimpers chanted, "Get a room!"

Cat Nips: Catastrophe

~*~

THE NEON ORANGE handbill glowed on the apartment door when she arrived home. "What's this?" Dropping backpack and grocery bags, she ripped it down and read:

NOTICE TO TENANT-- POLLY GRIGGS

Due to violation of terms of your rental agreement, you are hereby given 30 days written notice to vacate the premises. VIOLATION: Exceeding number of allowable pets. You must vacate the premises no later than NOON, February 8....

She couldn't bear to read the rest. Instead, her back and arms aching from her heavy backpack and bags, she opened the door to a chorus of meows, mrrks, and yowls. "Yes, yes, my pretties, I'm happy to see you, too."

Streams of multicolored fur swirled around her legs.

"There you are, Tabbish." She stroked a raggedy-looking, ancient cat sitting on the arm of a chair. "You're still with us, I see."

A small, three-legged cat hopped up on the chair with Tabbish and rubbed her hand with his head.

"Tiny Tim! You know I wouldn't forget to say hello." She picked up the little tabby and put him on her shoulder, where he sat like a parrot. "Happy now?"

He purred and butted her ear in response.

As she unpacked the plastic grocery bags in the galley kitchen, she greeted each cat by name.

"Abbott and Costello, how are you today? Miss Marple, where has your nose been? Sherlock, what have you been investigating? Sir Spots-a-Lot, Harry Spotter, did you tear up that plant?"

She glanced out at her living room.

"Okay, which of you knocked over the stack of books next to my reading chair? Was it you, Little Jack Horner? Mitzi? Faith? Come on, now, 'fess up! Belinda, Peter and Martha Cratchitt, where is your mother? Is she under the couch again? David Copperfield, where have you disappeared to? Oliver Twist, leave that plastic bag alone."

She put away cans of cat food and continued to chatter to her adoring audience. "There was a sale on Friskies, Pip. You and Miss Havisham will be delighted to hear that we are stocked up on the beef and turkey combo. Mrs. Joe, let me get to the tea, please."

She lifted the old calico cat off the counter, away from the cabinet that held her teas. It was one of her few indulgences: beautiful, aromatic teas with glorious flavors. She opened a tin and inhaled the smoky aroma of lapsang souchong. "Huckleberry and Jim, you have to move. I don't want to catch your tails on fire."

A one-eared brown tabby and a balding black cat hopped down from the counter with twin thuds. She opened another cabinet to get sugar. A cat sat there, staring at her.

"Tom Sawyer! Have you been in there all day?" She laughed and shook her head.

The large, one-eyed, black and white cat leaped down onto the counter. "Mrrp?"

A loud thumping at the door nearly made her drop her mug.

"I KNOW you're in there, Polly Griggs!"

She tiptoed to the door, careful not to step on tails or paws. The landlord's lumpy, bulbous nose was magnified by the fisheye peephole. When he drank, it was bright red. Like now.

"What do you want?"

"I want you and your cats out!"

"I saw the notice, Mr. Greeley. I have thirty days."

"Out, out—out!" He pounded at the door.

"You have no right to yell at me. I'll call the police."

"I *own* the police!" The door shuddered with each blow of his fist.

Her heart responded to the hammering with an erratic thumping. She felt lightheaded and sat down hard in the armchair, startling Tabbish. Then, she heard a young man's voice.

"M-Mr. G-Greeley, you know, you're b-bothering the b-building."

"I'm the landlord, Stutterin' Simon. She's got all those damn cats and she has to get OUT!"

"L-leave her alone, or I'm c-calling the p-police."

Greeley's harsh laugh echoed in the hallway. He cursed, mumbled, and at last was silent, as his footsteps thudded down the stairs.

A light tap sounded, and Polly opened the door to allow the tall, muscular young man into her apartment.

"P-Polly, are you okay?" He stood looking down at the floor.

"Yes, thank you, Simon."

Every time she saw him, she found herself taking quick, shallow breaths as butterflies flapped in her stomach. He had beautiful wavy dark hair, a handsome symmetrical face, and large blue eyes. *His name should be Adonis, not Simon,* she thought.

"D-drunk."

"Again."

"Wh-what are you going to d-do?" His eyes were closed.

I'm a fool, she thought. *A dumpy, frizzy-haired fool. I disgust him so much, he won't even look at me.* "I don't know. Where can I go with all my babies? Who would take them? They're all old, blind, or crippled, all trying to survive, no thanks to Mr. Greeley."

"B-bully."

The teakettle whistled.

"Cup of tea?"

He nodded.

"Milk and sugar?" She opened the refrigerator.

He nodded again.

"Have a seat. Just move Mitzi off that chair."

He picked the cat up, put her on his lap and rubbed her ears. Mitzi closed her eyes and purred while Simon looked around Polly's immaculate kitchen, at the walls covered with vintage anti-war posters and photos.

"Neat p-pictures."

She smiled. "My mother was quite a hell raiser in her day. Child of the sixties."

"Drugs?"

She frowned and shook her head. "Never. She taught high school civics. Loved her job." Sadness welled up in her chest. "My father died in Viet Nam, when I was tiny. My mother was devastated and protested against the war. Even chained herself to the White House fence. That's her in that photo. See the baby in her arms?"

He nodded.

"That's me." She paused and sipped her tea from a chipped mug. "The school board said she was a bad influence on children. They sacked her."

"N-no!"

"Took her a year to find another job. A year of hand-to-mouth poverty, my mother said." Polly gazed at the photo in silence for a moment. "She died of breast cancer when I was a freshman in college. She's the reason I majored in Political Science and became a high school teacher. But, enough about me. How are your classes this semester?"

He swallowed hard, looked at his teacup, and spoke as he inhaled.

"Speech class is b--bad. I n--need it to g-graduate. Have to g-give a talk the first week in February."

"Have you met with the teacher?"

He shook his head.

"If you go see her, maybe she'll give you some help."

"Y-you? Wh-where to?" His sky-blue eyes made direct contact with Polly's.

She felt like a deer in headlights. Flustered, she looked away.

"I don't know. Not too many places allow pets, much less twenty-three cats. The so-called Humane Society will kill them. The no-kill shelters are full. I need a farm, but I can't afford one on my teacher's salary."

"W-wish I could h-h-help."

"I wish you could, too, but you already have Ebenezer, Marley and Bob Cratchitt. That's all you can take. Otherwise, you'll get evicted, too."

He finished his tea and lifted the cat out of his lap as he stood up. "G-g-good l-luck."

"Luck? I need a miracle."

~*~

Polly came home the following evening after a hard day in the teenage trenches. A gaily wrapped package sat in front of her door.

The label read: *From your secret admirer.*

She flushed with pleasure and smiled. *Could it be from Simon?*

She looked up and down the hallway, saw no one, and entered her apartment. Savoring the anticipation of opening the package, Polly made a cup of tea to prolong the pleasure, and at last sat down. With her heart doing the cha-cha, she opened the gift with loving care—And screamed, while brown-stained knife fell to the floor.

The note attached to it said: *Here, Kitty, Kitty!*

She ran around the tiny apartment, calling names and counting heads.

"Twenty-three! Thank God, you're all here!"

She called a locksmith, and the police.

The next day, Polly came home from work and found the greasy-haired landlord waiting by her door. He wore a dirty, sleeveless tee-shirt and was digging at his belly-button through a large tear.

"You changed the lock. You're not allowed to do that."

She took two steps backward, out of range of his boozy breath.

"You're not allowed to be in my apartment without my permission. And, you threatened the life of my cats. I know you left that bloody knife. You're nothing but a drunken bully."

His piggy eyes narrowed and his nose glowed like a hot coal.

"At least when I wake up in the morning, I'm not *ugly!*"

"B-b-bastard!"

Greeley whirled on Simon.

"Well, if it ain't Stutterin' Simon. Here to see your ugly girlfriend? Don't worry. I was just leaving." He stumbled down the hall.

For once, Polly was relieved Simon didn't make eye contact.

"Thank you, Simon." Hot tears of humiliation spilled down her cheeks. "I'm afraid when I leave in the morning. And I'm terrified when I come home. The police said there was nothing I could do."

"C-call me." Simon looked at the ceiling. "I'll l-look out for G-Greeley."

"Brilliant! I'll call from outside to make sure the coast is clear. If only there was some way I could make the bastard pay for terrorizing me and my cats."

And if only I were your girlfriend, she thought.

~*~

In the following weeks, Polly racked her brains for a solution. What could she do? If only her mother were still alive. *Mom would have never gone without a fight*, Polly thought. She'd taken care of her helpless baby and stood up for her beliefs. It hadn't been easy, but nothing worth doing was ever easy, her mother had always said. It was time for Polly to stand up for her helpless creatures. But how?

As she had done each day after her confrontation with the obnoxious landlord, Polly called Simon when she rounded the corner to her apartment building. "Is he around?"

"N-no sign of him," he said. Barking erupted in the background as he spoke.

"What is that?" Polly asked, walking and talking on the cell while juggling bags of homework.

"N-new d-dog in the b-building, I guess."

"Jeez, it sounds like a wolf!"

Simon laughed and said, "W-wait till G-Greeley hears him!"

"Maybe it'll distract him from my cats." She said good-bye and climbed the stairs to the building.

Simon was waiting by her door. "N-n-need help?"

"Thanks," Polly said. She offered him a tote bag and placed the key in the lock. Simon's hand touched her, and a spark of static electricity popped.

"Youch!"

He dropped the bag, and grabbed her hand, looking at it intently. "D-did I hurt you?"

"No, I'm more startled than hurt," she said with a little laugh. "I'm fine."

Waves of warmth rushed from her hand up her arm, to her neck, and face. She could feel herself taking quick, shallow breaths, the butterflies somersaulting in her stomach.

He reached up, placed his fingertips on her cheek, looked directly into her eyes, and said, "Y-you sure?"

"Yes," she answered. "Better than fine. I'm, I'm—wonderful."

He touched her hair and whispered, "I l-l-love the way your curls b--bounce when you m-m-move."

"Simon, I--- "

"There she is!" Greeley screamed from the end of the hall. "Kill her cats!"

A frenzy of barking erupted in the hallway and echoed off the hard walls. It sounded like a pack of wild dogs racing toward Polly. As she whirled to face the attack, Simon leapt in front of her.

"No!" Simon shouted at the approaching gray blur. "No!"

The dog came to a halt in front of Simon and gave a deep throaty growl.

"Simon, no!" Polly cried.

"Sit!"

The dog sat down with a loud thump.

"Lie down!"

The gray creature flopped to the floor.

Greeley lumbered toward them, nose bright red, breathing labored. He shook his fist at the dog. "I told you to *kill her cats*, you moron!"

Simon knelt down and whispered in the creature's big floppy ear.

The dog rolled over on his back and whimpered.

Polly could have sworn the dog was apologizing.

"Dammit," Greeley shouted. "Do what I tell you to do!"

The dog ignored Greeley, and began licking Simon's hand.

Polly moved closer to Simon, placed her hands on his shoulders, and said, "I don't think he's your dog, Mr. Greeley. I think he belongs to Simon now." She pulled out her cell phone. "If you don't leave us alone, I'm calling the police and telling them what you did."

Greeley's face turned beet red. He sputtered and spat out a particularly vile curse, and stomped away.

"Good r-riddance." Simon rose and turned to face Polly.

Before he could say another word, she threw her arms around his neck and hugged him. He wrapped his arms around her waist and it felt like she was home. "You could have been killed," she said and choked back tears.

He shrugged. "D-d-dogs like me."

Polly pulled back and looked down at the dog. The tamed canine yawned, thumped his stub of a tail, and looked up at Simon with adoration. She knew the feeling.

~* ~

At eleven in the morning on the date of her eviction, after everything was in place, Polly Griggs made a few phone calls. An hour later, curious onlookers craned their necks, shook their heads, and thronged in front of the apartment building.

It was a blustery gray day. Polly dressed in a black down coat, a dark green hat and matching scarf and mittens, faced them all.

"Ms. Griggs, there's gotta be a better solution than this," a red-faced police officer said.

"Polly, what made you decide to chain yourself to the fence around this apartment building?" An attractive brunette television reporter held a microphone out to Polly, trolling for sound bites.

"I want to protest how the world treats people who love their pets. My only sin was that I cared for too many unwanted cats. Their only sin was that they were old, blind, crippled, and tossed aside."

All the cats were in double-occupancy, towel-bundled carriers at her feet, labeled with their names. A yowling, meowing, howling din came forth from under the covers. Each cat carrier had a sign on it that said, "Homeless, thanks to Mr. Greeley." And each cat carrier was chained to the fence.

Polly heard Greeley cursing and saw him pushing his way to the front of the crowd.

"I got a call to bring my tools," he said to the police officer. He stopped at the sight of Polly, the cat carriers, the signs, and the chains. "You *bitch*! You can't do this to me!" His nose was bright red, as he ran at her, raised a bolt cutter on high, and struck her.

The police mobbed him before he could hit her again.

Cuffed and pushed into a cruiser, he was still screaming about "the ugly bitch" and "her damn cats" as he was driven away.

Bright red blood trickled into her eye as the police officer keyed his radio. "Get an EMT here *now*!"

She struggled to remain conscious, but she felt so tired. Her head dropped onto her chest. There was a dull roar, then a murmur. She opened her eyes and thought she saw the sea of people part in front of her as if she were in a Cecil B. DeMille movie.

Then Simon was in front of her, calling her name. "Polly!" He grabbed her mittened hands. "Polly, can you hear me?"

She nodded, thinking it was a dream—he wasn't stuttering.

"Look!" He pointed at a group of young people standing behind him. An older, gray-haired woman stood in their midst. "They're from my speech class. That's my professor."

Polly stared at him, head throbbing, struggling to understand.

"You told me to talk to her, remember? She said I should speak on something that I'm passionate about."

Polly could feel a warm trickle on her chin as she gazed into his beautiful, sky-blue eyes.

An EMT pulled her hat off, put a bandage on her head, and called for a gurney.

Simon tightened his grip on her hands.

"I'm passionate about you, Polly. I gave the whole speech about you and your cats."

She looked past him at the crowd, then back again at Simon, confused. She heard metal crunching and the clank of chains falling on the sidewalk. "Wh-wh-what…?"

"I was so inspired by you—I forgot to stutter! And they were so moved by my speech, they're here to adopt the cats. Every single blind, old, crippled cat will have a good home."

His classmates began to gather up the carriers. She heard them discussing where they'd meet to divvy up the cats.

Not my babies! No, no, no, no….

"Not Tiny Tim. Not Tabbish. Too old." She struggled to get the words out. Soon, she'd have no one left in her life.

"Don't worry, Polly. I'll get them," Simon vowed. "We'll find a new place to live, with some of the cats and the dog, away from this bully."

She shook her head, weeping, struggling to believe his words, afraid that Simon would disappear into the crowd with her cats, leaving her all alone.

He leaned down, kissed a tear off her cheek and whispered, "I love you, Polly Griggs. Do you hear me? I love you, and I'm never letting you go."

Shocked, Polly stared into his beautiful eyes, and all she could do was stutter, "Wh-wh-what?"

At her cute new stutter, Simon rolled his eyes and shook his head with a smile."Oh, boy."

Hot Lips: The Lake Placid Cure

~✶~

KILLER KISSES

✳

SANDRA BLAKE RADCLIFF climbed out of her Toyota Highlander Hybrid, while a star-studded sky and a full moon shone over the quiet village of Scarsdale, New York. Her shoes crunched as she walked across the snow and ice-encrusted parking lot behind the converted Victorian home, and climbed the steps to the law offices of "Big" Jim Radcliff. Despite having been sent home by her husband earlier in the day to get some rest, she'd decided to get up and go back into the office.

Pre-trial jitters, she thought. *One more look at the files, then home to bed.* Despite all her work at prepping their client's daughter, a teenager with nails bitten to the quick, Sandra worried the kid would fall to pieces under cross-examination. The father, claimed he'd been at home with his daughter, watching television the night of his ex-wife's murder. Sandra's gut told her the client was lying, a concern she had shared with her husband. As a defense attorney, Jim was obligated to defend the man to the best of his ability—but he didn't need to be blind-sided.

He had listened to her, nodded and said, "Don't worry. I've got it under control."

But the nagging concern that something wasn't quite right in the case forced her out of bed and back to the office.

The building was dark, the back door locked. Had Jim gone to his club for a nightcap? As she entered the foyer, a distant thumping sound came from the direction of her husband's office followed by a loud groan. Visions of her spouse being beaten and struggling for his life raced through her head. Had a homicide victim's family member, enraged by a not guilty verdict, finally gotten revenge?

"Jim!" She raced down the short hallway to his office, threw open the door, and froze. The dim light from the computer screen clearly outlined the appalling scene.

A naked, thirty-something, visibly pregnant blonde sat on a man's lap, facing the door, her mouth an "O" of surprise. "Oh, my God! It's your wife!" Her partner's face, contorted with shock, rested on her shoulder.

Sandra flipped on the overhead fluorescent lights. "Not again," she said exhausted by his constant philandering. "What's this make? Bimbo number fifteen?"

Red-faced and short of breath her husband said, "What are you doing here?"

"Working." She turned her attention to the bimbo. "Strange to see you here, Ms. Cain. Or should I call you Assistant District Attorney, since you're supposed to be preparing to prosecute our client?"

The woman jumped up, attempting to cover herself while struggling to pull on her panties.

"It's not what you think," Jim said in a tone usually reserved for hostile witnesses.

Sandra pointed at his crotch. "I'd say I have a smoking gun right here--so to speak."

He jumped up, grabbing a file folder to cover himself.

"This is a new low, even for you," she snarled. "Now I understand why you weren't worried about this case. But, please, do go on, oh great defense counsel. Try to talk your way out of this one."

"Candi's the real deal."

"Your first name is Candi?" Sandra asked the now weeping younger woman. "What were your parents thinking?"

"Leave her alone!" Jim shouted, reaching for the other woman's hand.

With Candi at his side, Sandra had a sudden mental image of Adam and Eve being expelled from the Garden of Eden. An irresistible urge to giggle overwhelmed her.

"I love her."

Sandra stopped and stared. "What did you say?"

"I love her. She's carrying my baby. We're getting married."

"No, you don't mean it. *You never mean it.*" She couldn't take her eyes off the woman's swollen belly. It felt as if someone had reached into her chest and slapped an iron fist around her heart. *His baby.*

He slipped an arm around Candi, then kissed the top of her head. "We wanted to tell you, honest. But not this way. I didn't intend to hurt you. It's over. *We're* over."

Vision blurred, breath ragged, she stumbled backwards, and nearly tripped over a briefcase. As she righted herself on the door jamb, she saw the look of pity on Jim's face. Turning on her heel, she bolted.

~*~

The expensive Manhattan hotel offered all the amenities, including an honor bar, stocked with mini-bottles of booze. Pulling out the first four her hand touched, she lined them up by height on the nightstand, then placed one of Jim's sleeping pills in front of each bottle.

One pill for every miscarriage she'd suffered through.

Her wedding band landed at the end of the line-up. Kicking her shoes off, she sat on the edge of the king-sized bed, and flipped through the television channels, stopping when she came across, *The Women.* Joan Crawford, wife of a philandering husband, stood in a department store dressing room confronting the *other* woman about their affair—only to have the hussy announce the husband planned to divorce her.

It was as if her very life was being replayed before Sandra's disbelieving eyes. "Son of a bitch," she yelled, and chugged the scotch to wash down a pill. "How dare he do this to me?"

She hurled the empty tiny crown-shaped bottle across the room, anticipating the satisfaction of shattering glass—and watched it bounce harmlessly off the wall.

"Dammit! I can't do anything right!" She punched the pillow, then kicked at the dust-ruffle, only to hit something hard beneath. "Ow, ow, ow!" She grabbed her foot, flopped onto the bed, and sobbed. As she drifted off to sleep, the television whispering in the background, she heard the wronged woman's friends coaxing her to go with them to a resort to get over her broken heart.

Hours later, as she emerged from a dream of slapping Jim an infomercial for, 'The Cure Center, a MediSpa in the beautiful resort town of Lake Placid' commanded her attention while a flood of memories washed over her.

In 1980, she and a group of college friends decided to drive from the State University in Albany to Lake Placid to take part in the biggest party Upstate New York had ever seen during the 1980 Olympic Games. A pre-law student, working part-time as a secretary in a law firm, Sandra scrounged together enough money to buy two tickets to most of the events and stay in a cheap motel. When they arrived in Lake Placid, they went straight to a bar, where her wallet was stolen. Fortunately, she'd listened to her granddad and put the tickets in a money belt. Too bad she hadn't put her money there, too.

The next day, bundled in layers of wool and down, and forcing a big smile, she stood on a street corner in downtown Lake Placid holding a cardboard sign that read: "Will Sell—Figure Skating, Ski Jump, etc."

A large, handsome man in his thirties stopped in front of her, took a picture, and said, "I'll buy all your tickets—but only if you go with me."

Days later, in the middle of a crowded tavern, Jim and Sandra screamed and cheered with the euphoric crowd as the U.S. hockey team roared into history. When television announcer Al Michaels crowed, "Do you believe in miracles?" Sandra screamed, "Yess!" and hugged Jim.

He leaned down, kissed her, and shouted, "Marry me!"

That was more than twenty years ago, when she'd been young, beautiful, and built like Raquel Welch. Now a paralegal and soon-to-be ex-wife, she was still taller than her peers. Gray hairs had begun to silver her auburn brown strands, and she longed to recapture the time in her life when anything had been possible—even miracles. She turned up the volume, listened to the hypnotic spiel for the medical spa that promised rejuvenation, and dialed the twenty-four hour number plastered across the screen.

~*~

The next day, shards of pain shot through Sandra's head—either from the rough van ride, the scotch and sleeping pill hangover, or a combination of both. Jim had always said she couldn't hold her liquor. *I guess the S.O.B. called that one right.* She pressed her sunglasses firmly in place, and glanced around the vehicle.

The driver stared ahead at the road, wearing head-phones that blasted music so loud she wondered how much hearing loss he had. The big man with the crew cut sitting at the end of bench seat had helped her into the van at the Westport train station after she'd arrived from Grand Central with little more than the small overnight case she'd packed for the hotel. *What was his name? Bert? Bud?*

A young copper-haired girl whom Sandra guessed to be about twelve or thirteen sat between her and what's-his-name. Dressed in a faux-fur trimmed navy-blue parka, hands clasped in her lap, the girl stared straight ahead, her face an immobile mask. With her attention riveted on the child's strange affect, Sandra's headache was all but forgotten. "Who is she?"

"Shhh." What's-his-name stroked the girl's hair. "Her name's Erin. Sweet thing's had a terrible time. Her mother was murdered in front of her. Police had a time of it getting her out of the crawl space under the house, half-frozen, mute. She's practically catatonic." His hand lingered a bit too long, fingers played a tad too sensuously with tendrils of hair that trailed down the girl's neck.

He licked his lips, as if anticipating a special treat. Revulsion shuddered through Sandra, setting off a relay race of adrenalin from her heart to her head and mouth. "Take your hands off her."

Startled, the man jerked his head in Sandra's direction; his hand not moving from the girl. "What are you talking about?"

"If you don't take your hands off her *right now*, I'll call the police." She pulled her cell phone out of her pocket and flipped it open.

The creep slid away from Erin and pressed against the sliding van door. Sandra put her arm around Erin's shoulder, pulled her tight against her side, and glared at the man.

He muttered something that sounded like "Bitch!" And pulled the hood of his jacket up, hiding his face.

Forty minutes later, they arrived in the Village of Lake Placid. The Adirondack Mountains rose up around her, seeming to touch the sky. In the distance, a tiny gondola crawled up a cable. Normally, the sight of the picturesque village and its colorful shops would have excited her, filling her with the urge to visit all the places she'd been during that eventful time when she met Jim.

Her mood now, however, was anything but festive, and she wondered what had possessed her to come here. Was it a search for another miracle? A last stab at youth? An attempt at closure? What *should* one do when a marriage is over?

The van pulled into a parking lot next to a path that led to the front door of an old-fashioned camp cottage with a screened-in porch. Despite the sunglasses, the glare of the morning sun off the snow-covered lake beyond the cottage hurt her eyes. Using one hand as a visor, she focused on the building, and watched a pinch-faced woman dressed in a puffy black coat step off the porch, walk to the van, and open the door.

The creep hopped out and mumbled something indecipherable to the woman.

"I'm Louise Carson, Nurse Manager." She reached for the girl's hand, and led her out of the van, handing her over to the waiting man. "Take her in house. We'll be right there."

Head down, Erin obediently went along.

"*No!*" Sandra shouted. "He shouldn't be alone with her."

Carson took what felt like a proprietary hold on Sandra's arm. "Not to worry, Ms. Blake. Bob will take care of her. She's in good hands."

Bob. That was the pervert's name.

"His *hands* were all over Erin in the van. No matter what I said, he *kept touching her.*"

The nurse sniffed. "Bob's an excellent mental health aide. Now, let's get you into the cottage."

An arctic gust blasted across the lake and up the hill to the cottage, its temperature close to the iciness in Sandra's voice. "Listen to me. I'm a CASA volunteer and a Court Appointed Special Advocate for kids. I've seen a lot of creeps in my time, and I don't like the way he---"

Louise cut her off mid-sentence. "We'll get you a bite to eat and settle you into Cottage A. There'll be plenty of time this afternoon to talk about your stay with us." Iron-handed, she half-dragged Sandra along the icy sidewalk. Her breath came out in white puffs in the sub-zero air. "Here we are. Watch yourself. We need to get some salt on these steps."

Sandra stopped at the door, teeth clenched in frustration. "Your *excellent employee* is a pedophile."

"Ms. Blake, *please,*" Louise huffed. "All our staff have impeccable credentials. You have my word on it."

With a short honk of a horn, an SUV with LAKE PLACID POLICE printed along its side pulled into the parking lot. The driver's window rolled down, revealing a handsome, middle-aged man with salt-and-pepper hair and matching mustache. He removed his sunglasses and yelled, "Hey! Nurse Carson! You lose someone?"

Louise stiffened. "What did you say?"

"Looks like you lost one of your patients. We found her on Main Street. In pajamas. Barefoot. Incoherent."

Louise picked her way down the stairs, stepped over to the squad car, and stared through the rear window. After a second, she muttered, "She's ours."

First the creep in the van, now this? Sandra thought. *What the hell's going on here?*

"Second one this week," the cop said in a voice sharp with annoyance. "You guys having problems?"

No sooner were the words out of his mouth, when the sound of a man's scream came from inside Cottage A.

Already at the door, Sandra raced inside with Louise not far behind. Sandra found Bob in a bedroom, on the floor, sobbing and moaning. Blood oozed through the fingers of his hands covering his mouth and his panic-stricken eyes bulged out of his pale face.

Gaze locked on bright red trails on Bob's hands, Sandra heard Louise in the hallway, talking to someone. "We've got a situation here. No, not a patient. That new mental health aide. Yeah. I need an administrator here ASAP. The police chief is outside. I think he's calling for back up."

Movement caught Sandra's eye. The girl, Erin, sat in a corner with her head on her knees, hands inside her jacket, rocking. Years of working as a CASA never prepared Sandra for this. She knelt beside her. "He can't hurt you anymore, Erin. Why don't you give me that?"

Louise shrilled from the doorway, "Get away from her! She might have a weapon!"

The girl looked up, her beautiful face smeared with red streaks. She took her empty hands out of her pockets, smiled, and spat a chunk of pink flesh into Sandra's open palm.

~*~

While the EMTs attended to Bob, a patrolman took Louise to a separate room, leaving a female uniform behind to stand guard. Erin refused to let go of Sandra's arm and remained glued to her side while they sat on a couch in the waiting room.

Sandra thumbed through spa and tourism pamphlets with her free hand, and a wave of melancholy swept over her when she came to a glossy brochure advertising guided tours of Olympic sites.

"Ms. Blake?"

Sandra had to tilt her head back to see who was speaking.

The man from the squad car stood in front of her, a cowboy hat tilted back on his head, wearing a dark blue uniform beneath a shearling jacket. The heavy coat accentuated a pair of broad shoulders. His V-shaped torso tapered to a fully loaded Sam Browne duty belt, sans shoulder strap. His light blue eyes seemed to pierce her protective aura, an impression heightened by his furrowed brow.

Even as she studied him, she realized, he was examining her. Refusing to remain in a subordinate position, she stood. Erin, making soft grunting sounds, clung to her arm with one hand while patting her shoulder with the other. "It's okay, honey. I'm here. I'm not going anywhere."

"Ms. Blake?" he repeated.

At five-feet ten inches, Sandra was taller than some men—but not him. "Yes, that's me," she said. "And you are...?"

"Chief Doug Harrington, LPPD. I need a statement about the incident."

"That's a delicate way of putting it."

He nodded at Erin. "Is this the young lady you found with the victim?"

"I'm not sure the term 'victim' applies to Bob. He's lucky she only bit his tongue."

The Chief lifted an eyebrow and his lips quirked. He took a pen from behind his ear, pulled a small notepad out of his shirt pocket, and stood with pen poised over paper. "Could you describe what you heard and saw—minus the editorials?"

While the Chief scribbled, she described Bob's behavior in the van, then the scene in the cottage bedroom, careful to delete the *editorials*.

"What brings you to Lake Placid?"

She raised her hands and gestured to the walls of the small room. "We're standing in a world-renowned spa. I'm a woman. You do the math." She knew she was being a smart-ass. She couldn't help it. Inane questions always annoyed her.

"Were you under the influence of any substances?"

She shook her index finger at him. "I had *one* scotch and *one* sleeping pill—over eight hours before I arrived here. I know what I saw," she paused. "As soon as I got here, I told Louise I didn't like the way that creep had touched Erin in the van. She refused to listen."

"Okay. Go on." He stared straight into her eyes, giving her an even stronger impression of being inspected. She stared right back at him, silently dared him to blink.

"If this nurse was so concerned about her employee, why'd she call her boss *before* she gave Bob first aid?"

"Louise Carson says you were drunk and combative."

"Bullshit!"

"She also says Erin's a person of interest in an ongoing murder investigation. Father stashed her here to protect her. Maybe she's just pretending to be mentally ill to avoid jail time?"

Sandra fought back the urge to punch him right on his way-too-perfect-for-a-real-man nose. "Are you out of your mind? *Look* at her."

Harrington studied Erin for a moment, as did Sandra.

Boney hands. Torn, bitten cuticles. Dirt under her nails. Hadn't anyone bathed the child after they dragged her out from under the house? By this time Erin was rocking side to side, shifting from one foot to the other. A sweater and jeans bagged on her too thin body. Sandra had to wonder whose clothes she was wearing. Her dead mother's, perhaps? She shuddered at the thought.

"Look at her face." She tilted Erin's head in the Chief's direction, so he could have a better look at her empty eyes and vacant expression. "Some might argue she acted in self-defense against a sexual predator. Others might conclude she's suffering from post-traumatic stress disorder, secondary to witnessing her mother's murder. The fact that this Bob person went after a vulnerable, *mute* girl in full view of a witness is disgusting. And, re-victimizing the victim by suggesting she's feigning her symptoms to avoid prosecution is *doubly* disgusting, Chief Harrington."

He gave her a long, assessing look.

Sandra stared right back, locking on those unsettling blue eyes, waiting to see who blinked first. Butterflies ice-skated in her stomach. Warmth rushed up her neck. Her knees started to knock.

Whoa! The last time she'd felt this way had been in 1980—here, at the Olympics.

He sighed before glancing around the tiny room. "Are you a lawyer, Ms. Blake?"

"Paralegal. And a CASA volunteer."

He nodded. "How long have you've been a CASA?"

"About ten years." Starting two months after the doctor told me I'd never be able to carry a baby to term, she thought. "It's not a hobby; it's a calling. I've worked with hundreds of kids who have witnessed brutal crimes against family members." She tipped her head towards Erin. "Just like her."

"Interesting."

Afraid her knees might buckle under the weight of his attention, she sank to the sofa. Erin floated down alongside her.

Harrington made a few more notes and snapped his notebook shut. "We'll be in touch."

He turned on the heel of his cowboy boot, and strode away in a slightly bowed stance, as if he'd just gotten off a horse, taking the two uniforms with him.

Louise entered the waiting room, reversing Sandra's good mood. "Time to get you to bed, Erin."

Putting a Vulcan grip on Sandra's arm, the girl shrank behind her. "Tell you what, Louise. Why don't you show me where we're going? Looks like she and I are joined at the hip."

~*~

Sandra had to admit that the ambiance of her suite in Cottage A, decorated in soothing shades of aqua-blue and greens, was relaxing. An in-room snack bar offered bottled water, juices, organic fruit and cookies and Swiss chocolate. A young woman in a turquoise one-piece ski uniform and matching hat delivered breakfast on a white tray. The smells of piping hot bread, chocolate, and rich, dark coffee provided a perfect wake up call for Sandra's taste buds.

Sated on croissants and coffee, she shrugged into a thick, white terry-cloth robe and wandered across the hall to check on Erin. *Still sleeping.* When awake, if Sandra stepped out of her sight for more than a few seconds, Erin would become agitated, rocking and grunting.

After my shower, I'll try to coax her to eat some breakfast. Maybe she'll like the pastry. The poor kid didn't touch her dinner last night.

Louise whispered in Sandra's ear, startling her out of her reverie. "We'll have to sedate her to keep her calm, so you can begin your deluxe treatment regimen," Louise said. "That's what you're paying for."

Sandra closed Erin's door, and motioned to Louise to step into her suite. "Who's paying for Erin? What's she really doing here?"

The nurse picked a piece of lint off her slacks, avoiding eye contact. "That's none of your concern."

"How on earth will a seaweed wrap help this child?"

"Don't be ridiculous." Bright red spots rose on Louise's cheeks. "The psychiatrist will be up later this week to conduct an assessment."

"You've got to be kidding!" Sandra's voice, laden with anger and disbelief, rose to a near shriek. "This kid's been doubly traumatized, and she needs an emergency psych evaluation. What kind of operation are you running here?"

"We're a fully licensed mental health and substance abuse treatment center—as well as a MediSpa. Erin will receive psychotropic medications, electro-convulsive therapy—whatever she needs—when her *own* psychiatrist sees her, someone with whom she has a therapeutic relationship."

"Shock therapy? That's barbaric! I can't believe anyone does that anymore."

Louise's beady black eyes glared at Sandra. "It's an excellent treatment for depression."

Appalled at the prospect of someone passing electricity through anyone's brain, Sandra snapped, "It's a great way to get brain damage and memory loss!"

Crossing her arms over her breasts, Louise's lips thinned. "Since you're not a physician, Ms. Blake, your opinion isn't relevant. Now, if you don't mind, I'll give Erin her medication, so you can get some time for your own *much* needed therapy."

Sandra followed the nurse across the hall, and watched her remove a zip lock bag containing a pre-filled syringe from the pocket of her turquoise smock. As Louise approached the bedside, Erin woke up and began to wail, eyes wild with fear.

"For God's sake, woman, let me by!" Sandra pushed Louise aside. Erin threw her arms around Sandra's neck and howled. She loved kids, but hadn't signed up for a baby-sitting job. It looked as if she'd unwittingly become Erin's surrogate mother.

She pointed at the syringe. "What is it?"

"Just a little sedative to calm her down," Louise retorted in a brisk, no-nonsense tone of voice. "Doctor's orders."

"Let me see it." She reached for the medication. "Now, or you'll have to get past me first."

Louise shrugged and handed her the medication.

"Vistaril?" Sandra recognized the mild anti-anxiety drug from her post-partum depression days, when she'd been so agitated she thought she'd jump out a window. "Don't you have this in pill form?"

"This is the route the doctor prescribed." Sandra could have sworn the nurse was smirking.

Holding the quaking girl, Sandra said, "Hang on to me, honey. This will be over in a moment."

Torn between remaining with the teenager and going to her scheduled appointment, Sandra stayed at Erin's side until she fell back to sleep.

~*~

Louise offered to call the van to drive her to her appointment, but thinking a walk in the fresh air would do her good, Sandra declined. A slow-moving maintenance worker was shoveling a footpath through the snow-covered walkway, but didn't seem to be getting very far. As she stood on the curb, eyeing the pavement with trepidation, a police SUV pulled up alongside.

"Ms. Blake?" Chief Harrington beckoned to her. "May I speak with you for a moment?"

"I'm already late for appointment. I'm supposed to be at Cottage D right now."

"That's over a mile from here. Hop in."

Sandra debated for a tenth of a second, thought about how cold she was, and slid into the warmth of the car. She turned sideways to face Harrington, and noticed a zigzag scar along his strong jaw line.

"What can I do for you?"

Rather than detracting from his good looks, the scar added to his rugged appeal. A sudden urge to reach over and trace the path of its smooth whiteness nearly overcame her. Instead, she unbuttoned the top of her coat, pulled off her knit hat, and brushed strands of hair out of her eyes.

What was wrong with her? She felt like a high school cheerleader with a major crush on the star quarterback.

"You were right," he said. "Bob is a registered sex offender."

She allowed herself to gloat—just a little. "I'd say 'I told you so,' but I'm too busy trying to understand why they hired a creep like that."

"Seems Louise Carson was short-handed, in a rush to fill the position, and skipped the criminal background check," he said. "Which explains why she called her boss before giving Bob first aid."

"Told you so. Sorry. I *could* help that, but decided not to."

Harrington smirked.

She was a sucker for men with dimples. A tingling sensation emanated from a region of her anatomy that hadn't been excited in years. Her inner cheerleader shouted: *"Not dead yet!"* Her rational, sane self said: *Sit down and shut up!*

"Erin's not off the hook. Detectives are coming up from Long Island tomorrow with her father. Any chance you'd be willing to sit in on the interview with her? With your background as a CASA, you're the perfect choice to be her advocate, help her feel safe. I bet you're a pit bull when it comes to advocating for your kids, beating people up until you get what the child needs."

Sandra stared at him, shocked by his laser accurate assessment of her personality and work style. "Who have you been talking to?"

He gave nothing up. "Consider it a good deed and say yes."

"Hmmm." She took a moment to consider. "That would mean you'd be indebted to me, right? I might need a favor from the local PD, just in case I punch Louise Carson in the face the next time she talks down to me."

Harrington laughed. "Getting an assault charge dropped might be beyond the scope of my duties. How about dinner instead?"

Her stomach flip-flopped while her inner cheerleader performed an intricate tuck and roll.

"Why, Chief, for all you know, I could be a serial killer."

"I'll be sure to carry my sidearm. Here's your stop. Watch your step."

A tall, handsome, and funny guy had just asked her out for dinner. Lake Placid was suddenly looking better and better.

~*~

A wall of framed diplomas attested to Allison, 'call me Allie', Johnson's education in counseling.

"After what you've told me, and based on today's battery of tests," Allie said, "my professional assessment is that you need extensive talk-based therapy and good, old-fashioned pampering. Lucky you saw our ad and called. Tell me about you and Jim."

Allie was half Sandra's age. Would she understand why she'd put up with his *wanderlust* for so many years when Sandra wasn't sure she understood it herself?

"If it was just about sex, I could have dealt with it. He's had plenty of affairs. After a month or so, he'd get tired of his latest fling and come back to me. But this woman is different. He's been with her almost six months. And now I know why: she's pregnant."

"How does that make you feel?"

"Depressed and humiliated. Like I let us both down. He's ten years older than me and wanted children. I wanted to be a mother, but I've had four miscarriages. I can't carry a baby to term. Seeing her *so* pregnant with *his child*—well, it was the final straw. He's gone for good. For the past ten years, I've deluded myself that we had a good marriage. I guess you could say I've bottomed out."

Allie nodded. "Understandable. But, what do you want to do with the rest of your life?"

The question caught Sandra off-guard. "I hadn't even thought past this afternoon's manicure and pedicure."

"Can you consider this a time to regroup and work on a plan?" Allie tapped a pen against her milk chocolate-colored cheek. "Today's Wednesday. Let's get together again on Monday. Is that okay? You'll have time to get a massage, maybe a seaweed wrap and facial. The plastic surgeon comes on Fridays to do Botox injections and implant assessments. I see Louise made an appointment for you."

"You know what?"

Allie looked up from her notes. "What?"

"I'm going to hold off on injections and surgery for a while," Sandra said. "If I don't know what I'm doing with my life, what difference does it make what I look like?"

"All right." Allie nodded in understanding. "You're a pretty woman. You don't need all that stuff. Just don't tell anyone I said so. Management likes us to push services." She shrugged and rolled her eyes. "It is a for-profit clinic, after all."

Sandra walked back to her lodging, admiring the converted cure cottages along the paths. Long open porches spoke to the genteel days of old, when locals opened their homes to men, women and children suffering from Tuberculosis who came to the Adirondacks, hoping for a cure. They spent months, sometimes years, living on the porches, eating nourishing meals, allowing fresh mountain air and sunshine to heal their bodies. The Cure Center was built on the local history of spas and sanatoriums, only on a cash or credit card, no-insurance-accepted basis.

She paused for a moment, took a deep breath of the biting cold air, and considered Allie's question. What *was* she going to do now? She couldn't bring herself to hate Jim. True, the humiliation of seeing him with his pregnant mistress ripped a big hole in her self-esteem. Her volunteer work with CASA, looking out for other people's kids, had been satisfying—but hadn't assuaged the grief over her inability to have children. Perhaps she'd been blind to Jim's sorrow and greater need. She was jealous he'd have a baby to enjoy, and saddened that she would never be a mother.

Picking up the pace, she decided she'd pitied herself long enough. No more self-delusions. She and Jim had been friends and co-workers over the last years, but the love needed to sustain the relationship had long been extinguished—and both were culpable. Her priority now was to figure out how to make a fresh start.

~*~

The next day when the Long Island detectives arrived, everyone crowded into an overheated conference room in main building of the spa.

"Ms. Blake, nice to meetcha. I'm Tom Jones. This here's my partner, Vic Martinez." The Long Island police officer bore no resemblance to the popular Welsh singer. With his build and pure Bronx accent, Jones looked like a former football player. His partner nodded, but didn't say a word.

Erin continued to cling to Sandra's arm, but pulled back when her step-father, a weasel-faced man named Webster, tried to kiss her cheek.

Louise's eyes flicked back and forth between the detectives, Chief Harrington, and Webster. "Ms. Blake, we don't need you here during this interview."

"Yes. I demand that you leave," Webster said waving Sandra away. "This is a private matter."

"Okay." Standing with some difficulty, she peeled Erin's hand from her arm, then headed for the doorway.

With a shriek, Erin threw herself at Sandra.

"What the hell have you done to my step-daughter?"

Sandra turned and glared at the man. Harrington gave her shoulder a light squeeze. Suddenly she didn't feel so alone.

"As I said before, Mr. Webster," Harrington replied, "Erin has bonded with Ms. Blake. If you want to determine who killed your wife, you'd best let her stay."

"Very well, then. She can stay, but that woman." He pointed to Louise. "Has no need to be here."

Sandra wondered why the three cops were allowing this weasel to run the show. Was this a set-up?

The nurse marched from the room, slamming the door behind her.

"Officers, let's proceed," Webster said. "I'm wasting time, and time is money."

Jones started off. "Let's begin with the night in question. Please tell us what happened."

"I've already been through this a hundred times," Webster whined.

Jones pulled out his notepad and pen. "I know, but not with your step-daughter present."

Webster sighed. "I'd been out to dinner with some clients. My wife had a migraine and couldn't come with me. When I arrived home, the first thing I noticed was that our front entrance lights were out. I thought it was odd, because we always leave them on. After I pulled my car into the garage, I saw those lights were out too, and I began to get concerned." He took a deep breath. "I noticed the door to the kitchen was damaged—there were marks around the doorknob, like someone had used a screwdriver to open the door."

Erin dug all ten fingers into Sandra's arm.

"I ran into the house, calling my wife's name—'Rose! Where are you? Are you okay? Rose!' No answer. I found my wife on the floor of the study, a fireplace poker next to her. Her face was broken—like a porcelain doll—and covered in blood. She took a few breaths as she lay in my arms. I called 9-1-1, but by the time they arrived, she was gone. My beautiful Rose was dead, killed by an intruder. I think I must have surprised him, and he took off when he heard my car."

He pulled a crisp white handkerchief out of his pocket and mopped his brow.

Staring at Webster, Martinez asked, "Where was Erin during all this?"

"She wasn't my concern at that moment," Webster snapped. "I needed to attend to my wife."

"Your thirteen year-old step-daughter may have been in danger, possibly raped, possibly kidnapped by an intruder whom you say killed your wife." Martinez leaned down to get into the weasel's personal space. "Weren't you worried about her whereabouts?"

"I wasn't thinking about anything but my wife, and the fact that she was dying." He pursed his lips and stared at the girl. "I'm sorry, Erin. I should have looked for you sooner."

The girl buried her face into Sandra's shoulder and dug her fingers deeper into her arm. Her little body shook so hard that Sandra began to shudder, too.

Martinez plowed ahead. "Weren't you, in fact, in the middle of making arrangements to send Erin away to a boarding school for the emotionally disturbed? Weren't you and your wife fighting almost nightly about this?"

Erin started to grunt in a rising scale of notes. "Unh, unh, unh, unh!"

Webster clenched and unclenched his hands with each grunt. "Have you no mercy? She's just lost her mother. Now you're coming after me. You're upsetting her!"

"One more question, Mr. Webster," Martinez said. "We've been doing a little research. Seems your wife has no other living relatives. Who becomes the beneficiary of her estate if Erin is declared incompetent?"

Webster glared at him. "What the hell is going on here?"

"We checked with the restaurant." Martinez again, put his face close to Webster's, nearly nose-to-nose. "They confirmed you left at half past ten. Your 9-1-1 call was logged in at five minutes before midnight. The restaurant is only ten miles from your house. What took you so long to get home?"

Webster looked close to losing it. Red-faced and sweating profusely, he roared, "I thought we were here to see if Erin could assist in the investigation. You obviously have a different agenda. I'm done here. You can speak to my lawyer."

Erin continued to sob and grunt, while Sandra wondered if she'd ever be able to peel the girl off her arm. Putting together the pieces of what she'd just witnessed, she said, "You guys think Webster killed Erin's mother for her money. You wanted to see what she would do while you interviewed *him*. Am I right?"

"Bingo," Harrington said. "This young lady is the key to the case—if she could talk."

"Don't you think you took a huge risk she'd be driven further into her shell?"

"That's why you're here," Harrington said.

"I can be her advocate, but I'm not a shrink." A queasy feeling came over her. "I'm worried about leaving Erin alone now. Webster is pissed enough to try something."

"Don't worry." Harrington gave the Long Island cops a meaningful glance. "We've got an undercover cop to watch over her when you have other things to do."

"Then, gentlemen, if you don't mind, my best girlfriend needs to get some food and rest. Maybe Erin will eat some of those little chocolates." Sandra moved toward the girl's suite with Erin still attached to her arm.

"I owe you," Harrington said when she passed him.

Sandra nodded and replied, "You bet your ass."

~*~

"Where are we going?" Sandra asked as she climbed into Harrington's beat-up, non-LPPD Ford Explorer on Friday evening.

"Call me Doug, please. We have reservations at a quaint little place called The Veranda. If it was good enough for President Clinton, it's good enough for us."

"Are you sure Erin will be safe? I don't trust Louise to protect anyone but herself," Sandra turned in her seat to look back at the cottage. "On second thought, maybe I should go back."

"Relax. She's covered."

"Don't you ever get upset?"

"The last time I got upset was two years ago, when my wife left me. She claimed I was married to my job, not her. She never understood that a police chief—especially on a tiny force—is always on call. She remarried a younger guy, a nine-to-fiver, who comes home every night for dinner."

"Oh." She settled back to enjoy the scenery as he drove around Mirror Lake to the restaurant. Snow-covered pines blazed with red, pink, and purple tones from the setting sun. She made out the trails of cross-country skiers in the wide-open spaces. The road wound around the lake, which was frozen in pristine beauty and unmarred by the sound of snowmobiles.

When Doug broke the silence, his voice gave Sandra a little frisson of anticipation. "In the daylight, there's a pretty view from the deck. You'll have to take my word for it tonight."

"I'll use my imagination."

A fireplace blazed in the restored wood and high-beamed Adirondack manor, filling the intimate dining room with warmth. Conscious of Harrington's physical proximity with each bump of his knee under the small table, Sandra perused the menu while hoping the butterflies in her stomach would eventually cease the downhill slalom course they'd been taking for the past hour.

"You a meat eater?"

"Love it."

He ordered for both of them: A Chateaubriand for two, accompanied perfectly by a bottle of Merlot.

As they speculated about what would happen to Erin, she realized that his knee was resting on hers—and that it felt natural. Where had he been all her life? How had she missed him that fateful day in 1980? Or had he not been in Lake Placid then?

She glanced around and noted they were the last two people in the dining room. A fleeting vision of making love to him in front of the roaring fireplace danced through her mind. She started to suggest they should think about leaving and caught him staring at her left hand. "Something wrong?"

"You tell me. Why didn't you mention your husband is Big Jim Radcliff?"

Sandra froze, the fantasies about bedding him coming to a screeching halt. She felt a rush of heat into her face; her ears burned with anger as she glared at him. "Why is that any of your business?"

"Let me see." He tilted his head and put his finger to his chin in a pose of mock puzzlement. "You arrive in the middle of a series of unusual events. You become a mother-bear for a girl involved in a murder investigation. And, it just so happens you're a CASA. I'm a cop. You do the math, as you told me once. I made some phone calls, to see if you were legit and not some wacko."

Sandra lowered her eyes and stared at her bare left hand.

"As of this week, he and I are through. Long story short: I caught him in our office with another woman. Another *pregnant* woman." She let the statement hang out there for a few moments before looking up to catch his gaze. "I'm over forty, have had multiple miscarriages. My husband never kept his pants zipped, but as long as he kept coming home, I pretended we were okay. He's not coming home anymore."

Hot tears filled her eyes. She was *not* going to cry. She tossed back the rest of her wine and thumped the glass down on the table.

He grabbed her hand. "I'm sorry. I've met so many women who come up here for the spa, get Botoxed, and conveniently forget they're married. I was afraid you might be one of them. I like a woman with a few gray hairs and laugh lines."

Sandra wasn't sure if he'd just complimented—or insulted her. "Are you saying I look like I *need* Botox?"

"No, that's not what I meant!" He motioned the server for the check.

Maybe this date wasn't such a good idea. Here she was rushing into another relationship, and she wasn't even legally separated, much less divorced.

The ride back to the cottage was frigid, and not only from the temperature. He pulled the car next to the curb. "Let me walk you to the door."

"I'm fine, thank you." She pushed the door open to cut off further conversation.

"God, you're hard-headed."

Screams cut the air. Sandra bolted out of the car only to fall on the icy walkway. Harrington pulled her to her feet before they raced up the stairs. More screams came from the back of the cottage. They ran toward the sounds and slammed into a locked door.

Harrington pulled his revolver, pushed Sandra away from the door, and flattened himself against the wall. "*Police. Open up.*"

He kicked in the door; Sandra raced in behind him. Strapped to a table, Erin struggled and kicked at Louise's attempts to restrain her feet. A man in a white coat stood at the head of the table, holding a paddle over Erin's head.

"I said shock her, God Dammit!" Webster shouted from the corner of the room.

"Nobody move!"

Ignoring Harrington's order, Sandra slipped to Erin's side to remove the restraints. She was only able to loosen one wrist before someone grabbed her arm and twirled her around.

"You interfering bitch!" Spittle hit her face as Webster shook her hard enough to make her teeth rattle.

"Don't hurt Mommy! I'll be good! Don't hurt Mommy!"

Everyone froze.

Between sobs, Erin repeated, "Please don't hurt Mommy! I'll be good!"

Webster shoved Sandra out of his way, before bolting for the door.

Arm extended, Harrington stepped in and clothes-lined him, then pinned him to the wall. "C'mon. Gimme a reason to kill you."

Webster's eyes bulged—but he didn't move.

~*~

On Monday, Sandra walked over to Cottage D to see Allie Johnson one last time, before she departed. The walkways were cleared now that the real maintenance man, not the undercover cop, had returned from vacation. Friday evening, once all the excitement had worn down, Harrington had found the cop, unconscious and duct-taped, in a closet.

Webster was under arrest. The local court refused to set bail. Louise Carson was also under arrest for an assortment of crimes, including assault for drugging the police officer, and false imprisonment. The unlicensed psychiatrist, along with the shock therapy paddles, awaited deportation back to his home country somewhere in the Balkans. The Cure Center was closed indefinitely, pending further investigations.

Erin had recovered the ability to speak in complete sentences. She was going to make an excellent witness for the prosecution.

"Enough about everyone else," Allie said as she filled a box with personal items. "What about you?"

"I have a plan." Sandra was both relieved and excited by the prospect. "My soon-to-be ex-husband has agreed to help me apply to become Erin's legal guardian. He's so happy I'm only asking for the house, my car and money to cover my living expenses, he's promised to pull some strings to expedite the process. She's about the age of one of the children I would have had, if I hadn't miscarried, and she already calls me Mommy."

Allie nodded. "What about the rest of your life? Children grow up and move away, you know."

"When Jim and I married, I gave up on law school, became a paralegal, and helped him build his practice. I've decided to pick up where I left off." She smiled. "I've become very attached to the Adirondacks. With any luck, I'll be accepted at Albany Law School. Jim has offered to pay my tuition. Can you believe it? He said it's an investment in *his* financial freedom."

A horn honked. "There's my ride. Thanks for everything." Sandra walked outside into the diamond bright sunshine, squinting at the outline of a man leaning against the limousine—and felt a sharp pang of disappointment when she realized it was only the chauffeur.

Did you really think he'd be here to see you off?

"Ready to go, Ms. Blake?"

"Yes, thanks. You have all my things?"

He nodded.

She turned and took one last look around Lake Placid as her eyes welled up with tears. *Damn, damn, damn the man!* He had really gotten under her skin. "Let's go," she choked out.

The chauffeur opened the back door and Sandra slid into the dark leather interior, eyes blinded, head bowed as she wept. Needing time alone, she pressed the button and closed the divider. Too soon, the car stopped. Despite pressing all the knobs in the back seat, the divider wouldn't go down.

The back door flew open; Harrington stood on the curb.

He reached in to take her hand. "Come with me."

"What's going on?"

He led her up the steps of the gray courthouse, through a metal detector, and into a judge's chambers—all without a word.

A gray-haired man in black robes looked up from a stack of papers. "Ms. Blake?"

"Yes," she answered, anxious that something had gone terribly wrong.

"I've spent the last two hours on the phone with Family Court judges in New York City, each and every one of them singing your praises. A bossy lawyer named Jim Radcliff has called here so often, I've told my secretary not to put him through anymore. And this fellow—" the older man shook his finger at Harrington. "Has been badgering me to death."

Sandra looked back and forth between the judge and Harrington, and opened her mouth. All that came out was a weak whisper, "Why?"

"Because a certain young lady needs a foster parent, and everyone in the State of New York seems to think *you* are the best person for the job."

Erin burst into the room, leaped into Sandra's arms and hugged her, rocking and repeating, "Mommy, Mommy, Mommy!"

"I thought you'd like some company on your trip back to Manhattan," Harrington said with an enormous smile.

Eyes swimming, Sandra took the pen, and signed the paperwork with shaking hands.

As the beaming judge looked on, Harrington embraced Sandra and Erin in a giant bear hug.

"Do you believe in miracles?" Sandra whispered.

"Yes, I do," he replied, and sealed her destiny with a kiss.

French Kiss: Pigmalion

~✳~

✳

BALTIMORE METROPOLITAN UNIVERSITY'S football stadium thundered with the footsteps of homecoming fans rushing to get out of the torrents of a heavy late November rain. Car horns honked, and revelers shouted a drunken chorus of, "BMU BEAT YOU! WILDCATS RULE!"

Levisa Harris and her best friend, Claire, crowded under the eaves, pressed back against the closed concession stands with what seemed like hundreds of other fans who peered glumly out at the rain. A post-game ambiance of hot dogs and beer, mixed with the smell of wet wool, swirled around them.

Hair soaked, Levisa attempted to push her flattened copper-colored curls out of her eyes and noted Claire's short blonde hair hadn't fared any better. "We look like drowned Wildcats." Levisa glanced at the unending rain and hoped it would stop soon.

Claire looked at her friend and laughed. "Thank God, for hair dryers and flat irons." A young man jostled up against the petite blonde. "Hello, I'm standing here!" Claire shouted.

"I know," a man wearing a nautical windbreaker retorted with a soft southern drawl. "We came over to offer ya'll a lift."

Levisa spoke without thinking. "Richmond, Virginia."

"Beg your pardon?" A look of surprise crossed his clean-shaven face.

"You're from Richmond, right?" Levisa noted he was attractive in an old money, preppy kind of way, but he didn't appeal to her at all.

"Yes, but how'd you know?" He leaned in a tad too close, expelling beery breath as he spoke.

Levisa leaned away, seeking fresh air as Claire spoke up. "She's an expert on accents."

"Parlor tricks! Oh, this is fun!" the Virginian said. "Sam, say something."

"Chip, we need ta go." Sam's deep voice held a note of irritation. "I have ta study fer my CPA exam."

"Baltimore—Pigtown." Levisa looked at Sam with interest, and not just because of his accent. High forehead, half-covered with a shock of black-brown hair, he possessed long straight nose and full lips. A small scar curved around his strong chin.

She touched the scar on her own chin and wondered if he had fallen off his bicycle as a child, too. She pulled herself up short. Stop thinking about how adorable he is. Focus on the brass ring: finish the research project, graduate, and get a good job. "You'd be perfect for my Speech-Language Pathology Master's research project."

"I ain't no guinea pig." Sam pulled at Chip's arm.

"One quick question—Sam, is it?"

He turned and faced Levisa directly, towering over her, his broad shoulders and wide chest straining at his ratty sweatshirt.

An image of him without his shirt, all rippling muscles, flashed into her mind. She forced herself to look directly into his deep-set eyes the color of dark chocolate. She swallowed hard, and asked the sixty-four-thousand-dollar question. "How far do you think you'll get with that accent in an accounting firm?"

Sam's face flushed. "I'm really good at numbers. That's what matters in bidness."

He was so good-looking, but he wouldn't be hired, much less promoted, with that accent. Why didn't he get it? Frustrated, she heard herself blurt out, "What company wants a CEO who sounds like a hick?"

He glowered at her. "Yew callin' me a hick?"

Claire stepped between Sam and Levisa. "Please don't be offended. She's saying she can help you get a better job—if you reduce that Bawlamer accent, Hon!"

"It's not nice ta make fun of people," Sam snapped and grabbed Chip's arm. "Let's go."

She felt short of breath, as if she'd run up a flight of stairs, instead of standing here, arguing with this hardheaded man. "If you change your mind," Levisa shouted after him, "come to the Speech, Language, and Hearing Clinic. It's in the middle of campus."

As the two men walked off, collars pulled up against the wind, Claire turned to her friend. "You know, he's not half-bad looking."

"Chip? The preppy? Not my type," Levisa watched the two men climb into an old Ford Taurus and focused on the back of Sam's head and the way his dark hair tapered down his neck.

"No, the other one—Sam, with those dreamy brown eyes and that wavy black hair. Whew!" Claire fanned her face. "I'd love to give him a few private lessons, if you know what I mean!"

"Put a lid on your id, girl!" Levisa laughed and shook her head in an attempt to dispel her own disturbing responses to Sam. "I don't have time for a man in my life. If I don't finish my research, I won't graduate in spring. All I need is one more Pigtown subject for the study and I'll be done. Too bad, he's the one that got away!"

~*~

"Look at this email." Levisa pushed away from the computer, so Claire could read the screen.

"Dear Levisa—I hope you don't think me too bold, but I can't stop thinking about you since we met at the stadium on Saturday. You are the most interesting woman on this campus. Would you please meet me for coffee at the library? I'd love to get to know you better.

Warmest regards, Chip."

"You have an admirer. Isn't that sweet?" Claire giggled. "I wish I had someone who wrote me fan letters."

Levisa strummed her fingers on the desk. "How'd he get my email address?"

"The clinic website?" Claire suggested.

"If it was Sam," she murmured, "I'd be there in a heartbeat."

Claire smirked at Levisa and harrumphed.

She caught herself, and put on her studious face. "No— Not that. I'm still short one subject." Levisa looked at the calendar over her desk with the days numbered in a countdown to graduation. "I'm running out of time."

"So, are you going to meet Chip?"

"No. It wouldn't be fair to lead Chip on just to try to get to Sam. I'll write back and tell him thanks, but I'm too busy with my research."

Levisa spent the rest of the day working with her clients and entering data for her project.

At five in the evening, Claire stuck her head in the doorway. "Ready to go?"

"One sec. I'm going to check my email before I leave." Levisa logged in and gasped.

"What's wrong?" Claire peered over her friend's shoulder. "Oh, Chip's AHOY!"

"I have over thirty emails from him—one every fifteen minutes!" Levisa clicked the mouse, scarcely able to believe her eyes. "Look at this! They all say the same thing—*Please reconsider. I'll just keep begging until you give in!*' This is creepy, I'm blocking his messages."

"Wow!" Claire exclaimed. "How come I never get a guy that's mad about me?"

"This is the wrong kind of 'mad'! Let's go to the Rusty Bucket. I need a drink."

~*~

The next day, Mrs. Pierce the receptionist, called back to Levisa's office. "There's someone here to see you."

"Does he have a Pigtown accent?" Levisa crossed her fingers, sat on the edge of her seat and hoped it was Sam.

Mrs. Pierce chuckled. "Always on the lookout for good material, aren't you? No, he's just the usual."

Disappointed, she wondered who would ask for her by name. Levisa walked out to the front counter, scanned the noisy waiting room crowded with mothers and preschool children and stopped short.

"I'm so glad you can see me." Beneath his open nautical windbreaker, a tiny polo player raced across Chip's shirt. As he placed his hand over his heart, the Virginian extended a small bouquet, and the scent of roses wafted her way. "Darling, these are for you."

She ignored the flowers and took a step backward. "Chip, I'm sorry. I thought I was clear in my email. I don't have time for dating now, I have to finish my thesis."

He dropped to his knees in front of the desk, much to the amusement of a nearby child playing with a toy truck on the threadbare carpet. The little boy giggled and ran to his mother, pointing at the 'funny man.'

"Please go out with me!" He clasped his hands to his chest, still holding the flowers. "I think about you constantly. I can't sleep—I can't eat. I must be with you."

Levisa's face burned with embarrassment. It seemed as if people were coming out of every nook and cranny to watch the dramatic scene. If she heard one more woman say, "Isn't that romantic!" she was going to scream.

"Get up!" Levisa seethed between gritted teeth. "I'll have a cup of coffee with you, but that's it." She grabbed her raincoat. "Let's go."

All the way to the café, Chip jabbered about his admiration for her profession, how dedicated she was, how lovely she looked, and how brilliant she must be to be able to identify all those accents. By the time she got into line, Levisa was exhausted. She looked at her watch for the fourth time.

"Did I tell you how much I admire you?"

Levisa gave Chip a weak smile and answered, "Yes, many times."

For heaven's sake! Why did it take so long to make a latte?

The preppy leaned his head close to hers, the smell of mouthwash heavy on his breath. "I must tell you, Sam Parker is driving me mad with his practice. Did you tell him to put marbles in his mouth?"

"What? No, I never even saw him in the clinic!"

"Gotcha!" Chip guffawed. "The look on your face! If only I had a camera."

The milk steamer hissed in the background, matching Levisa's slow burn. "That's not funny." She turned her back on the snickering man.

"Oh, come on. It was just a joke!"

Maybe they should play rock-n-roll instead of jazz to make the lines move faster! One cup of coffee with this jerk and she was gone. A second register opened and the clerk motioned to Levisa to approach.

"Let me get that," Chip interjected.

"No, thank you." She reached out to give the clerk a five-dollar bill.

"Really, I insist." He flashed a perfect smile and grabbed her wrist, pulling her hand away from the barista.

"I said—No— Thank You!" Levisa wrenched her hand away from his viselike grip. He was beyond a jerk, and had moved up to the jackass category.

"Oh, you are a vixen! I like it when a woman has fight."

Coffee in hand, she backed towards the exit. "Get away from me. I never want to see you again."

Everyone in the coffee shop stared at her.

"Levisa, darling! Don't do this to me," Chip called, following her out the door. "You know how much you mean to me." He reached for her arm.

Could it get much worse than this?

She turned to flee, felt her footing slip on the wet concrete steps, and tumbled through the air.

~*~

"Are yew okay?" Sam's face came into her field of vision, a worried frown creasing his handsome features.

"Why am I on the ground? What happened?" Oh, my God! Of all the times, of all the places to run into him again! She attempted to sit up, but he placed a gentle hand on her shoulder. She felt heat rush to her neck and face. Was his hand really that hot? Or, was it just that the ground was so cold and damp by comparison?

"Yew fell down the stairs. I think yew got knocked out. Stay put. The police are on their way."

"I just had the wind knocked out of me." She took a deep shuddering breath and lifted her head. Flashbulbs went off in her skull and the crowd of students surrounding her began to spin. She closed her eyes to keep from getting sick.

"Let me put this under your head, Hon. Then yew can tell me what you remember." The pleasant scent of a spicy aftershave wafted up from his jacket, as he tucked it in place. He brushed her hair back on her forehead, and his fingertips left a blazing trail on her skin. She blinked and found herself staring into his warm brown eyes. Her stomach dove in a long, lazy somersault. Yes, maybe she should stay put for a little while longer.

She took a deep breath. "Your buddy, Chip, he's a weirdo." She related how he had emailed her so often she'd had his email address blocked, then his embarrassing behavior in the clinic. "I thought if I got him out of where I worked, I could reason with him, but he wouldn't give up. The last thing I remember was him trying to grab my arm. Which reminds me—where is he?"

Sam shook his head and frowned. "He ain't my 'buddy.' We just live in the same apartment building." He glanced around the crowd of students, his hair ruffled by a light breeze. "I don't see him."

The BMU Police and EMTs arrived, took reports from Sam and Levisa, and placed her on a gurney. She clutched Sam's jacket to her chest, intending to return it to him, but when she looked around, he was gone. A pang of disappointment surprised her. *What's happening to me? I'm a scientist, cool, calm, rational. But when he's around, I'm a quivering toy poodle!* She closed her eyes, breathed in his scent, and dozed off to sleep.

~*~

A week later, arm in a blue sling, Levisa stood behind the counter at the clinic, reviewing her caseload for the morning. Holiday garlands of green, red, blue and silver decorated the crowded waiting room, and the scent of pine filled the air. Senior citizens played musical chairs with one another, each vying for a seat closer to the intake room.

Levisa hummed, and headed for her office, juggling coffee and client files with her good hand. She was going to try to reach Sam again—this time through the Accounting Department. Maybe they'd know how to find him.

"BMU Department of Accounting, how may I help you?"

Mouth dry, she tried to sound businesslike. "Yes, I'm looking for a student in your department. His name is Sam— Sam Parker, I think. I'd like to return his jacket."

"Certainly. I'll put you through to his office voicemail."

Office voicemail? For an undergraduate? How odd.

"Hi! Yew've reached the voicemail of Sam Parker. I'm not available rate now. If yew are calling about tutoring, I have office hours Mondays and Wednesdays from two to four in the afternoon. Please leave a message and I'll get back to yew."

"Sam, this is Levisa Harris." She hoped she didn't sound too anxious. "I'd like to return your jacket. Please call me at the clinic." She placed the phone on the receiver, puzzled. He had an office—with voicemail. Only graduate students and faculty had those perks. And he tutored people. Sam Parker, Pigtown man of mystery.

Mrs. Pierce stood in the doorway, her plump cheeks flushed.

"There's someone here to see you."

Levisa felt a surge of fear. "Chip?"

"Heavens, no! I'd call the police if it was him."

"Does this one have a Pigtown accent?" Levisa held her breath, hoping for the answer she wanted, and the right man to go with it.

"Oh, yes!" The receptionist smiled. "If he didn't speak he'd be adorable. Puppy dog eyes..."

"Sam!" Levisa exploded out of her chair and pushed past the daydreaming woman to the front desk. Sam stood at the counter, looking around as if he was in a foreign country.

"Am I in the rate place?" Sam lowered his voice to a whisper. "What's wif all dem old folks?"

Levisa suppressed a smile. "Free hearing tests." She pressed her good hand on the counter to keep it from trembling. No man had ever affected her this way before. Could he tell? "I was just trying to reach you. I have your jacket. Come around, so we can chat in private." She led him to her office and handed him his coat.

Their hands touched and a spark of static electricity flashed between them.

"Ouch!" Levisa jumped back, caught herself, and laughed.

Sam smiled and said, "Sorry 'bout dat. How's yer arm?" He pointed to the sling, a worried look on his handsome face. "And head?"

"Sprained. Mild concussion. It could have been worse. Thank you so much for all your help." Her gaze traveled along his strong jaw to that oh-so-kissable scar. "Is there anything I can do for you?"

Sam looked at the floor. "Yes." He looked up and made direct eye contact. "Yew were rate." I had an innerview at the Career Center. The guy didn't unnerstand me. Told me ta get rid of my accent. I need your help."

Moved by his beseeching look, she fought back the urge to hug him and tell him everything would be all right. "First of all, you can probably reduce your accent, but I can't promise you'll be completely rid of it."

"Okay, I can live wif dat," he nodded and a shock of black hair flopped into his eyes.

"When do you want to start?" One-handed, she pulled out her phone to look at her calendar. If only her fingers would stop tingling, she could get the darn thing to work.

"Now. I have an innerview wif Ernst and Young in April. He sighed. "I really want a job wif dem."

Levisa looked at his forlorn expression, and realized how hard it must have been for him to swallow his pride, and come to the clinic to ask for her help.

"The good news is, if you're willing to do the work, that's half the battle."

He nodded.

"The bad news is that we need to get you ready soon—it's only four months away. Henry Higgins had six months to transform Eliza Doolittle. And she lived in his house, practicing twenty-four seven." Unbidden, an image of Sam practicing his speech exercises while lying in bed with her flashed through Levisa's mind. She ducked her head down, pretending to look closer at her calendar, and hid her smile. "Can you can meet with me three times a week, an hour each time? And are you willing to work on a computer program two hours a day on your own?"

"I'm ready to work like a dog!" He gave her an enormous smile—then his face fell. "Is it expensive?"

Levisa pounced on the opening. "Not if you agree to be in my study."

He hesitated for a moment, then said, "Tell me more."

Pulling a sheaf of papers out of the stack of folders, she slid them across her desk. Their fingertips touched, sending waves of longing up her arm, and Levisa became flustered. Tongue-tied, she headed for the safe territory of her research spiel. As always, she concluded with, "These are the informed consent forms, including a description of the research project. This study is completely voluntary, has been approved by the Human Subjects Protection Committee, and you can stop at any time. Any questions?"

He transfixed her with a stare. "How old are yew?"

Taken aback, she blushed and stammered, "Tw-twenty-three. Why?"

"Talkin' about your work, yew sounded older." He cocked his head and grinned, showing perfect teeth—all except for a dear little crooked one on the bottom row. No expensive braces for him as a kid. "But we're the same age."

She felt her pulse kick up a notch and took a deep shuddering breath. "May I ask you something personal?"

He smiled and settled back in the visitor's chair, long legs stretched out in front. "Fire away."

"Why do you have an office and voicemail in the accounting department?" She watched him swallow hard and lick his lips, his pink tongue darting in and out.

"I'm workin' on a big project. And I tutor students who're havin' trouble wif accounting." He tapped his temple. "I told yew, I'm good wif numbers."

Not a full answer. He was hiding something, of that she was sure. But what?

Claire sailed around the corner just as Sam was leaving the room with Levisa. "Well, hello!" Claire stood with a perfectly manicured hand on her hip, swaying back and forth. She twirled her hair with her other hand, in blatant flirt mode. "I see you found us."

"Yep." Sam shifted his weight from one foot to the other, brushing Levisa's leg as he did so.

Claire gave Levisa a sly look, and then turned to Sam. "Did she offer you private lessons?"

Levisa glared at her friend and wished she could kick her in the shin. "Sam will be here three times a week for the next four months." She had to remain cool and professional in front of Sam, or she'd never hear the end of it from Claire.

"Oh, good!" the blonde replied. "I'm happy to hear that, Hon."

After Sam left, Levisa yanked Claire into her office. "*Hon?* What's wrong with you?"

Claire batted her eyes and fluffed her bangs. "Whatever do you mean?"

She felt her face and neck get hot. "The guy is already mortified that he's been told to 'get rid' of his accent, and you do that?"

"I was just speaking his native tongue. Don't get all bent out of shape." Claire raised an eyebrow. "If I didn't know any better, I'd think you were sweet on the guy, hmm?"

Levisa stepped back and shook her head. "Don't be ridiculous. I'm grateful to him, that's all." A swarm of butterflies flapped into formation in her stomach, spelling out the word: LIAR.

"Methinks the lady protests too much!" Claire stepped closer to her friend. "You're blushing! I do believe Sammy Boy got through your intellectual armor!"

Levisa put her hands up. "Stop! I have my work to think of—that's all. He agreed to be in my study in exchange for free sessions." Those beautiful eyes! Every time she thought of them, those butterflies spelled out much more interesting things...

"Do you really think you can help him sound like an executive job candidate in four months?"

A shadow of doubt crossed Levisa's mind, and her stomach plummeted. Could she do it? Or was she being arrogant?

"I bet a 'Day of Beauty' at Spa Du Jour that you can't do it," Claire challenged.

Levisa stood up and straightened her shoulders. "You're on."

~*~

"I know the National Anthem, Hon," Sam protested, after the first month of sessions with Levisa.

She smiled. "Yes, but do you know how to say it without Bawlamerese?"

He began to sing. "Ao say can yew see by don's early late..."

"Oh, say can you see by the dawn's early light?"

"That's what I said!" Sam glared at her.

"Okay, let's try this: Oh, oh, oh!"

"Ao, ao, ao!"

Levisa held her head in her hand, her temple throbbing. *What was I thinking? I'll never get him ready in time.*

He touched the back of her hand, setting off tremors in her legs, in spite of the fact that she was sitting down. "Are yew okay, Hon?"

She looked up, fell into his eyes, and her headache receded. *I am so much better than okay.* She smiled. "I'm fine. Let's try again."

~*~

I brought yew some chocolates." Sam held out a heart-shaped satin box, looking like a little boy bringing his teacher a gift.

Levisa stared at the gift, surprised and pleased at his thoughtfulness, her breathing unnervingly uneven, her heart doing a cha-cha. "Why?"

He looked puzzled. "Didn't yew look at the date?"

She glanced at the calendar. "February—oh!" How had she forgotten, with all the cupids and hearts in the waiting room!

An amused look crossed his face. "Balentine's Day."

"Valentine's Day."

"Just what I said." Sam smiled.

"Just what yew—you—said." Levisa smiled back, feeling flushed and lightheaded. "Thanks, Sam. I think I need a piece of chocolate, right now."

~*~

"Oh, say does that star-spangled banner yet wave, over the land of the free and the home of the brave! Play ball!"

"Excellent! 'I do believe you've got it!' to quote Henry Higgins." Levisa nearly crowed with delight. Sam was a quick study and had an excellent ear. She was going to win her bet with Claire, she just knew it. "How about the next one?"

"I'm going to Bel Air to the library."

"Fantastic! Next one?" She decided he was her best student ever, but maybe she was just a teeny bit biased.

He strutted around the little room, threw his chest back, and roared out the words, "Don't open the window, it's too humid."

Levisa clapped her hands and cheered. "Keep going, you're doing great!"

He stopped, turned and stepped close to her. "Do you know what day it is, Hon?"

Confused, she looked down at her clipboard. "That's not on our list, but good try. Don't say 'Hon'."

"Do you know what day it is?"

Levisa glanced up from her notes. "You're asking me a question?"

He sighed. "Yes, I'm asking yew—you—a question."

She checked her watch. "April first."

"It's a week before my big interview with Ernst and Young." Sam reached for her hand and took it gently into his large warm one. "Will you go out to dinner with me? I'd like to thank you for all your hard work."

She stared at his fingers, wrapped so softly around hers. A thrill of electricity raced up her arm to her neck and she could feel herself blushing. She flashed onto Chip at the coffee shop and mentally compared his rough touch to Sam's. She hadn't seen the preppy, thank God, for months.

His touch made her feel wired, as if she would jump out of her skin. "Yes! I'd like that." Like it? I'd love it. She restrained herself from jumping up and hugging him. Slooow down, girl. Put a lid on your id, Levisa!

"Good." A look of relief was followed by a big grin. "Ah'll—I'll meet you at seven? Is the Rusty Bucket okay?"

"Perfect." After she closed the door behind him, she let loose with an unbridled happy dance, complete with arm waving.

That evening, as Levisa locked the clinic door, she worried about Claire. Ever since Levisa's fall and subsequent beginning of work with Sam, Claire had been distant and aloof toward her. Today, the blonde had spritzed herself with too much perfume, and then run out the door saying she was meeting someone for lunch. She hadn't returned and didn't answer her cell phone. Sometimes, she could be such a flake. Luckily, the threat of a snow squall had caused several patients to cancel their appointments, or Levisa and her coworkers would've never finished today.

Loud music and laughter poured out of the Bucket as Levisa pulled into the parking lot. Jeez. What a zoo. Couples lined the entryway, waiting for tables and swigging bottled beer. She gave her name to the hostess, took a lighted pager, and joined the line. She couldn't believe she was actually going out on a date with Sam. All these months of one-on-one sessions in close quarters with electrifying looks and tentative touches, and now here she was waiting for the man of her daydreams. She checked her watch and cell phone, looked up and down the line, and wondered where Sam was. What on earth is going on?

"Levisa?" A man called to her, barely audible over the background noise of bar televisions and couples' chatter.

She turned, hoping Sam would be waving to her from the door, but instead it was Chip. She felt her smile freeze in place. Ugh. Of all the people she did *not* want to see.

He pushed his way through the throng until he stood in front of her. "Sam sent me to tell you he changed his mind."

"What?" Was he standing her up?

The preppy made a sad face, a messenger with bad news. "Yeah, he realized he'd made a mistake asking you out. I guess I'm your consolation prize."

Booby prize is more like it. How could he do this to me? And send Chip? Of all people! Furious, she thrust the pager into his hand. "Here, you won't have long to wait." As Levisa turned on her heel and headed for the exit, the crowd moved back to allow her to pass, and tisks of pity followed her.

When she reached the dark parking lot, tears blurred her vision, and she leaned her head on the side of her car.

"Hey, don't cry, darling." Chip grabbed her arm, whirled her around, and pressed her back against the car. "I'm here to show you a good time."

He shoved his hand between the lapels of her coat, pawed at her breasts, and planted a beery kiss on her lips. She struggled to get away from his groping fingers.

"You are so hot! I love a girl who fights back!"

"Get off me! Stop it!"

She looked over Chip's shoulder and saw Sam on the sidewalk, peering into The Rusty Bucket.

"Sam? Help!" Her voice didn't carry over the booming music. Sam headed into the restaurant.

"You frigging cock tease! You're just like that bitch Claire."

Fear jolted Levisa into action. She kneed him in the groin. When he yelped and grabbed his crotch, she kicked him in the shin—then ran like hell for the restaurant and Sam.

The police responded to Levisa's call in three minutes, but Chip was long gone. Holding Sam's hand, she gave Chip's description between sobs and gulps.

"He lives in my building, one floor up," Sam said. "I ran into him at the convenience store on the corner when I stopped on my way home to pick up some..." He paused and blushed. "He slapped me on the back, said, 'Way to go!' and took off without buying anything. When I left the apartment to meet you, my car had a flat and my cell phone was missing. He must have picked it out of my holster in the store. I spent the last hour trying to get my tire fixed, and I had no way to reach you."

"Claire had a lunch date with someone—and never came back to the clinic." Panic-stricken, her voice rose. "Tonight, he said I was a bitch—just like Claire. We've got to find her!"

Sam reached out and stroked her cheek with trembling fingers, his warm touch soothing her jangled nerves. "We will, I promise." He looked up at the police officers. "The apartment complex has a gym, but it's not used much. Chip calls it his private play room."

Levisa put her head on Sam's shoulder and broke into tears. As the squad cars peeled out of the parking lot with their lights going, she prayed they weren't too late.

~*~

Levisa stood at the side of Claire's hospital bed, grateful that her friend was still alive, knowing full well that she herself could have been Chip's next victim. She leaned into Sam and squeezed his hand. He pulled her close, his arm around her waist. She felt as if she'd known him all her life, not just four short months.

"The police have him in custody," Sam said. "You're safe now."

"Aren't I just the great judge of character?" Claire tried to smile through her swollen lips, but winced in pain. She had two black eyes but, amazingly, no broken bones. Speckles of dark-brown blood stood out on her champagne-blonde hair, telltale signs of her abuse.

Levisa didn't know what to say. She had told Claire she thought Chip was a creep. She reached for Claire's hand—the one that wasn't bandaged—and squeezed it.

"I wanted someone who would adore me." She shifted in the bed and groaned. "Dumb, dumb, dumb. I should have listened to you." Tears shimmered in Claire's blue eyes and Levisa handed her a tissue. "After I pretended to pass out, he was really pissed. He wanted me to fight back. He said he was going to find another playmate—you. I put you at risk."

"No! Don't say that. Your quick thinking probably saved your life."

"I'm positive Chip sliced my tire." Sam shook his head. "I never saw this coming. I'm so sorry."

"It's not your fault. I was a fool." Tears welled up in Claire's eyes. "Go home, you two. Get some rest. I'll be okay—now that I'm here and he's in jail."

In the elevator, as Levisa reached to press the button for the ground floor, Sam turned her around and pulled her close to him. The sound of his heart thumped in her ear as she pressed her face into his chest.

"This will sound selfish—but I'm so glad he didn't hurt you." His voice hitched. "I would never have forgiven myself."

She tilted her head up to speak and his soft mouth was on hers, taking her breath away. Lips parted, she responded with equal ardor, tasting him, dizzy with wanting him, and forgetting her vow not to allow romance to get in the way of her work.

"Sorry—"

"I'm not," she said. "Kiss me again, and don't stop until morning." She held him tighter, closed her eyes, and for the first time in her life, felt herself relax into the free fall of her emotions. As his tongue explored her mouth, she arched her back and felt overheated—then as if from far away, she heard a soft whooshing sound. The elevator doors? Eyes open, she jumped away from Sam, and turned around to see a little old lady standing in the entryway.

"Well, well, well!" She smiled, and then joined them in the elevator. "You two should get a room!"

Levisa and Sam looked at each other and giggled. His face looked as flushed as hers felt. He grabbed her hand and nodded vehemently. "Yes, ma'am. You're absolutely right."

~*~

Levisa opened her apartment door. "Come in. I'll make us a snack. We never did get dinner."

"Mrrp? Mrrowp?" A large black-and-white cat with a half-black, half-white mustache demanded her attention.

"Oh, so sorry, Colonel Pickering." She threw her coat on the back of a flowered sofa and picked up the purring cat. "Your dinner first, then ours."

Jacket off, Sam stood in the middle of the small living room, slowly turning in a circle, staring at the posters. "So, how long have you been obsessed with Audrey Hepburn?"

Levisa laughed. "Not just her—the most amazing story of all time—My Fair Lady."

"And that's how you became interested in studying speech?"

She straightened up from placing a can of food in the Colonel's dish. "Well, that started in high school when I read

George Bernard Shaw's play, Pygmalion. The movie sealed the deal."

Sam nodded, looked thoughtful and said, "The only thing I ever really liked in school was arithmetic. I've always been good at it. Surprised the heck out of everyone, especially my teachers. They thought I'd just be another loser."

"You? Never. You're one of the hardest-working students I've ever had." His eyes snagged hers, and she felt her stomach begin to drop—but now the sensation rivaled what she had felt on her one terrifying ride on Space Mountain.

Just as she began to wonder if she was doing the right thing by having him in her apartment, he reached over and took her cold hand in his warm one. His gentle touch extinguished her doubts. Instinctively, she knew this man would never hurt her.

"You're the best, the most beautiful teacher I've ever had." He wrapped his long, muscular arms around her shoulders, pulled her close, and stroked her head. "I love your hair. So soft." He nuzzled her neck and nibbled on her ear, his spicy aftershave tickling her nose, reminding her of his kindness when she fell. "I've wanted you ever since we met."

"I thought you hated me when we met," she murmured, her arms around his waist, lips brushing his.

"No. Just angry that you hit on the very thing I wanted: to be an executive in an accounting firm." His fingers traced her spine, lightly caressing the small of her back, then pulling her snug against his growing hardness.

She rubbed against him, and her legs felt weak. "I've been struggling to keep my hands off you for four months," she whispered,

"We've waited this long, this is going to be special—for both of us." He nibbled at her shoulder, and began kissing his way down to the base of her neck. "Time to take this off." Her turtleneck sweater slid up over her long curls, exposing her black camisole. "Next." He peeled the spaghetti straps down, removed the silk lingerie, then her bra. His lips hovered over her breasts, his breath warming her, thrilling her nipples.

Levisa moaned and shuddered with anticipation. She cupped her hands under her breasts, offering them up to him with abandon. She had never been this free with a man before. She'd always felt like an observer, not really involved, when she'd made love. But this time, this man, this aching need was different.

Oh my God, I'm so in love with him!

In a nearly hypnotic state, she watched him lightly lick her left nipple and then take it into his mouth, sucking and pulling. She groaned and grabbed his firm butt, pressing hard against the outline of his erection.

"Now?"

"Not yet." He took her nipple between his teeth, tugging lightly. Levisa gasped as his hands slid up her skirt, between her legs, and stroked her thigh a torturous inch below her silk thong. She pulled at his waistband and unzipped his pants, barely recognizing her own voice thick with lust, "My turn to drive you wild."

"I like the sound of that."

"Get over here," she ordered. Slowly, intent on teasing him, she eased his jeans down. As he stepped out of the pant legs, she tiptoed her fingers down his back, beneath the waistband of his underwear, and grabbed his butt. "Did I tell you, you have a perfect ass?"

A look of surprise flickered across Sam's handsome face; then in a in a flash, still watching his expression, she yanked his briefs down to his ankles. His beautiful penis stood at attention, long and hard, waiting to be of service.

"Oh my," she whispered in awe. "I admire a man who's happy to see me. Now we get in the shower."

Walking backward, giggling and kissing, she led him into the bathroom, turned on the water, and adjusted the temperature. "Do you have protection?"

He smiled. "Always." As if by magic, a metal streamer of condoms appeared in his hand.

She laughed. "Expecting a busy night?" She stepped into the shower and crooked her finger at him. "Well, I'm going to put you to work." She handed him her coconut-scented shampoo. "Use your imagination."

Levisa closed her eyes as Sam poured a drizzle of shampoo on her hair, the tropical scent mixing with his spicy aftershave and male musk in a heady blend. As Sam massaged her scalp with slow, firm strokes, she relaxed, practically melting under his tender touch. While the warm water sprayed over her, his fingers traced soap bubbles down her neck to the base of her throat, and rubbed lazy circles around her nipples. He increased the speed and intensity of his touch, finally leaning down to take her eraser-hard nipples in his mouth. She moaned, grateful that the running water covered the sounds of their lovemaking.

She returned his caresses with increasingly firm strokes on his back, then his buttocks, between his legs, soap bubbles rising up and bursting under her watchful attention. He groaned as she fondled his penis, lightly running her thumb across the opening, soaping up. Then down. Up and down again, the size and thickness of his shaft mesmerizing her. He stilled her moving hand and pulled her in for a long hard kiss.

Then, he turned her around and placed her hands against the wall, saying, "Don't move." Foil crinkled. His fingers explored her, and then he pressed his erection between her now exquisitely sensitive thighs. She squirmed, trying to rub her clitoris along his shaft. His voice was firmer. "Don't move." His right hand pulled at her wet nipple, while the fingers of his other hand probed the folds of her vagina and found her clitoris. At last, he slid his enormous shaft deep inside her.

She gasped and he stopped moving.

"What's wrong?" She panted and wriggled against him, wanting more.

"Nothing, I want to enjoy the moment."

It felt like all the air was sucked out of the steamy shower. He stayed still, holding onto her until she couldn't take it any longer.

She wriggled against him, begging, "Don't stop, please, don't stop!"

At last, he resumed his long, slow lovemaking, each stroke, each touch, driving her further up the spiral of passion until she climaxed and shuddered to a halt. Weak-kneed, she fell against the shower wall and gasped for air. "I can't move."

"Don't worry, I'll carry you to bed and finish ravishing you there." He hugged her with a towel, lifted her off her feet, and placed her gently on the bed. He opened the terrycloth wrap and gazed down at her, and licked his lips as if she were a tasty morsel.

"You're beautiful all over. Every inch of you." He kissed her breasts and continued kissing his way down to her belly-button and the silky red triangle below.

She grabbed his thick black hair, opened her quivering thighs, and pressed his face between her legs. He licked her tender skin, teasing his way upward, making slow circuits, tantalizing her, until she pushed his head down, and whispered hoarsely, "If you don't take care of me right now, I'm going to scream my lungs out."

After hours of lovemaking, Levisa fell asleep in Sam's arms and did not awaken until the bright morning sun pushed its way around the window shade. She looked up and saw her cat leap onto the bed, then stroll over to Sam.

"Mewrp?" Colonel Pickering stood on Sam's chest, looking at him with intense green eyes.

Sam blinked and laughed. "Well, good morning, Mr. Kitty Breath."

Levisa glanced at the clock. "Is it really eight in the morning? I'm going to be late."

"No." Sam chuckled, taking her in his arms. "You're going to be *very* late."

~*~

The following week, on the day of Sam's interview, Mrs. Pierce dragged Levisa out of a speech lesson with a lisping child and thrust the phone in her hand. "It's him!" Mrs. Pierce smiled and gave Levisa a thumbs-up sign. Claire and the receptionist looked on with barely suppressed excitement as Levisa sat down and took the call.

"Sam?"

"I got the job of my dreams!" He voice shook with excitement. "My parents are going to flip!"

"That's wonderful news!" She high-fived the receptionist and mouthed to Claire, "I won!"

"It is. But they're sending me to Europe to finish my project—effective immediately."

"What about—?" She stopped herself. She almost said us. Had she misinterpreted? She'd thought they had more than just great sex.

"I'll see you at Commencement." The phone clicked and he was gone.

"He has to leave town," Levisa said, a hollow feeling forming in the pit of her stomach. "Said he'd see me at graduation."

Mrs. Pierce looked concerned. "It seems so abrupt."

"That's it? He blew you off? After all you've done for him? What a jerk!" Even under layers of makeup Claire's face looked the worse for wear, but her cocky attitude hadn't been damaged.

"Maybe he got a better offer." Levisa knew she was grasping at straws. He got a great job, and she got her heart broken.

"Like what? Vice President of Ernst and Young?" Claire's voice rose. "The least the bum could have done is send you flowers!"

Levisa sat down and covered her face with her hands. She'd thought they had something special. Unlike any other man, he had gotten through her intellectual armor, as Claire called it, and she had fallen in love with him. Damn the man! She never should have let him get under her skin.

The door to the clinic opened, and cool air whooshed in.

"May I help you?" Mrs. Pierce asked.

"Is Levisa Harris here?" A uniformed delivery man held a large vase of red roses.

She sniffed and wiped her nose. "That's me."

"These are for you. Have a nice day."

She looked for the little white card and was surprised to find a larger envelope instead. The front of the card showed Rex Harrison in a top hat with Audrey Hepburn on his arm in a scene from My Fair Lady. Inside, in small, careful letters was a note:

"I saw this and thought of you.

You've been Henry Higgins to my Liza Doolittle. I hope our story has a happy ending, too. Please wait for me. Hugs and Kisses, Sam."

Levisa started to cry and laugh at the same time.

~*~

Every day, for four weeks, Sam sent her emails telling her how much he looked forward to seeing her. But he had something very important to finish first.

Her advisor and the department finally approved her research project, and with the May commencement close at hand, Levisa wandered through the BMU bookstore, marveling that her journey to her Master's degree was almost complete. Shelves overflowed with black caps and gowns, invitations, diplomas, rings, and memorabilia of idyllic times at the university.

"May I help you?" A silver-haired woman peered over her glasses at Levisa.

"Yes. I'm here to pick up my cap, gown, and Master's hood."

"Your name, Hon?"

Levisa almost giggled. Hon. How she missed hearing Sam say that to her. "Harris. Levisa Harris."

"Let me see. Harris, Harris, Harris. There a lot of people with that last name."

Levisa watched the woman flip through the pages, then gasped. "Stop! Please, wait a minute."

"Something wrong?"

"Sam Parker—is he really getting a doctorate? Am I reading that right?"

"Shhh. I'm not supposed to share this information, but yes. He's the youngest PhD in accounting we've ever had. Just passed the CPA exam with a perfect score, too. And, he's one of the student speakers this year."

Levisa flushed and her legs felt like rubber. She clutched the edge of the glass counter to keep from swaying. What had he said? I'm really good at numbers. That's what matters in bidness. The little sneak. All the times they'd been together, she had yakked about her research, and not once had he told her he was working on a PhD. The only thing he had spoken about was getting the job of his dreams. What else hadn't he told her?

~*~

With six tickets for graduation, Levisa had been limited to bringing her parents, brother, sister, and grandparents. But that was plenty. The first person in her family to graduate with a Master's degree, Levisa basked in the glow of their love and pride.

"When will we get to meet your young man?" her grandmother asked for the fiftieth time.

"Soon, I promise. Dad, could you stop with the photos? I have to get in line." She craned her neck, looking around for Sam. He had to be here, but in this mob of black caps and gowns, everyone looked alike.

"We're buying the DVD, too," her mother called across the crowd. "We're getting everything about your graduation!"

Colorful medieval banners designated colleges, and an array of flags from every country represented in the student population lined the back of the stage. The president, provost, deans, and faculty entered to the BMU orchestra's rendition of Pomp and Circumstance while undergraduates jostled and called out to one another and their professors.

When she reached her seat and looked up, she saw Sam on the stage in the front row, sitting next to the provost. She found herself taking quick, shallow breaths and had to tell herself to breathe more slowly. How had she not known? She had assumed that he was an undergraduate in the five-year program for the CPA. She'd never bothered to ask him about his studies, or his life outside the clinic and his speech lessons. She really didn't know him. So why did her throat constrict, her legs shake while a bevy of ballroom-dancing butterflies did the quick step in her stomach when she saw him?

The president welcomed the graduating class, the parents of the graduates, the grandparents, the brothers, sisters, family and friends of the graduates, asking each group to stand up and be recognized, all to wild applause. The provost spoke about outstanding professors and star students, then introduced this year's 'most amazing young man', a role model for all, Dr. Sam Parker."

"Thank you, Provost Charles. Every student who graduates from BMU has a story. My story is about a man who began in Pigtown, Bawlamer, land of dem O's and Hons."

Laughter greeted his words, and Levisa clutched her clammy hands in her lap, fearing she would clap too soon.

"My parents worked hard, so I could come to BMU, and I worked hard. I was able to get scholarships, grants and part-time jobs. It was a dream come true. I was so afraid to fail that I didn't tell many people that I was working on a doctorate. After all, I was just a poor guy from Pigtown."

The crowd laughed and a spattering of applause burst out from the parents' front row.

"Thanks, Mom and Dad!"

More laughter.

"I thought I had it made, until I was told by a young woman, and I quote: 'What company wants a CEO who sounds like a hick?'"

Levisa covered her face with her hands, flushed with shame. Coming from his mouth, her words sounded cruel. Had she been that harsh?

"I was really angry at her for saying this—until I went to an interview at the Career Center here and was told to get rid of my accent, or I wouldn't land a job with a Big Eight firm."

She lowered her hands from her face, and looked at this amazing man, this honest man, who spoke from his heart to the full arena. The crowd was quiet. Even the undergraduates paid attention.

"I'm here to tell you that I now have a job with Ernst and Young. They hired me as their Vice President for Research. I know that I wouldn't have gotten that job without the resources of this university and without the hard work and honest feedback from a great teacher."

He paused and Levisa realized she was crying, her chest tight. She was so proud of him. He had exceeded her wildest dreams, and she'd helped him get there.

"I'd like to ask my speech coach to come up on the stage with me. I know you're here, Levisa."

She felt people patting her on the back, reaching for her hands, guiding her along the path, and up the shaking stairs. Or were her legs shaking? Sight blurred with tears, she crossed the stage to stand in front of Sam.

"I want to take this moment to publicly thank Levisa Harris for making me into a new man. She believed in me and worked with me when others laughed and ridiculed me. She saw through my Pigtown accent to my potential and helped transform my life. I am eternally grateful."

Applause and cheers filled the arena up to the rafters with sound, until Sam held up his hand for them to stop. Rooted to the spot, unable to speak for fear of blubbering, Levisa smiled and nodded, then turned to go.

"One more thing."

She turned back to him, his black hair slick and neatly placed under his cap, brown eyes bright, and a broad smile across his face. Then, before all and to her breathless amazement, he got down on one knee and said, "I love you, Levisa. Will you marry me?"

She froze. The arena fell silent and she could hear her breath coming in short, shallow puffs. The butterflies in her stomach quivered in a question mark, her hands and legs trembled, and her field of vision compressed to a tunnel, with Sam at the end of it. She stared into his eyes and saw the depth of his passion—and her future. The trance broke.

Levisa reached for his hand, pulled him up to standing, and said, "Yes, Sam Parker of Pigtown, Bawlamer, I will marry you."

Cheering and stomping roared from the crowd.

A Sizzling Smooch: Bonded for Life

~★~

�֍

CHAPTER ONE
~*~

LOLA GETZ CLIMBED out of the salt water pool and shook out her long black tresses. Every man standing guard around the compound stood at attention--above and below the waist. And she knew it. Pretending not to notice the looks of lust, she toweled off her legs with upward languid motions. When she reached her hot pink bikini bottom, she wrapped the terry cloth around her butt and slowly rubbed it back and forth.

A new guy groaned and his peers laughed, and then fell silent, when the head guard ordered them to shut up.

She threw a leopard cover over her lush curves, prompting sighs of disappointment. She smiled. "Show's over, *muchachos.*"

As she sashayed into the stucco covered mansion, curses swelled behind her—all aimed at the new body guard. She knew they'd straighten him out, or kick him to the curb.

Flora, her loyal housekeeper, greeted Lola with a hot cup of coffee and a gap-toothed smile. Lola had offered to buy the gray-haired woman new teeth, but the elder had declined, saying at her age she wouldn't be around long enough to enjoy them. Aztec blood ran through Flora's veins, so it was hard to tell if she was sixty, or six-hundred years old.

Lola took a sip of the scalding *café con leche*. "Has the mail arrived?"

"*Sí.* On the front table." Flora handed her a cloth napkin and stared at the floor.

"*Lo que es?* What is it?"

"*Lo siento,* so sorry. The envelopes were *all open* when the mailman he gives them to me." Flora shook her head and sighed. "Things are getting worse, *Senora.*"

Dammit. What was wrong with the mail service? Hadn't she just paid an exorbitant 'service fee' to the post master to keep her mail private? Ever since her husband died last year, things had been going downhill.

When they had married ten years ago, Rico was an ambitious young car salesman. Over time, he became a wealthy dealer, catering to those who wished to travel in style and safety. The specialty of the dealership was protection: bullet-proof cars with tinted windows. He began with Mercedes, then moved into Hummers, just like the ones used in the wars in the Middle East, minus the camouflage. These big rides were tricked out in metallic colors and artistic detailing that corresponded with the tattoos preferred by each cartel.

Perhaps he'd still be alive today, if he'd used one of the custom vehicles himself, instead of run off the road on his beloved Harley.

Lola *knew* it was the work of a rival car dealer, someone who paid a mobster to kill him. But, of course, there were no witnesses. And the corrupt cops just shrugged when she went to them crying and screaming for justice.

After she buried Rico, she sold the car dealership to her wealthy cousin, Isabel Ramirez, for a pittance. In exchange, Izzy provided twenty-four/seven bodyguards for Lola's estate. Her cousin warned her to be vigilant; kidnappings of family members of affluent families for exorbitant ransoms were rampant in the province. Izzy insisted Lola keep a 'go bag' packed and a throw-away phone pre-loaded with a list of emergency phone numbers. In addition, the same paranoid, the end-is-near-cousin helped her set up safe houses in and outside Mexico. For the past eleven months, Lola had felt protected in her fortified enclave—until today when the mail arrived, already opened.

A little shudder ran up her spine, but Lola was not about to give in to her cousin's paranoia, and told herself she was chilled from the cool marble foyer and nothing more.

She set the coffee cup down, before picking up a large envelope covered with grubby fingerprints. The pig that opened her mail must have been eating chocolate at the same time. She stared at the postmark, it had been mailed months ago. God only knew how long it had sat in the Mexican post office.

Summerville, New York? It couldn't be. She tore off what was left of the paper and read the invitation, squinting at the words half-hidden by a large smudged thumb print.

Dear fellow alumna,

Hard to believe it's been 25 years since we last walked the halls of Summerville High. Wouldn't you like to know what's going on with former classmates? The Reunion Committee has worked hard to plan a fabulous, fun-filled three day celebration on the last weekend in June at the historic Summerville Inn.

Come for one day or all three—but register early for the SHS package discount. Bring your spouse or come stag. You won't believe the surprises waiting for you!

RSVP to BethandRich@heade.com

How had they found her? Damn the Internet and its googling eyes. One of the New York galleries that showcased her work must have given them her address. Was there no way to escape from the assholes of high school past?

Unbidden, hot tears welled up in her eyes, then spilled down her cheeks. That year, her senior year, without a word of explanation, and despite her protests, Lola's parents shipped her off from the exciting city of Chihuahua, Mexico to the boring town of Summerville on the shores of Lake Ontario in Western New York State.

The cheerful wording better described an invitation from hell that would occur ten days from now. With the anniversary of her beloved Rico's death approaching, the last thing she wanted was to relive wretched memories of Summerville, New York.

Never—Ever, again.

"Flora, where's the shredder? Didn't I tell you to leave it there?" She pointed at a spot to the right of the table.

"Ah, *Senora*, don't you remember, you asked me to move it to your office? So you could get rid of your husband's old business papers?"

Lola bit her lip. "You're right. *Gracias.*"

Flora bobbed her head and hurried toward the kitchen.

Aromas of cinnamon and chocolate wafted in the air. Was chicken mole on tonight's menu? Lola's stomach growled. She needed to get the salt water off her skin and hair before dinner. She grabbed her mug, stuffed the invitation into the pocket of her leopard cover up, and headed for the shower.

~*~

Packed with every self-serving merchant in Summerville, the community center room was so hot and the air so charged, it felt as if a thunderstorm would break at any moment. First dabbing at the sweat dripping into his eyes with a monogrammed hankie, then removing his expensive tailored suit jacket, Richard, aka Dickhead, Heade blathered on.

"And as you can see from this diagram, the band will be on the stage, facing the head table," Chief of Police Heade paused in his Power Point presentation. "Get it? Head table?"

A few suck-ups snickered; one woman, who laughed like a chicken, clucked along with them.

Dick's shoulders shook with laughter. "Ahh, I kill myself."

Webster Bond covered his face with his hands and moaned. If he had to sit through one more of these reunion planning meetings he'd eat his sidearm. Thank God, the nightmare would be over in ten days.

"You got a problem, Dweebster?" Dickhead's whine had all the charm of a droning buzz saw.

Web leaned back in his chair and crossed his arms over his chest. "Oh, no, I *love* going through the same slide show over and over *and over* again, all for a frigging high school reunion. The only thing we're missing, Chief, is the picture of you in your *awesome* 1985 mullet."

Chicken woman commenced clucking and the snickering grew to roars of guffaws.

Heade's cheeks reddened. "So, do you believe you're too *good* for this committee, Dweebster?"

"It seems to me, the SPD has matters that should take a higher priority, like aliens slipping over the border from Canada."

"Trafficking of illegals belongs to ICE, not SPD."

"So as the Chief of SPD, that's your *official* position?" Web tilted back, lifting the front feet of his chair off the floor. "Seems to me, we just got a BOLO for a delivery of Chinese packed in hidden compartments in cement freighters out of Toronto."

As Heade's face flushed a deeper shade of red, he strode to Web's chair, reached out and gave it a yank. Web leaped to his feet just in time to avoid toppling to the floor. Under his breath, Heade murmured something for Web's ears only. "You'll pay for that, Bond."

Web stared at him. On any day, Chief of Police Heade was a manipulative charmer, especially for the public. This display of teenage crapola went outside the box. *What's going on here?*

He flipped into cop mode, conducting an almost instantaneous visual assessment. Bloodshot eyes, dilated pupils and hand tremors. A runny nose?

Oh shit. This was worse than Web originally thought. He kept his hands at his sides, not moving a muscle. If he flinched, the former school yard bully—now town bully, would win. The room went silent, including chicken woman.

"I'm not one of your rookies," he retorted, "scared of their own shadows. Go back to what you do best—blowing hot air."

Dickhead's eyes bulged; a slow trickle of blood oozed from one nostril. Very smoothly, he lifted the silk handkerchief from his vest pocket and covered the end of his beaked nose. Just then, his over-dressed, over-endowed wife stepped between them.

"Boys, for God's sake." As Dick continued to dab at his nostrils, Beth Heade yanked at her husband's arm. "We have more important things to work on than some juvenile pissing contest."

Heade lowered his fist and allowed himself to be led away, all the while glaring at Web. "I'll make sure you're on the night shift the rest of your life, Dweebster."

Web shrugged. There were worse things in life—like being married to Dick Heade, for one. He sat down and listened to Beth pick up where her husband left off, her high-pitched voice artificially cheerful, as if she was on the Home Shopping Network hawking a particularly garish lot of jewelry.

"Okay, then," Beth pointed the remote control and clicked to the next slide, showing downtown Summerville. "It is going to be *very* busy time. Between the reunion and the Arts Festival, every hotel room in town and in the neighboring villages are booked. This is a great opportunity for homeowners to rent out rooms to our visitors."

The next slide showed Beth's downtown real estate office. Web assumed she couldn't resist the opportunity for a bit of shameless self-promotion

Despite the fact that their rival hogged the spotlight, two other local realtors, Susan Cloutier and Sam Kruger, seemed unperturbed by Beth's hype. Web knew for a fact that many clients defected from Heade Real Estate when they grew tired of Dickhead's intrusions into his wife's business dealings. His overbearing boss just *had* to be in charge of everything and everyone in his realm.

"As always, I'm *happy* to help with rental agreements," Beth announced. "Let's not forget that in addition to catching up with our old or shall we say, *mature* colleagues, we have a wonderful marketing opportunity for Summerville. Some folks might decide they want to move back here to be among their friends."

A photo of sail boats gliding across the white capped surface of Lake Ontario came up on screen. "Or they might want a summer home." Beth flipped to a photo of a brick town home on Lake Shore Boulevard. Thanks to the wonders of cosmetic surgery, the perpetual look of false surprise on her face grew to clown-like proportions. "We have *everything* here in Summerville!"

Web couldn't decide which was more annoying. Dick's nasal annoying bombast ego driven dribble, or Beth with her incessant chirping. If it hadn't been for his mother, Web would have escaped from this boring little burg a long time ago, and moved on to more exciting places where he could make a difference, instead of spending weekends arresting underage drinkers at the U.

The death of his father in a car crash when Web was sixteen sealed his fate. He stayed in Summerville to become his mother's scrawny, but determined protector. Her slow descent into Alzheimer's Disease, turned his role into a permanent one.

His mind drifted back to those dreadful adolescent years when, all arms and legs, he was known as the Dweebster. He'd spent a lot of time stuffed into hall lockers by his constant tormentor, the same back then as now, Dick Heade. The only good thing that ever came out of it was meeting Lola Getz the day she opened her locker and he fell out—right on top of her luscious curves.

They both went down, him flailing, her squealing. Then, she'd dissolved into laughter. He'd been mortified, but would never forget what she said after they finally got back to their feet and he told her his name.

"Webster Bond."

"Hmm. Stirred but not shaken. I like that in a man."

Her Mexican accent sent a thrill down his spine and elsewhere. Thankfully, the class bell rang before he could say anything terminally stupid.

After high school, with no money for an out of town, much less out of state university, Web enrolled at Summerville University. Knowing he wanted to get into the police academy, his Criminal Justice Studies advisor took him under his wing to mentor him. Over time, with the help of the professor, puberty, and pumping iron, Web morphed from a scrawny kid into a lean, mean muscle machine.

From that point onward, women fell over themselves to get him into bed. He'd even been told by the same professor, still his mentor, the local co-eds had a running contest to see who could get arrested by the 'hunky cop'.

He came back to the present and tried to focus on a new slide, allegedly of Doogan's Pub, but with the Heade Real Estate sign clearly visible next door. Talk about shameless self promotion. He closed his eyes and wondered if the years had been kind to Lola, or if she'd turned into someone like the overly surgerized Beth.

Web shook his head to clear his mind of the revolting image of Lola with artificial body parts. The *only* person he was remotely interested in reconnecting with from that era probably didn't even remember him. Besides, after what happened to her, he doubted she'd ever want to see Summerville again.

CHAPTER TWO
~*~

Ravenous, Lola slipped into a plush terrycloth robe and wrapped a towel around her thick hair. She couldn't wait to sink her teeth into that chicken mole. It had been calling her name for the last thirty minutes. She slid into a pair of flip flops and flapped her way to the kitchen, the tantalizing aromas growing stronger with each step.

"Flora?"

She pushed the swinging door inward and paused to admire the room. Aside from the minor work she'd had done on her studio behind the house, the kitchen had been the last renovation on the old *casa* before her husband's death. Outrageously non-Mexican, its white tile floors, black granite counters dotted with opal inclusions and white cabinets with glass fronts gave the room a clean, modern look.

Lola's marketplace paintings, much sought after in the United States and elsewhere, imbued the space with splashes of color and contrasted past with present. Mexico, with all its turmoil, crime and corruption was still a beautiful country replete with the contradictions of modern day life and a foundation of ancient civilizations that still could be seen in the faces of the common people.

A covered dish sat on the stove; the table was set for one. A glass of red wine awaited her, along with a note. She opened it. Large block letters spelled out "LO SIENTO. FLORA." How odd. Flora *never* left notes. Lola had no idea the woman could even read or write.

What the hell was going on?

She looked out the kitchen door, searching for the telltale glow of the night watchman's cigarette. *Nada.* She ran to each exit, trying to find signs of the usual cadre of gunslingers assigned to stand at each of her entryways.

Nada, nada and nada.

Panic bubbled through her chest. She ran to her bedroom, locked the door behind her, and picked up the house phone.

It was dead.

Her cell phone wasn't safe. Izzy had told her that anyone with a Bluetooth headset and a computer could listen in on her conversations, worse yet, they could track her movements using the GPS in her own phone. She grabbed the 'go bag' from the closet shelf, threw in the leopard cover for sleeping, tossed the throw-away phone into her large purse, and opened the hidden wall safe. Stacks of US currency and jewelry went into her bag next, along with passports from two different countries. She hesitated for a moment when she reached for the next item.

She wouldn't get across the border if she took it with her. On the other hand, there was a good chance she wouldn't make it out of the compound if she *didn't.*

Lola took a deep breath. Enough waffling. Her life was in danger.

She grabbed two boxes of ammo and the Glock. Good thing she'd practiced with it during the last weeks. She might just need to kill a few *coyotes.*

~*~

After the room emptied, Web collapsed the folding chairs and placed them into stacks along the beige cinder block walls. With a little paint and care, the community center could be transformed into a real community jail. *Yeah. That's the ticket.* He chuckled, then Beth Heade's chirpy voice broke into his thoughts.

"What's so funny?" She stood with her fist on one hip, her head cocked at a bird-like angle.

Web shook his head. "Nothing you'd want to hear."

She sighed as a curtain of blonde hair fell across her eyes. "Honestly, don't you think it's time you guys buried the hatchet?"

Oh, yeah. He was willing to bury it. Right into Dick's head. He cleared his throat. "Let the record show I did not lift a hand against your husband."

"No, but you deliberately provoked him. You know better. He has a short fuse, and you lit it."

Web glanced around the dingy space. It was just Beth and him now. Time for a private conversation. "No, he was lit before he came to the meeting."

Her head snapped back and she glared at him, all signs of friendliness gone into the blue permafrost of her eyes. "How dare you?"

"I dare, because I'm the adult child of an alcoholic. All you're doing is enabling him with cover ups and denial, Beth. You have to open your eyes."

She wrapped her arms around her super-sized chest. "He's just a heavy drinker. Like his dad."

"Yeah. Just like his dad's drinking buddy, *my* dad. Except my dad drank and died in a car crash. Thank God he didn't kill anyone else, but my mother and I are still paying for it. You should be thinking about the consequences for your family."

Her eyes glittered with tears. "We don't have any kids— you know that."

"Kids or no kids, you owe it to yourself to get help…get him help and we're not talking about alcohol, are we? I think he's into coke."

Beth's gaze darted around the room. "He's not an *addict.* He just uses it *recreationally.*"

Web opened his mouth to respond, only to be interrupted by Dick's bellow. "Beth, where the hell are you?"

Dick charged into the room, his custom-made suit looking uncommonly wrinkled. "What's taking you so long?"

Beth grabbed her bag and a stack of handouts. "I'm all set. Why don't I drive home?"

Dick turned and glared at Web. "What've you been saying to my wife?"

Web didn't respond.

"Okay, Dweebster. That's it." Heade put his arm across Beth's shoulder. "I'm making sure you're on night shift for the next month. Your job will be to patrol all of Summerville, keeping our streets safe for the Class of 1985. No Eastman Awards dinner, no dinner dance with the Harbor Lights, but look at the bright side. You *might* make it to the baseball game."

"I have seniority. I'll be talking to my union rep."

Heade placed a hand on his chest and feigned a look of surprise. "You do that, and I'll just have to declare a state of emergency, what with all the mobs of folks coming into town with Art Fest."

"That seems a bit over the top, even for you, Dickie."

"Did I do that?" Heade snickered. "Let's go home, Beth. I have big day tomorrow."

Waiting until he was certain to be alone, Web slammed a chair against the wall. Now he wouldn't even have a chance to see if Lola showed up for old times' sake.

~*~

Lola made one more trip into the house from the garage. Her hair still damp, clothes stuck to her wet skin and the gun irritated the hell out of her lower back. How did gangsters keep the stupid things jammed into their waistbands? She loaded a cooler with ice, cold drinks and the chicken mole that she absolutely refused to leave behind. There were limits, after all. And she was *starving*.

The lights went out.

Praying and moving as fast as she dared, she felt her way along the walls, silently cursing her choice in building materials when she bumped into the corner of a granite counter.

Breathless and hands shaking, she found her way into the garage, then to the car. She fumbled miserably to get the key in the ignition and waited for the propane generator to kick in, so she could open the garage door.

Nothing. Had they shut off the gas line?

She called on all the saints she could remember.

She heard a loud thump and the lights came back on. Lola hit the remote and the garage door began to rise in slow motion. She bit her lower lip, drawing blood.

Vamos. Madre de Dios, vamos!

She heard men shouting and saw small flashes of light.

"Ooh, *mierda!*"

She floored the gas pedal and the armored Hummer flew out, the roof rack scraping the door with a shriek. The sounds of fire crackers followed, pinging the car. Tires squealed and dark forms leaped out of her path. If she could make it to the border into the US, she *might* avoid being kidnapped—or worse. Just as she thought she was clear of obstructions in the driveway, a boom rattled the windows of the car and a burst of light erupted in her rear view mirror.

~*~

Web sat in his mother's room at the Victorian style assisted living facility and played with the remote control for the television. "What would you like to watch, Mom?"

"Is that you, Webster? When did you get here?"

"An hour ago, Mom." He sighed. It was the same thing with every visit. "How about the news?"

"Your father said he'd be coming in from the garden soon. Go get your dad, tell him to wash up for dinner."

"We had dinner, Mom."

"We did?"

"Yes, chicken and green beans. Very tasty."

"I used your grandmother's secret recipe." She waved at him to come closer and whispered. "It's the cinnamon. Don't tell anyone I told you."

"My lips are sealed." He pretended to lock his lips with a key. "Our secret."

"Time for sleep, Webster. It's a school night. You have to be up early if you want to catch a ride with me."

He shook his head, sighed and stood. "Get some rest. Don't stay up all night watching TV."

"Pshaw! That's your dad. He loves all the old movies." She pointed at her cheek. "Now, give me a kiss and run along to bed."

"Yes, ma'am."

"That's a good boy." She looked up and her tone shifted. "Whatever happened to that Lola gal, the one you had the crush on?"

Startled, Web stepped back a pace. "What's that, Mom?"

A vacant expression came over her face. "Good night, dear. I love you, too."

What on earth had made his mother ask about Lola? And how did she know that he'd had such a major crush on the girl? Sure, Mom had been the Secretary for the Counseling Department back in the day, but he could have sworn he'd kept that secret to himself. He shook his head. Even though she was demented, his mother was still able to spook him.

Lost in thought, Web closed the door, strolled past the nursing station and said goodnight to the African American woman at the desk.

Beverly gave him a warm smile. "Will I see you the same time tomorrow?"

"It's a date. But I've got to be at work by ten-thirty, so don't you even think of trying to get me liquored up."

She giggled. "Go make Summerville safe."

"You been talking to my boss?"

He heard her giggles all the way out into the parking lot.

Dickhead was driving everyone crazy. He'd even posted a countdown calendar in the station. "*Only Five More Days!*" one sign proclaimed while another read, "*Keep Summerville Safe!*"

With the U on summer break, incidents of underage drinking were way down, and not a single unexplained Chinese person had arrived under cover of night, except for the occasional guy delivering take-out. If the little burg got any safer, it might as well be a morgue. He yawned and glanced at his watch. He had just enough time to grab a cup of coffee, before he reported in for another mind-numbing night at work. Maybe it was time to put in for a lateral transfer to the Staties. Perhaps Rory McDaniel had spots open in the County Sheriff's Department.

~*~

On the seventh morning, there still was no rest for Lola. She rolled over in the no tell motel's rickety bed and tried to remember where she was, and what day it was. Picking up the disposable phone, she couldn't believe so many days had passed. Her mind still reeled in disbelief and shock from the whole chain of events.

From the narrow escape and harrowing drive down the Mexican mountain side, to driving straight through for forty-eight hours, fueled on Flora's chicken mole, coffee, and pure, unadulterated fear.

When she caught herself nodding off and driving on the shoulders of the highway, she pulled the Hummer behind a sleazy motel and checked in. Twelve hours later, she hit the road again, not stopping until after dark to check into a series of roach ridden rooms. Just one more day, one more leg of the trip and she'd be at the safe house.

The phone buzzed, jangling her nerves and shocking her into hyper vigilance. She didn't recognize the number. It stopped buzzing. Then a text popped up:

Call # on your phone.

Izzy.

Lola's hands shook as she hit the call-back button, then almost cried with relief when she heard the familiar voice. "Izzy! What's going on?"

Her cousin's husky voice rumbled in her ear. "Inside job. Your maid set you up. Someone must have made her an offer she couldn't refuse."

"No! That can't be." Her stomach knotted. "Flora's been with my family, since I was a child. She was my rock when Rico was killed."

"Rock or no, she's definitely the one who told the guards she saw lights in the hills. Classic diversionary tactic."

"All the shooting? The flashes?"

"My guys returned just in time to see you flying down the mountain in your Hummer. They tossed in a flash bang, so you could get away," Izzy paused. "I lost a couple good men, but we returned the favor and captured some of theirs. Extracted information out of them the old-fashioned way."

Lola didn't want to know what that meant.

"They definitely said Flora?"

"The guy wasn't talking too well at that point, but yeah, he said, *Vieja*. The old lady."

Lola swallowed hard. "Any idea who she was working for?"

"Someone big enough to have the *cojones* to try to take me on." Izzy snickered. "I'm looking forward to cutting them off."

"Jesus." As Lola sank back on the creaking bed, the room began to spin. She closed her eyes and the open envelope with chocolate finger prints danced before her, taunting her.

The chicken mole. *Mierda. How could she have been so stupid?*

Lola took a shaky breath. "What about—about Flora?"

"In the wind. Her, I'm not worried about. It's the guy she was working for that has me concerned. You could have a tail, someone looking to make some money on you."

Lola felt as if she was going to be sick. "What should I do?"

"Get out of harm's way."

"The safe house?"

"Go there, get what you need, but do *not* stay there. Flora was in your house twenty-four/seven and could have found your instructions. Go somewhere *you* can blend in, where an outsider will stick out like a sore thumb."

Feeling uneasy, Lola glanced around the room, checking the curtains and the chain on the door. Her gaze fell on the chipped Formica coffee table, reminding her of her front hall table in her home, and the invitation that arrived seven days ago. "I have an idea."

"Don't tell me. I don't want to know."

"Izzy, I really owe you."

"Family sticks together. Get going. Find someplace safe."

Lola jumped up and threw her belongings into her bag. A high school reunion in Summerville. What could be safer than that?

CHAPTER THREE
~*~

On the Thursday before the reunion, Web sat in his cruiser on a side street, radar gun pointed toward Lakeshore Boulevard. The Art Festival crowd, nicely tucked in bed at this hour, was pretty tame. So far, the biggest news this week came out of one of his fellow officers arresting two septuagenarians for smoking pot. Rumor had it the administrative judge could barely keep a straight face during the proceedings and released the gomers on their own recognizance.

Now *that* would have made a nice human interest piece for the *Summerville Gazette,* but he doubted it would ever surface. The pristine image of Summerville had to be maintained, at all costs.

Web sipped his third coffee of the night and tried to think about what he had to do the next day.

Sleep.

Shower.

Clean the house.

Pick up some food and wine.

Visit Mom.

Go back to work on the graveyard shift.

He groaned. He had to *do* something, *change* something or he'd turn into a lush like his Dad—or worse. He'd almost gotten married once, until his footloose bride-to-be realized he would never abandon his mother. She took off with a long-distance truck driver and left a note saying she was going to be "Queen of the Road." He shook his head. He hoped she was happy in her mobile sovereign nation. She just never got that above all, family sticks together.

A black Lexus drove past his hiding place going five miles *below* the posted speed limit. Web's pulse quickened and his mind switched into full alert. He tossed his iced coffee out the window and put the cruiser into gear. At two in the morning, going under the speed limit could be a sign of a drunk driver—or a careful coyote. With the largest trunk space in a luxury car, that Lexus could hold at least two, maybe three illegals, if they were small.

He pulled onto the road behind the vehicle and noted a busted tail light. *Excellent.* He turned on his overhead lights, automatically activating the video camera mounted over the dash. A small pang of disappointment coursed through him when the car immediately pulled over to the shoulder at the first blink of his strobe lights. He'd been half-hoping for a chase.

He assessed the situation as he approached the car, considered calling in for back-up, but decided he wasn't in the mood for Dickhead's nasal whine of, "What's wrong, Dweebster? Afraid some little old lady's going to pull a gun on you?"

The tinted windows on the Lexus offered no sense of the driver; all he saw was a dark shape moving within. He tapped on the window with the butt of his Maglite. The window slid down in slow motion.

Well, Dickie *would* have had a heyday. It *was* a woman.

Beneath a baseball cap, black hair cascaded down her back; she made no effort to brush long bangs away from her eyes. "What is the problem, Officer?"

Her husky voice sent a frisson down his spine. She sounded familiar. He had to be so buzzed on caffeine and adrenaline that his mind was playing tricks on him. *Focus.* "Please step out of the car."

"What is wrong?"

She had a slight accent. One he couldn't place.

She *had* to be a trafficker.

He stepped back and turned his body at an angle, his sidearm *away* from the driver. "Just step out of the car, please. Now."

The woman scrambled at the door, then slid out. She was dressed completely in black. Black baseball cap pulled down over her face, black slacks, and blouse. Hell, even her flip flops were black.

In the summer. *Yeah, that's normal.*

"License and registration."

She reached into the pocket of her jeans and extracted both, as if she'd known she'd get pulled over.

He glanced at them briefly. Lara Spencer of Baltimore, Maryland. For all he knew, the documents were phony. He held onto them and motioned toward the back of the car.

She hesitated.

He stepped back a pace and gripped his sidearm in case she made a lunge for him. Instead, she shook her head, sighed and flapped to the back of the car.

Nerves tingling, sweat running down his back, he knew this was the break he'd been looking for. "Your tail light's out."

The woman stared at the light and her shoulders slumped.

Guilty as hell. "Open the trunk." His heart trip hammered and his hands shook.

Using the key fob, she popped the trunk.

He swept the dark space with his flash light.

An overnight suitcase and nothing more. He ground his teeth in frustration. *Something was off.*

"Ms. Spencer, what are you doing out at this hour? And where are you going?"

The flash of surprise crossing her lovely features sent an immediate jolt from his head to the toes of his boots.

"Webster? Webster Bond? Is that *you*?"

~*~

Strung out on caffeine, adrenaline and energy drinks, Lola's stomach had dropped at the sight of the police lights, a Pavlovian response to all the bad experiences she'd had with the corrupt cops in Mexico, including the ones she'd had to bribe at the border. From the moment she saw the cruiser in her rear view mirror, she thought she was going to be pulled over and gunned down. When he made her open the trunk, all she could think of was that this was the kidnapper she'd eluded for over a week—only to be caught by him in the safe, sleepy town of Summerville, New York.

Paranoia alarms screaming and jangling all fingers and toes, she almost cried with relief when she recognized him. "Webster! Oh, my God, it's so *good* to see you." She sagged against the armored Lexus, fatigue weighing down every muscle.

Web shone the light onto her face briefly, then lowered it. "Lola Getz?"

He sounded a little short of breath.

No, don't be ridiculous. She was hearing her own breathing, raspy and hard in her ears, as if she'd been running a marathon. "Webster Bond. The years have been *very* good to you."

What happened to that skinny boy who fell on top of her twenty-five years ago? This muscled hunk bore almost no resemblance to the Dweebster, except his eyes were still kind and he still had that adorable dimple. When he smiled. Like now.

His grin faded. "What's with the Lara Spencer ID?"

"I changed my name."

His eyebrows shot up.

"Legally. A Long story." She yawned. "I'd really like to get to bed. Am I under arrest?"

"No, you're free to go, but there are no hotels or B and B's available."

"The reunion is *that* big a deal?"

Web shook his head. "The Arts Festival. It's a three week event. People come from all over the country."

Mierda. So much for going someplace to blend in, where an outsider would stick out like a sore thumb. The place was *crawling* with out-of-towners. Not to mention the fact that one of the myriad of gallery owners who came to her studio to purchase her art might be in the crowd and recognize her. *Dos mierdas.* Exhausted, near tears, she didn't think she could drive much further.

The lights from the cruiser strobed across Web's face. When did he get that scar on his cheek? He looked so rugged. Tough. Like someone who could protect her. If she told him the truth, would he believe her? Would he help her?

After twenty-five years, they were really complete strangers to each other. Why should he believe her? And why should she trust him?

"What should I do? I can't sleep in my car." She could, and had, but it wasn't safe. Not now.

Web nodded. "You'll be picked up for vagrancy." He paused a long moment and at last nodded. "I have a guest room. You're welcome to use it."

Relief washed over Lola. "No, I couldn't impose on you like that---"

"Honest, it's no imposition. I'm working the night shift and sleeping during the day. You won't even know I'm there."

Barely suppressing a sob, Lola threw her arms around Web and held him in a fierce hug. "Thank you, thank you." He smelled like coffee and a spicy aftershave. His shoulder muscles rippled beneath her fingers. "You're a life saver. You have no idea what this means to me."

Clearly flustered, Web stepped back, breaking the embrace. "I'll take you there now. Just follow me."

Lola watched him return to the cruiser, his stride almost military in its precision. When did he get to be so buff? In some ways, he reminded her of Rico. Like the way he smelled and her body's response when she hugged him, her nipples pebbling at the rub of the rough cloth of his shirt against her thin blouse. But this man, so serious, all business, did he ever laugh like her husband had? She needed some laughter in her life right now.

Or was that gone forever, too?

~*~

Web leaped into the cruiser. If Dickhead saw the footage, the conversation and the hug would be fodder for constant jabs. If *only* he could erase the memory chip. Well, the rules were the rules and a traffic stop meant the recording would be maintained for two years.

In his defense, he'd only done what Beth Heade suggested to the group: rent a room to a visitor. The fact that the visitor just *happened* to be an SHS alumna who caused palpitations and erections in every human, bearing an iota of testosterone in high school would be the *piece de resistance* in his passive war against Dickhead.

Web put the unit into gear and pulled in front of the Lexus. His house wasn't far from the Boulevard. As he passed the gazebo in Dentzel Gardens, he thought about all the fantasies he'd had in his youth about taking Lola there, kissing her and running his hands over her luscious curves while the lake lapped at the shore.

The sands of time had left few marks on Lola. When she hugged him, her breasts pushed hard into his chest and her hips molded themselves against his. Terrified of an instant erection, he'd almost shoved her away.

He put on his blinker and turned down a side street, away from the elite section of town, toward the modest subdivision where he'd grown up. Pulling alongside the curb, he waved Lola into his driveway.

He called in to dispatch. "Forty-three-H to Summerville. I'll be on a meal break at my home."

Lola climbed out of the car, stretched and looked around.

Half-embarrassed that he'd never moved out of his house, even when he'd been forced to place his wandering mother into a nursing facility, he hoped she wouldn't be dismayed or disgusted by his home.

She pulled the overnight bag out of the trunk of the Lexus and looked around at him. "Are you coming in?"

"Just for a bit."

A streetlight shone on the driveway, illuminating the hypnotic sway of Lola's hips as she strolled ahead of him, her sandals flapping against the soles of her feet. He was a man, not a saint. And the feelings she stirred up in him roared back at him, twenty-five years strong. Good thing, he was working the night shift. Otherwise, just being in a bed in the same *house* with her would be torture.

She hesitated at the steps. "You go first, yes?"

He nodded, plucked his house key out of the thick ring in his pocket, and turned the knob. "Welcome to my humble abode."

She entered the foyer and dropped her bag. "*Madre de Dios.* I've been here before."

His tongue cleaved to the roof of his mouth. "Wh-what?"

"*That* day, your mother—brought me here. I couldn't go to my host family. The husband, he was a minister. I didn't want to hear about God taking people to a better place. Your mother held me. I sobbed, screamed and shouted at God. She was so kind." She turned around, tears streaming down her face. "Web? Where is your mother?"

He sighed and pointed toward the kitchen. "Let me make a pot of coffee and tell you about her."

Over a cup of scalding *café con leche*, Web told Lola about his mother's decline into the twilight of Alzheimer's.

"It's sort of like watching re-runs. She's in the past, reliving each day from over thirty or forty years ago. I'm a little boy some days, my dad on others, and---" He flushed at his mother's question about his crush on none other than the woman sitting right here, right now, at his kitchen table.

Lola placed her hand on his. Nails bitten to the quick, her polish chipped, it was clear she hadn't been living the grand life of late. "I'm so sorry."

He looked into her eyes and was suddenly reminded of spring grass and flowers. The fine lines around her eyes told him that unlike Beth Heade, Lola's body had not been surgically altered. "Thank you. Maybe—" He stopped. What would she think of him?

"What? Tell me."

"Would you like to visit my mother tomorrow? She probably won't know you."

"I *want* to see her."

He shook his head. "On second thought, no, that's not fair. You're here to have fun, go to the reunion, party with the in-crowd."

"Party with the in-crowd?" She giggled, a youthful merry sound that brought him back to high school. "That's why you think I'm here?"

"Don't tell me you're here to relive our special moment?" At her quizzical look, he felt his face warm. "Me falling out of the locker on top of you?"

"Webster Bond. Stirred, not shaken." She burst out laughing and he joined in.

When was the last time he'd laughed in this house? Sitcoms didn't count as genuine mirth.

The timer on his cell phone buzzed. "Time to get back to work." He led her to the guest room, just down the hall from his. "Use whatever you want. The computer's in the den. Laundry room is off the kitchen. Sorry, the house is a mess. I planned to clean tomorrow. Eat, drink whatever you can find. The grocery store was on my list of things to do, too. Here's a spare key for the house." He handed her a

Cougar key chain, a leftover from high school. "My shift ends at seven-thirty. I'll see you then."

She stood in the doorway to her room. "Web?"

"Yes?"

"Thank you. You have *no* idea how much this means to me." Two steps and she was at his side, up on her tiptoes, giving him a kiss on the cheek. "I look forward to seeing you tomorrow. Stay safe."

A question niggled at the back of his mind. "Can you tell me about your name change?"

"Tomorrow, I promise."

CHAPTER FOUR
~*~

Lola waited until she heard the squad car pull away, then raced down the hall to the computer. She shot an email to her cousin, letting her know she was safe without giving her whereabouts. Still wired, she surfed the Internet for information about the Mexican drug cartels and found an article in the *New Yorker* by William Finnegan, "Silver or Lead."

As she read, she berated herself for enjoying the lifestyle the gangsters had given her through her husband's *legitimate* business. She could no longer pretend that her life was not connected to these thugs and that being a famous artist allowed her to turn a blind eye to the war going on in her country. Her head-in-the-sand approach to life in Chihuahua had been a façade, until Rico's death. It was time to pay attention—or die.

She studied the article. In the west of Mexico, Finnegan wrote, the Sinaloa cartel ruled, while the east coast was run by the Gulf cartel. Oozing between these territories were the Beltran Levya, *La Familia* and Zetas. The profit from organized and brutal crime wove across countries and around the world, all the way to Italy's mafia.

Under two Presidents, the US had clamped down the borders, but the American appetite for drugs and the willingness of the cartels to feed this appetite, meant extraordinary measures would be needed to defeat these crime lords who had become folk heroes among poor and disenfranchised Mexican youth.

Despite a fondness for 'corpse messaging' *La Familia* made explicit statements that they *never* hurt women. Okay. That ruled them out. But according to a *New York Times* article, the other cartels did not seem to have such a code of honor, one even threw children of a rival cartel, off a bridge. Several fought with each other over turf for setting up cottage industries to manufacture *cristal* or methamphetamine.

But at this point in time, with the exception of *La Familia*, it appeared that all of the other cartels were happy to use the kidnapping and ransom signature. If a family couldn't raise the ransom money, the loved one was never seen again. Cousin Izzy wouldn't let that happen. And what if Flora had hired a drug lord wannabe, a young man with no morals, a lot of ambition, and a posse of eager thugs-in-waiting? Lola hoped it wasn't one who would kidnap, rape, torture, maim— and then *finally* kill you.

She erased her browsing history, shut down the computer and headed for the bedroom. Four in the morning. She had to get some rest, but couldn't stand the thought of one more night in that leopard print cover-up. Tomorrow she'd do laundry, eat without bolting her food, and take a long bubble bath. Right now, the pillows beckoned to her. Praying she wouldn't have nightmares, she peeled off her sweaty clothes and fell into bed naked.

~*~

Simultaneously exhausted and exhilarated, Web ended his shift with no further incidents. The formerly boring Summerville seemed to twinkle in the early sunlight, a jewel along the shore of Lake Ontario. Whistling, he stopped at a convenience store, picked up eggs, bread, bacon and milk for breakfast and, on a whim, grabbed a *Gazette* which ran a '*Remember Them?*' column in honor of the reunion. He wondered if they had a photo of Dickhead in his mullet. Web would have paid double for that issue.

When he placed the pile of purchases on the counter, Bob, the gray-haired store owner, gave him a puzzled look. "What's up with you?"

Web stopped whistling. "What's that supposed to mean?"

"This is you, normal." Bob made a poker face and nodded. "This is you, today." The man grinned from ear to ear and waved his hands. "Not to put too fine a point on it, it looks like you got laid last night."

"Well," Web laughed. "Wouldn't you like to know?"

"Yes, I would."

"A gentleman never tells." Web began to whistle again, paid and waved good-bye. He jumped into his Chevy pick-up and headed home. The old neighborhood had never looked so good.

Juggling bags of groceries, he let himself into the house, and winced. Dishes were piled up in the sink, laundry sat in mountains by the washing machine and he thought he saw a herd of dust bunnies hop by. Sleep first, then clean. Shoes off, Web tiptoed down the hall and froze.

The door to the guest room was wide open and Lola lay on her back, her arms above her head. A sheet covered her breasts—just barely. Unconsciously, his feet took him in the direction of the object of his instant arousal. She sighed and rolled over. He pulled the door closed and headed for a cold shower, and tried not to think about his lips on her breasts.

~*~

Lola waited a few moments after the door closed, then sat up. He had passed the first test with flying colors. If he could resist coming into her room with *that* kind of invitation, Web must be the only man she'd ever met who didn't need to have a gun pointed at him to keep his hands off her tits. *A man of honor. What was the world coming to?*

She heard the shower running and for a split second imagined joining him. Would he be shocked? What did he look like naked? She closed her eyes and thought of water and soap bubbles coursing down his back, to his tight—the water stopped running. He took quick showers. Lola shook her head and sighed. A year without sex had made her horny. She flopped back on the bed and fell into a deep sleep.

She was running, trying to escape from an army of shouting men and barking dogs. They were closer, she heard the roar of a jeep coming over a rise, closing in. She took cover behind a pile of boulders, but the man in the jeep found her. She fell to her knees, weeping as he brandished a machete. As the blade fell, he shouted, "Vieja sent me!"

She screamed,

And found herself in Web's arms, his kind brown eyes filled with concern. "Wake up."

"What?"

"You were screaming, 'Not my hands'." He pulled the sheet up over her shoulders and stood. "Was it only a nightmare? Or is someone really after you?"

She sighed. He had passed the first test of her trust. But was she really ready to tell him the whole story? Would he blame her? Or help her?

"A nightmare. Nothing more."

"You seemed pretty terrified."

She tried to laugh. "It was a very real dream." She glanced up at Web. He was fully dressed, but not in uniform. His jeans hugged him in all the right places and his polo shirt revealed a modest amount of chest hair, not shaved like a younger man's style, but in keeping with his age. She liked that. "What time is it?"

"Noon. I thought you needed to sleep." His brow furrowed. "Sure, you're okay?"

"Yes, yes. Absolutely, and starving. Is that bacon I smell?"

He smiled. "The house specialty: coffee, bacon, eggs and toast. Why don't you grab a shower, get dressed, and I'll give you a great home cooked meal."

She wrapped the sheet around her like a toga. "My clothes are filthy. I can't stand the idea of putting them on.

Can I borrow a tee shirt maybe and some shorts? And do a load of laundry?"

His eyes seemed to glaze and he licked his lips. "You got it." He left the room for a few minutes and returned, holding the requested items. "Here you go. I have no doubt they'll look better on you than on me."

"I think that depends on your point of view." She arched a brow at him. "I bet you look great in these."

Beet red, Web turned on his heel and closed the door behind him.

She sighed again. Damn, he was an honorable man. She was really getting to like him *and* she liked making him blush.

~*~

Over a third cup of coffee, while Lola's clothes rolled around in the dryer, Web tried his question again. "Why the name change?"

She put down her mug and raised her hands. "See these?"

He nodded, puzzled.

"These are insured by Lloyd's of London." She sat back and eyed him.

"I'll bite. Why?"

"The name Lara Spencer doesn't ring any bells for you?"

"None."

She stood, shoved a damp curl behind her ear, and crooked her finger at him. "Follow me."

Anywhere. And she really *did* look hot in his boxer shorts and wife beater shirt. Web stood behind her as she sat at his computer, shaking his head to clear the fog of lust.

Lola entered Lara Spencer into the search engine and ten-thousand websites popped up—all with photos of a blonde who looked not at all like Lola.

"*Mierda.* I forgot about her." She refined the search to Lara Spencer, artist. The page populated with hundreds of art galleries and snap shots of colorful work. "There. That's me."

Web leaned over her shoulder and tapped a particularly intriguing photo. The touch sensitive monitor enlarged the picture. "That is stunning. Yours?"

"Yes. Years ago, I began with street scenes, marketplaces, and the like. When I started experimenting with abstract interpretations of the same scenes? Well, things got *un poco loco.* Art critics called me 'a female Leonardo Nierman.'"

"And the crazies started coming out of the woodwork?"

"You could say that. My agent thought I was *loco* to change my name, but I needed my privacy, or I couldn't work."

"What about the IDs? Are they legit?"

"Very. I was born in Texas, my mother was visiting relatives and I arrived a month early. I have dual citizenship. My Baltimore house is the address I use for my fans. The US mail is much more trustworthy than the Mexican post office." She grimaced. "In my little village, I must pay the postmaster to *not* open my mail. Fat lot of good—" She stopped. "Anyway, I go to Maryland when I need some space."

He leaned over her shoulder again, ostensibly to tap another picture, but really to inhale her floral scent, and sneak a peek down her tee. He was human, after all.

She leaned her head back into his chest and closed her eyes. "You're a good man, Web. I wish I'd gotten to know you better in high school."

He placed a tentative hand on her shoulder, willing it to stay there and not to head south. "We have all the time in the world to get to know each other, unless you're already taken?"

Her shoulders shook and huge tears ran down her cheeks.

Web pulled away as if burnt and he stepped out of her personal space. "I'm sorry. I didn't mean to upset you."

She wiped her face with her palms. "I lost my husband a year ago today. He was riding his Harley, someone ran him off the road." Her shoulders hitched and a little sob escaped her lips. "The police told me there was nothing I could do. No witnesses."

The dryer buzzed and a clock ticked loudly in the office. Her artwork blazed on the computer screen, mute testimony to her enormous talents. Web didn't know what to say. Her grief was palpable and now he felt like a horned toad. Only a perve would even think of taking advantage of this stunning widow.

Without warning, Lola leaped to her feet and threw her arms around him. She kissed him hard and full on the lips. He pulled back, stunned by the intensity of her passion, and fearful that his response, already noticeable would be rejected when she regained her senses.

"Make love to me. Right, now," she whispered hoarsely,

All at once it seemed like the air had been sucked out of the room. Rooted to the floor, he could only shake his head in dismay. "No, not now. It's not right."

"I've been alone for a year, with no one to hold me." She wept harder. "I'm so lonely."

He carefully put his arms around her, and gave her a hug. "You're having an anniversary reaction, it's completely normal."

Her response was to bury her face in his chest and cry harder.

"You're vulnerable now. You'd hate me for taking advantage of you," he paused. "If and when we do make love, I want it to be because you want me. Not because you're missing your husband."

She raised her head, and despite her eyes being puffy from crying, she was *still* stunning. Always would be in his eyes.

"You are the most honorable man I have ever met." She patted his chest. "Thank you—for saving me from myself."

He gave her forehead a chaste peck. "Get dressed. We're going out."

She gave off a deer in headlights look. "Where? Why?"

What was she so afraid of? There had to be more to this than just bad dreams. Something wasn't adding up.

"We're going to go see an old friend. My mother."

"Oh." She smiled and let out a long, slow breath. "Family first?"

"Always."

CHAPTER FIVE

~*~

Bouncing along in Web's truck, Lola tried to recall the Summerville from twenty-five years ago, but came up short. The shoreline was the same, but the houses, once run-down, had been yuppified and the business district was beyond quaint. It looked like a real estate brochure.

"I forgot about the Arts Festival," he muttered. "This is taking twice as long to get to Summerville Cove, my mother's nursing home."

As if to underscore his point, a police officer blew his whistle, then stepped in front of Web's vehicle, so a throng of people could cross the street to get to the easel-lined sidewalks along the shoreline. He rolled his window down and waved at the cop. "Get a better whistle. That one's not loud enough."

The uniform laughed and waved Web along.

Lola shivered. "Friend?"

"Pretty much every cop on the SPD is a friend, except Richard Heade."

"*Madre de Dios!* Dickhead is still here?"

"Yup, and just as charming as he was in high school, married his high school sweetheart, Elizabeth Jayne Baumgartner. Now he's the Chief of Police." He pointed at Heade's storefront. "And she's into real estate."

"Ready Betty," Lola mused, and waved her hands as if she was holding pom-poms. "Always the cheerleader. Rah, rah and all that."

"She's still a cheerleader, but now she's urging people to buy houses, not win games. Careful, she doesn't corner you. She could talk the ear off an elephant."

"What about the others?"

"Lots of people never left Summerville." He turned into a tree lined driveway. "Some, because they wanted to stay and be big fish in a little pond. Others, like me, had family obligations." He parked the car in a shaded spot. "Now let's see if Mom remembers you—or me."

Beverly looked up in surprise when Web and Lola strolled in the door. "You're early."

"Brought a friend." He signed the visitor sheet and introduced the two women.

Beverly gave Lola the once over, her eyes shrewd, as if she could see into Lola's soul. She seemed to approve of Web's choice of friends, when at last she smiled.

"Mrs. Bond loves visitors, but she was pretty fuzzy this morning. Kept trying to wander past the alarm, saying she had to get back to work at the school." Beverly shook her head. "She kept me pretty busy. I think she got tired out, too. She's napping, but you can take a peek, see if she's up."

Lola marveled at the sterile white walls offset only by some bland paint-by-numbers mass-produced art pieces. If she lived in Summerville, she'd make sure this place had some *real* art, not this garbage. The décor was deadly boring. No *wonder* Web's mother kept trying to get out.

Web pushed the door open to a small, but well-kept room. "Well, look who's awake."

"Richard Heade, I *told* you not to come here without an appointment. The only juvenile delinquent I see right now is *you*. Honestly, don't you have homework to do?"

Lola and Web exchanged amused glances.

"Mom, it's me, Webster."

She reached over to her nightstand and put her glasses on. "Oh, heavens, I'm so sorry, dear. I can't believe I mistook you for that despicable Richard Heade. Loathsome toady."

Lola tried to suppress a giggle but failed.

"Who have you got with you, Webster? Come here young lady. Let me take a look at you."

Lola stepped from behind Web and stood beside his mother's bed. "Hello, Mrs. Bond. I don't know if you remember me."

Web's mother took Lola's hands into hers and stared at her for a long time. "Poor child. How will I tell her about the plane crash?"

Lola started, then looked to Web for help.

He raised his hands, palm up and shrugged.

"Poor Lola. All alone now. No parents. She even lost a sister."

"No, that's not right," Lola blurted. Even though she knew Mrs. Bond has Alzheimer's disease, she felt as if she had to get the record straight. "I never had a sister. I have no idea who that other person was on the plane."

The elderly woman stroked Lola's cheek. "There, there. In time you will heal. But today, it's okay for you to cry on my shoulder." Surprisingly strong, Mrs. Bond yanked Lola to her bosom and stroked the younger woman's back. "It's okay, let it all out. Just let it all out."

Twenty-five years of grief came roaring back into Lola's chest and cry she did. She sobbed until Web gently pulled her out of his mother's iron clutch.

Lola felt relieved when he took her elbow and led her to the door. Not only was it the anniversary of her husband's death, but now she was reliving her parent's death in their private plane crash the day they left Mexico to come to her high school graduation. *That terrible day.*

He went back to his mother's bedside. "Lola's had a tough day, Mom. I think I'll take her home now, okay?"

"Webster, you still have chores to do. Don't be late." A light seemed to dim in her eyes. "Tell your father to come in from the garden and wash his hands."

"Okay, Mom. I'll do that." He kissed her on the cheek. "Get some rest, okay?"

Just as Web was about to close his mother's door, the elderly woman called out, "Web? You take care and watch over Lola. She needs your help, her father was *not* a nice man."

Lola froze in place, her gaze locked onto Web's.

She walked back into Mrs. Bond's room, poised to ask her what she meant. But the old woman was already asleep and snoring. She bit her tongue to keep from cursing. *What did Web's mother know?*

She had never learned who the other person was on the plane in addition to her mother, father and the pilot. It was a woman, the police had said, but forensic investigations were rudimentary twenty-five years ago, and no further information had ever been forthcoming.

Plus, Izzy had insisted that the teenage Lola come live with her and forget about the crash, saying it was an accident, nothing more.

Had it really been an accident?

~*~

Web took Lola's hand and led her out to the car. She seemed dazed and he worried that she might wander off, like his mother. When he had her settled into the truck, he turned and said, "It's been a rough day for you. Let's get a bite to eat."

"I'm not hungry. And my clothes---"

"Well, I am, and I'd like some company while I eat. There's really cute place, very casual. Your jeans and tee shirt will be fine." He put the car in gear.

Lola stared out the window with glassy eyes.

He wanted to engage her in conversation, so he started with a softball question. "So, which name do you prefer me to call you?"

"Lola. Lara's for my art *persona*." She chewed on her lower lip. "I'm not feeling very artistic right now."

The crowd on Lakeshore Boulevard surged across the crosswalk, the police officer's whistle, shrieking at those cars trying to slide by.

Web turned in his seat and tried to make eye contact with the woman beside him. "Lola."

She glanced his way and their gazes locked.

"What's really going on?"

She shook her head and clenched her hands in her lap. "You wouldn't believe me, if I told you."

"Try me."

"No. Here in safe little Summerville, my story would make me seem more than *un poco loco*." She pursed her lips and stared out the side window. The conversation was over.

Through some miracle of timing, a mini-van pulled out of a parking place right in front of Sips Coffee Shop. Web searched his pockets for quarters, but stopped when he saw the parking meter had a bag over its head that read, "Free Parking for Art Fest."

Dickhead must be having fits over that. Heade looked forward to those end-of-the-month quotas and all the extra revenues heavy parking fines brought in to his piggy bank. To be fair, the levies did help to finance parking and road improvements, but it sure seemed like Dickhead owned more custom suits than the previous Chief.

Web shouldered his way through the jostling crowd, pulling Lola behind him. *Why was she being so secretive?*

A bell jangled as Web led Lola into Sips and Maggie LaMonica pointed to the only available table right by the window, facing Lakeshore Boulevard. Thinking she'd want to people watch, especially those who loved art, he moved the chair so she could have a better view. Instead, she turned the oak seat around, so she could face the restaurant.

Maggie stopped by the table and offered beverages and the special. "Art Fest salad, a colorful medley of local fresh spinach, strawberries and goat cheese, topped with a smattering of candied pecans, and dressed in a light mixture of balsamic vinegar. You can add grilled chicken, salmon, or shrimp for another five bucks."

Lola stared into space.

Web handed the menu back to Maggie. "Two iced teas, no sugar and two of the Art Fest salads with chicken. Thanks."

After Maggie left the table, Web grabbed Lola's hand. "I'm here for you. Ready to listen, when you're ready to tell me what happened."

A single tear coursed down Lola's cheek and she shook her head.

"Oh, my gawd! As I live and breathe, it's Lola Gomez with the Dweebster?"Beth Heade shrieked her way through the little shop to their table, only to grab Lola out of her chair and hug against her huge breasts. "I can't believe the invitation made it to you." Beth's tone of voice held a strong note of regret.

That it arrived, Web wondered, or that Lola had the nerve to accept it?

Lola flashed him a *Help Me* look.

"Lola's pretty tired from her drive, Beth. I'm sure she'll be glad to catch up with you later on. Maybe at the awards dinner?"

Beth gave him a piercing look. "That is a *black tie event*. We are filled." She focused on Lola again. "Sorry, honey, but the rules are the rules. We can't bend them even for *special* friends."

She tapped Web with a folded newspaper and said in a stage whisper, "A sworn officer of the court should be careful who he hangs out with." She dropped the *Gazette* in his lap and it flipped opened. He focused on the *Remember Them*, column which featured Lola and the story of her parents' fiery deaths.

"For God's sake, Beth. Lola is sitting right here. What is wrong with you?"

"We don't need *her* type here in Summerville."

Web jumped to his feet. "I never took you for a racist."

All heads in the restaurant turned in the direction of the argument. Web felt hundreds of eyes boring into his back.

"It's not about her being a Mexican," Beth mewled. "It's all her father, the head of a drug cartel. Who knows what she *really* does, who she *really* is? Read the article, Web. Ms. Lola has some 'splaining to do." And on that note, Beth turned on her heel and marched out the door.

Web wished for a bucket of water to throw on the witch.

Lola stood, glanced around the coffee shop at all the staring patrons and froze. A man in a baseball cap tipped his hat and returned her gaze with a smirk. Web wanted to punch the sneer off his face. The man threw a few bills down and sauntered out the front door.

Cringing, Lola pressed her face into Web's chest. "We need to leave. *Now.*"

Food untouched, he tossed money on the table and headed for the exit. Just as they were outside and away from prying eyes, Lola's phone buzzed. She yanked it out of her pocket and read a text message.

And fainted dead away into Web's arms.

CHAPTER SIX
~*~

Lola was aware of Web holding her hand before she even opened her eyes. *It couldn't be true. Her home—her studio. Torched? Everything destroyed.*

Someone pulled her eyelid back and shone a bright light. Right eye then the left eye. "Pupils equal and reactive."

She blinked and her tongue stuck to the roof of her mouth and finally, she freed it enough to speak. "Where am I?"

"Welcome back," a voice answered. "You're the guest of the Mynderse Memorial Hospital ER."

"I can pay my own way." She sat up and the room spun. "What do I owe you?"

Dr. Henry Cho gave her an odd look. "No one said anything about money."

She grabbed Web's arm. "Get me out of here. The longer I stay, the more danger—" *Mierda.*

Web looked at Dr. Cho. "Can you give me a minute, Hank?"

The white-coated physician nodded. "I'll just go check her lab values."

Lab values? She looked down. A piece of gauze was taped to her arm. *How had she not felt that?*

"Lola, look at me."

Her gaze met his and all she could think of, was how kind he'd been to her. He'd taken in a virtual stranger, and now she was bringing danger to his home. *It wasn't right.*

"I don't know what I was thinking. I should have never come to Summerville."

"Forget about Beth. She's an idiot. If we believed everything the *Gazette* published, then the Lake would have a

Loch Ness monster, Big Foot would jog down the Boulevard every third Monday, and UFO's would abduct Dickhead. Hold on—I like that last one."

She smiled in spite of herself, partly because he was working so hard at trying to cheer her up. "You're a nice man, a good man, Webster Bond."

He put his hand on his heart. "Is this where you tell me, you only want to be friends?"

"No!" She realized he was kidding. "You. How do you do that? I'm scared to death and you make me laugh."

"Don't you remember my title?" He smiled. "Class Clown? Ahh, how quickly we forget. The red nose? The squeaky shoes?"

She grinned and smacked his chest. "Stop. You're making that up."

"Yes, yes I am. So, seriously, while you were conveniently passed out, I read your text. Who the hell would torch your home and studio? What or who were you running from?"

Lola took a deep breath. *How many tests did the man need to pass in order to prove, he could be trusted?* She called on all the saints she could remember and began to spill her guts, starting with her swim in the pool. Just as she got to the part where Web pulled her over and she feared he was a kidnapper about to throw her into the trunk of her own armored car, Dr. Cho re-appeared.

"You look better." He waved a sheet of paper at Lola and read the discharge instructions to her. "And here, my dear, is your starter pack of iron tablets. *You* are anemic, which can be the cause of your fainting. Have you been doing anything strenuous lately? Working out extra hard?"

"Well, I've been running a lot."

"Aha. I *knew* it. You look like a runner. You need to see your primary care physician when you get home, have follow-up blood work. In the meantime, you're free to go."

"What about my bill?"

"Talk to the people at the desk. They handle all that." He waved good-bye.

Brow furrowed, Web appeared to be deep in thought.

Her breath caught in her throat. What if he thought she really was *loco*? "Do you believe me?"

"Yes, I do. I'm trying to put the pieces together."

They settled her bill and wandered out to the hospital parking lot. The sun had set hours ago. Soon, Web would have to prepare for work. Rather than go to another restaurant on a busy Friday night, they opted for drive-through.

As they unwrapped the largest burgers fast food could produce without requiring a forklift, Web probed for more information. "What are your theories about this, Lola? Who would want you kidnapped?"

She shrugged and licked mayonnaise off her fingers. "Narco terrorists run much of Mexico. With the exception of *La Familia* cartel, they all kidnap for ransom. If you don't pay?" She drew her finger tip across her throat. "You're dead." She stopped talking. "In my dream, the thug was about to chop off my hands, my livelihood—with his machete."

"Did the guy in your dream say anything?"

"*Vieja* sent me. That's it."

"Let's assume your cousin is correct. What motive would Flora have for having you kidnapped? Was she on drugs, in debt, trying to ransom a child or grandchild in exchange for you?"

She shook her head. "I've known the woman most of my life. She practically raised me. I think she might have had a child or a grandchild? Not sure if it was a girl or a boy. There was a period after I graduated from high school when I went to live with Izzy and I didn't see her."

"How did she come to work for you?"

"She showed up at my wedding and asked for work. Said she'd fallen on hard times and I was delighted to see her."

He put the car in gear and pulled into the traffic. "Not as delighted as she was to see you, apparently."

She rubbed her hands over her eyes and sighed. "I've been so paranoid. I thought I knew the smirking man at the restaurant. He reminded me of—*mierda*! He was one of my bodyguards! What the hell is *he* doing here?"

Web shook his head. "It feels like a vendetta."

Lola's stomach, which had been nice and full, now knotted. "Eye for eye, tooth for tooth. But why *me*? What did my family ever do to Flora to justify a blood vendetta?"

~*~

"Just do what I said, and you'll be fine." Web squeezed her hands and kissed Lola's forehead.

"What about you?"

He opened the gun safe and slid his sidearm into his holster. "I've got a job to do."

"Okay." Her voice was tremulous.

He knew she was trying to be brave for him. "Lock the doors. I'll see you soon."

~*~

A blanket of darkness settled over the house; only a small night light shone in the room, a minor concession. The house sighed as it settled. No. Wait. *That* wasn't a normal house sound. Those were footsteps coming down the hall toward the bedroom. A door opened and closed on squeaky hinges. Steps came closer to the bedside. The blanket flew off—

"Drop your piece or I'll blow your head off."

Mouth gaping, the thug dropped his gun. "Who the hell are you?"

Web swung his legs over the side of the bed. "I'm Officer Friendly and *you* are under arrest."

Bright lights glared into the windows and a thunder of footsteps shook Web's little house.

"Get on the floor. Hands behind you. Spread your legs." With a nod for the dropped weapon, Web sneered, "This ain't your first time at the rodeo, is it pal?"

The back-up squad crowded into the tiny bedroom.

Web kicked the creep's legs farther apart and pinioned his wrists with handcuffs.

"You know," he said in a conversational tone as he patted the man down, "some people have interesting hobbies..." He pulled roll of duct tape from one pocket. "Like fixing broken pipes with duct tape." A pair of metal handcuffs appeared from the other hip pocket. "And some folks, they like to play cops and robbers."

He tossed the manacles to a buddy in blue and ran his hand down to the left ankle, and removed a Bowie knife from a sheath. "Other people? Well, they like to go deer hunting." Web yanked up the cuff on the guy's right pant leg, and removed an ankle holster with a snub-nosed thirty-eight. "But, ya know, my friend, I think you have a different kind of hobby. Seems to me, you like to go *people* hunting." Web nodded at his team. "Get this scumbag out of here."

Two men in blue yanked the thug up to his feet while they read him his Miranda rights.

Web and his friends marched his captive out to the waiting patrol car, to Lola.

She threw her arms around him and exploded in sob. "Oh, thank God, you're okay."

He hugged her back. "I told you every cop on the SPD was my friend, even Richard Heade, much to my surprise. He pulled cops off the reunion to back me up." Maybe it *was* time to bury the hatchet.

Lola's pretty face creased. "You got one kidnapper. What if there are more?"

"That's what we're going to find out. I want you to come to the station and watch the interview. Think you can handle that?"

She flexed a bicep. "I've taken my iron pills. I can handle *anything.*"

He smiled. "Look who's making the jokes now."

~*~

The thug, whose name according to his Texas driver's license was Juan Santiago, sat in the interrogation room and stared at the glass.

To be fair, Web thought, with his hands manacled to the chair which was bolted to the floor, he probably didn't have much else to look at.

Web straddled a chair and stared at the man, and nodded to indicate the video recording should begin. "Let me get this right, Juan. Your plan was to grab Ms. Getz, duct tape her mouth, hands and legs, then put her in the trunk of your car and drive from Summerville to Mexico—in the summer," he paused for effect. "Does that about sum it up?"

The stocky man stared at him and smirked.

"Did you finish high school?"

Santiago curled his lip in a sneer. "I ain't never gone to school, and I don't need it for *my* job, *Senor Puerco.* I got all the training I need."

Web ignored the *Senor Puerco* comment. In his role as a police officer, he'd been called a *lot* worse than 'Mr. Pig'. "Sooo," Web drew the sound out as long as he could for effect. "You never considered the fact that she'd probably die, before you got her to Mexico?"

The boy who didn't go to school appeared to have a sudden brain attack.

Web let the thought swirl around in Juan's mind for awhile, then continued. "And, I suppose your *employer* wanted Ms. Getz alive and well? What if we sent a story out to go to all the newspapers, including Mexico, saying she cooked in the trunk of *your* car?"

The little man began to sweat.

Good. Now he was making progress. "Okay, well, as long as you keep silent, that's the plan. A reporter from *The Summerville Gazette* is on the other side of that mirror, just waiting for the sign. He's been dying for a good story." Web raised his hand and waved at the one-way mirror.

"No. Stop. Don't do that!" Juan began to sob. "Don't. Please don't. He'll chop me into fifteen pieces while I'm alive and feed me to his dogs."

Web dropped his hand. "What do you propose we do?"

"Arrest me. Jail me. Keep me away from him."

"I don't know." Web made a sad face and shook his head. "We're *supposed* to extradite you to Mexico."

The thug gave him a beseeching look.

"So, I'm sorry, *hombre.* We seem to be coming out short on this deal. What's in it for us?"

"I'll tell you who bought the contract, and why."

Web waved to his boss who stood beside Lola on the other side of the glass. It was time to bring in the big guns. Deal making was not Web's job.

~*~

Lola nearly exploded when she heard the man's tale. It was preposterous, outrageous and absurd. She ran out of adjectives. "Flora's daughter was on my parent's plane when it exploded? Why?"

Web took her elbow and sat her down on a chair by an old metal desk, and handed her a cup of coffee. "The *Remember Them*? Story about your parents? It was true."

She glared at Web, not believing her ears. "You said that newspaper was garbage, full of lies."

He shook his head. "While you were in the ladies room and weasel-faced Juan was whining at the DA, I did some checking of my own." He turned the monitor around, so she could see the face on the screen.

"Papa?" In the mugshot, her father wore a dirty, ripped tee shirt and looked much younger than she recalled. He held a card with a long number on it, and his name, Rosario Getz. "How could that be? He went to church? Gave to the orphanage---"

"That was the last mugshot ever taken of your father. He worked smarter and got others to take the fall for him, when things got tough. Your father *was* chief of an organized crime syndicate, well ahead of his time."

"No, that can't be." Her hand shook so badly, coffee spilled on her lap.

Web took the cup away from her and handed her a napkin.

"He trafficked in drugs, guns and women. He was going to sell Flora's daughter to a brothel in New York City—one that specialized in young girls."

Cold sweat dripped down her back; she thought she might be sick. Her father, a trafficker? How had she not known? Had she denied the truth? Repressed it all these years? No. He'd never, ever discussed business at home. He always said he was going to work. She assumed he had an office job, a good one. They lived nicely, had help, a walled compound. But so did their other friends.

The room began to spin.

She put her forehead on her knees. The daydreaming girl with her mind in the clouds, sketching, painting, dressing in expensive clothes and looking forward to her senior prom, never once realized where all their money came from.

Just like her life with Rico.

A sudden realization hit her and took her breath away. Flora had been plotting her revenge for *twenty-five years*? Then, when she saw Lola's wedding announced in the newspaper, opportunity knocked. What *was* the going rate of murder for hire? Chilled, she sat up and wrapped her arms around her chest. "Flora scrimped and saved every single *peso* she earned—to buy a contract on me, the daughter of the man who stole her child. Eye for an eye, tooth for a tooth."

Web put his warm hand on her cold one. "She was sick. Grief twisted her, made her lust for revenge for the loss of her one and only child. If it had been me, I don't know what I would have done."

Lola never had children. She had wanted them, but after two miscarriages, Rico told her enough was enough. He didn't want to see her suffer any more. She begged him to reconsider, but after time, she stopped arguing with him. Her heart twisted with fresh grief at the memory of the loss of her babies.

She choked back a sob. "I'm *glad* Flora torched my house and studio. I hope she felt some measure of recompense for the loss of her child. At least, up until the moment, when she caught on fire and died in the flames herself."

Tears running down her cheeks, she stood, rigid with determination and anger at the men in her life and the narco terrorists running her country. Her *former* life—her *former* country.

"You'd better get used to me being here in Summerville, because I'm *never* going back to Mexico."

Web stood and tipped her chin up and looked into her eyes. "Welcome home."

She sealed the deal with a kiss.

EPILOGUE
~*~

Lola walked among the older women, stopping on occasion to encourage a student to stroke the canvas with a bold color, urging another to soften her touch, then came to Mrs. Bond. Well, the *other* Mrs. Bond.

"How's it going, Mom?"

"Oh, dear, I'm worried the colors will clash with my curtains. Is that bad?"

"To heck with the window treatments. Do you like it?"

Her mother-in-law cocked her gray head and nodded. "Yes, I do. I like it very much."

"That's all that matters."

Web stood in the doorway of Summerville Cove's new art room. "Nice to see my girls getting along so well."

"Webster, what brings you here today?" His mother called out to him.

"I came to pick up my bride. It's time for our prenatal exam." He placed his palm on Lola's huge belly. "The baby kicked me. I'm not sure he or she likes the doctor's cold hands."

Lola smiled. "At my age, we have to make sure the baby is okay."

"Pshaw. I had Webster when I was forty-five. He turned out just fine."

Lola gave her husband a sly look. "I'm not so sure about *that*. He likes damsels in distress."

"You are the only damsel I'm interested in." He took her hand and gently led her toward the door.

"Webster. Lola. What are you going to name the baby?"

They stopped and turned. Mom's new medications seemed to be helping her with her memory, some of the time. But not with baby names, apparently.

Web squeezed Lola's hand. "Flora, if it's a girl."

His mother smiled. "Well, what if it's a boy?"

Lola squeezed back. "We'll name him after Webster's father." She broke into a huge grin and looked up at Web. "James—James Bond."

Delectable and Delicious:

An Inn Decent Proposal

~✳~

✳

CHAPTER ONE
~*~

JIM RAWLINGS PULLED his rental car into a parking space on the shady street in front of the Summerville Inn and gazed at the huge real estate sign posted on the rusted iron fence.

Public Auction
10 AM
October 31ˢᵗ

How appropriate, he decided, that the old girl would go up on the block today of all days—Halloween. She'd hosted some pretty terrific costume parties back in the day. Two decades ago, the Summerville Inn bustled with life and vigor, a vacation destination for the rich, famous, and wannabe famous. Now she looked like a decrepit old crone, suitable only for haunting or the latest in slasher flicks. He drummed his fingers on the steering wheel and worked the odds for getting her up and running.

With a degree from Cornell's School of Hotel Administration, he knew the hospitality business inside and out. Renovations wouldn't be cheap and repairs would take time. But, and it was a gigantic *but*, where would he find an executive chef? Not just any toque-topped slice-and-dice genius would do for this inn. No, he wanted, and the old gal deserved, a world-class *chef de cuisine* on a par with those found in the Big Apple or Vegas. No matter how beautiful the setting, the service and fine dining *always* drove the bottom line.

He watched people stroll the tree-lined streets and tried to remember the last time he'd been back in Summerville. Had it really been twenty-four—no, almost twenty-five years? Lucky for him the teachers had all liked him; otherwise, he'd still be the oldest senior in SHS. He rubbed the medallion in his pocket, a gift from an old friend, and winced as memories floated back, reminding him of his many screw-ups.

It wasn't as if he was stupid. Hell, he'd had nearly perfect scores on his SAT exams. But homework and classes took a backseat to more pressing matters of poker and ponies. Men with heavy accents had phoned his parents' house day and night, issuing thinly veiled threats about Jim and the money he owed their *associates*.

Over and over, his mom and dad begged him to stop, alternating between threats, tears and self-recriminations. When he learned his parents had put a second mortgage on their house to keep him safe, guilt and remorse overwhelmed him. He left town for good the night of his graduation from SHS, telling his teary-eyed mom and red-faced dad that he'd be back once he'd made a name for himself. That day finally arrived, but his folks were gone, taken in a head-on collision with a drunk driver three weeks after he left town.

He climbed out of the car, opened the shrieking gate and bent to pluck an empty cigarette pack from the overgrown weeds covering what once had been a beautiful plant-lined walkway. At forty-two, he wanted to travel back in time and smack sense into his eighteen-year-old self. *What was I thinking?*

A compulsive gambler, Jim had hopped from casino to casino, eking out a living as a waiter to support his mounting habit—until he hit his own personal bottom. And the rocks didn't get much harder than that. To this day, he could still smell the stink of an Atlantic City low tide as it washed over his nearly lifeless body while thugs in steel-toed boots tuned him up for not paying back his bookie in a timely manner.

Had it not been for the sudden appearance of an amorous couple under the boardwalk, he wouldn't be alive today. Later, he found out that the man who saved his life was in town for the Atlantic City Professional Body Building contest—and pissed as hell that he only came in third. Jim rubbed the scar on his eyebrow and mentally thanked the man who came in first that day.

He turned and eyed the object of his affection. The Summerville Inn, once a beautiful centerpiece of the little town, had fallen on hard times. The three-story brick building with a Federalist-style façade with its enormous front porches and overgrown ivy still enjoyed a charisma that hadn't faded, despite its age and disrepair. He climbed the front steps, avoiding broken rocking chairs, crumbling concrete, and detritus of days gone by.

Leaning on what appeared to be a solid railing Jim closed his eyes and recalled serving drinks and hor d'oeurves to well-dressed, well-heeled guests. He'd been shameless, telling them he was saving money for college. Little did the heavy tippers know they were supporting his expensive habits, not his higher education. He turned and patted the old gal's wall. Large chunks of peeling paint on the trim revealed pockmarks and pits beneath, damage from ice cold winters and blazing hot summers. He sighed. She needed a *lot* of work.

There were no twelve-step programs for run down hotels—but Jim had enough Gamblers Anonymous experience to share with everyone, including this dame. He'd done his homework, gotten an in-depth inspection report. Down, but not out, it was time to get her back on her feet. If he could do it for himself, he knew he could do it for her.

He crunched through weeds and kicked empty beer cans to the side on his way back to his car. The bank was still open. He'd bring a cashier's check for the largest amount of money he'd ever been able to save in his life—half a million dollars. He touched the medallion once more for good luck.

By noon tomorrow, the Inn would be his. No one in their right mind would out-bid him. The odds of that happening were a million to one—of *that* he was one hundred percent certain.

~*~

Genie King sat at her chipped Formica kitchen counter and ran her index finger down the spreadsheet for the fourth time in the last thirty minutes. The reserve price for the auction was two hundred and fifty thousand dollars. Knowing Beth Heade, Genie was certain that her obnoxious husband, Dick Heade, would be there as a plant in the audience to bid up the price. If she bought the Inn for three hundred thousand that would leave her another two hundred thousand to fix it up. But, if she had to go as high as four hundred, that meant she'd have to obtain a home equity line on top of the mortgage she'd already taken out.

She knew *all* about the cosmetic and structural issues at the inn, having already invested five hundred dollars for a top to bottom inspection. Replaced a mere ten years before, the roof was still in good shape, as was the foundation. However, everything in between and surrounding the Inn was a different story. From peeling paint and rotting interior wood floors to overgrown gardens, the old gal was going to be a major labor of love.

Genie had fallen head over heels for the Inn the first day she sat in the job interview with the owner. At the end of the meeting, her new boss had told her that she had a good feeling about Genie and her future in the hospitality industry. Little did her supervisor know that one day the girl in front of her would come back to claim the Inn as her own. She smiled at the thought—then gnawed at her bottom lip when the butterflies of worry crowded out those of excitement.

If *only* Mom and Dad were still alive. Five years had passed, but she missed both of them every single day. Mom had taken care of everyone; so much so that she never took care of herself. When she found out she had uterine cancer, the disease had spread so far and so fast, she survived only six months. Dad died six months later of a broken heart. They left everything to Genie, including the home she still lived in. She wiped a tear off her cheek. She could really use their advice, financial or otherwise.

Always supportive, Mom would have asked, "Will it make you happy?"

Always cautious, Dad would have asked, "Do you have an exit strategy, if it doesn't work out?"

Would it make her happy? Her life revolved around preparing and presenting food and—much to her chagrin— her waistline showed it. Tasting went along with cooking. How could *anyone* trust a skinny chef? Her education from the world's premier culinary college culminated in a Bachelor's of Professional Studies in Culinary Arts. A Culinary Institute of America, or CIA, graduate was *always* looking for an opportunity to be the head chef. Having her own restaurant would make her downright *delirious* with joy. Genie burned to find a showcase for her unique blend of French-Asian dishes which some likened to those of Roy Yamaguchi and Alan Wong. Given a chance, she knew she'd make it in New York—or Vegas.

Exit plan? Worst-case scenario, she'd go bankrupt and have to return to some other executive chef's kitchen as a Sous-chef. Her stomach knotted at the thought of working for yet another temperamental *bête noir*. The last one had thrown a large iron skillet at her. Lucky, she'd learned to dodge his temper tantrums—and pots and pans. The dent left in the wall was evidence enough that it was time to leave before that bad boss killed her.

What she *really* needed to find was someone with hotel management expertise. With Cornell's School of Hotel Administration within geographic striking distance, she expected to find a hungry young man or woman willing to start on the ground floor of the historic inn's renaissance. Once she had the title to the property in her hand, then she'd make a call to the career center and post a job description. She *had* to make this work. If she couldn't make a go of it with the inn, she'd lose everything—lock, stock, and cooking pot.

The living room clock cuckooed eight times. Her heart sped up. Almost time to go and she wasn't even dressed. Good thing she'd picked out her outfit for the auction the night before. She dashed to the bathroom and showered quickly. As she wiped off the mirror, a face surrounded by long ringlets of copper colored hair emerged from the fog. She aimed the hairdryer at the remaining mist and worked at pulling her unruly curls back in a ponytail. Or should she wear it down? After all it was an auction, not a kitchen. There was no hazard of hair falling in the food.

What the heck. It was a day for taking chances. She let her hair down, and began to work on her makeup. The woman at the cosmetic counter had assured her that the color palette in her hand complemented her blue eyes and freckled complexion. At this moment in time, Genie wasn't sure the bronze and blue shades were right, but she plunged on feeling daring and somewhat dangerous. The hardest part was yet to come.

Her new black suit and cobalt blue blouse awaited her in the closet. She'd been dieting, trying to lose the pesky fifteen pounds that followed her around like a faithful dog. The moment of truth was at hand. She took a deep breath and put on the blouse. *Holy crap.* How had she not noticed the low-cut neckline before today? Had the saleslady been holding the blouse up when she looked in the mirror? The skirt was a tad tighter than she had hoped it would be. *Dammit.* At least it zipped. She put on the jacket and faced the mirror.

Great. *Sweet Charity* meets *Wall Street*.

The clock cuckooed nine times. She slammed the closet door, stomped into the living room, and glared at the annoying timepiece. "Shut up, you stupid bird!" *Maybe it's time to rip the cuckoo out of the clock.*

Mortified that she would even *think* of destroying a memento her father gave her mother more than three decades ago, she whispered, "Sorry. I didn't really mean it. I'm just nervous." She thought she saw a glint in the old bird's eyes, but no, it was the tears in hers.

Time to go. Even though she wasn't Roman Catholic, she didn't want to take any chances today, of all days, and said a quick prayer to Saint Lawrence, the patron saint of chefs. She stopped mid-jog to the front door. Maybe Saint Rita, the patron saint of impossible dreams would be a better choice. On the other hand, why not pray to Saint Cayetano? After all wasn't she just about to take the biggest risk in her entire forty plus years of life? Surely, the patron saint of gamblers would hear her plea and help her get the winning bid—with money to spare.

CHAPTER TWO
~*~

Beth Heade paced the gloomy foyer of the Summerville Inn and for the tenth time that morning rearranged the brochures on the registration desk. Pausing to admire her reflection in the ceiling to floor mirror, she fluffed her short blonde hair, and touched up her blood-red lipstick. After a quick glance around the room to be sure she was alone, Beth reached into her bra and lifted her breasts for better display. She could have bought a friggin' townhouse with the money she spent on plastic surgery. For the price she paid, the girls deserved to be up and out on a silver platter.

Where the hell is Dick? He'd better not stand her up today. She needed him there to jack up the crowd into a bidding war. Not that *she* wanted the dump. She shuddered at the thought. Reeking of old cigars and older mold, the place gave her the creeps and made her itch. *Dammit.* She was breaking out in hives just being here. A car door slammed shut.

"Well, about time you got here," she called.

But the man who stomped into the front door wasn't Dick—in fact she wasn't sure he was even human. Short, dark, and hirsute with knuckles practically scraping the ground, the Neanderthal walked up to her and breathed garlic into her face. No, he could *not* seriously be thinking about buying the inn. He *had* to be lost, in search of a bar—or the zoo. She took a deep breath and gave her best sales person welcome. "Can I help you?"

He ignored her extended hand. "Yeah. I'm here to buy dis place."

"Pardon me?"

"Dis here is an auction, right?"

"Well, um, yes, yes it is," she stammered. *Oh, my gawd. This gorilla is a buyer?* She snapped out of her stupor and into sales mode. "Please take this brochure and feel free to wander around. The Summerville Inn is over a hundred years old and has a great history. F. Scott Fitzgerald and his wife, Zelda, summered here—"

"Zip it."

"Pardon me?" A warm flush ran up her neck and face, her *sang froid* threatening to reach the boiling point.

"I don't give a shit 'bout no Xena. When I want you to talk, I'll rattle your cage."

Suppressing the urge to tell the Neanderthal off, Beth's mouth snapped shut. *Where was Dick?* If she ever needed the Summerville Chief of Police at her side, *this* was the day.

As if on cue, Dick's voice boomed into the foyer. "Honey, I'm home." He bounded in the front door, dressed in a custom suit looking more like he was about to go to work on Wall Street, not on the SPD. "Ah, Tony, I see you found the place." He clapped the stocky man on the back. "Take a tour, it's gonna be all yours soon."

Tony's close-set eyes darted around the foyer and sitting area. "Dis place come wid a terlet?"

It took a moment for Beth to translate his request. "Yes, the men's room is down the hall, on the left."

As Tony shambled away, Beth grabbed her husband's arm and hissed at him. "Dis? Dem? Terlet? What kind of beast *is* he? And how do *you* know him?"

"Hey, you know what they say about judging a book by its cover," Dick chided. "Tony's got a lot of loot. After he sets up shop here, he'll be making generous donations to our favorite charity—us."

Horrified at the possibilities, she demanded, "And what *exactly* do you do in return for your new found friend?"

Dick glanced around, then gave her a wink. "SPD will give him, shall we say— certain considerations."

"And what *is* his business?"

"This and that."

"You have reached new lows—which I didn't think was possible." Dizzy with rage, Beth could barely speak. "My realtor's license is *not* going on the line for your latest scam. Everything that happens today goes *by the book*."

"Beth, c'mon, you gotta work with me."

Dick tried to wheedle her, but just then car doors slammed shut and a man's voice called out, "Hello? Anyone here?"

A throaty woman's voice responded. "I think we need to go inside. I doubt they'll have the auction out here."

Footsteps clomped up the stairs. A Nicholas Cage look-alike entered first, blinking rapidly to adjust to the gloom. *Well hello, handsome.* Beth shot a glance at her buffoon of a husband, now deep in a huddle with the returned gorilla, and made a mental comparison. Dick was coming up short.

Her attention shifted to the sound of high heels clicking on the hardwood floor. The woman who came in behind the hunk looked as if she belonged in an executive bordello. With bright red hair cascading over both shoulders and a low-cut blouse that exposed ample cleavage, it took Beth a full minute to realize who the curvaceous sexpot was.

"Genie King? Is that really you?" Beth adjusted the girls before bounding over to give the other woman a hug. "I didn't recognize you out of your work clothes."

Genie gave Beth an awkward smile. "I cleaned up for the occasion."

Beth extended one hand to the handsome man. "Beth Heade, Heade Realty. You are?"

The man's slow sexy smile had Beth's rarely used nether regions tingling. *Hubba, hubba. When is Dick's next business trip?*

"Jim Rawlings. You haven't changed a bit, Beth."

"Oh, my gawd! It's been so long. What have you been up to?"

Ignoring Beth's question, Jim turned to Genie. "You seem familiar—but I can't place you. Should I know you?"

~*~

Genie felt heat flush up from her breasts to encompass her neck and face. *Should he know me?* After working together every summer from middle school through high school, she knew everything about Jim Rawlings—where he lived, what car he drove, how many poker games he played a week—to name but a few of his favorite things. Today people would say she was *obsessed* with him, verging on stalker material. Twenty-four years ago, it was simply called a major crush.

Her normally throaty voice came out in a tremulous squeak. "You and I worked together here at the Inn. Every summer."

"Skinny, little Genie?" Jim stepped back, gave her a long head to toe look over and whistled. "You filled out in all the *right* places."

Heat flared in Genie's cheeks. He *liked* her curves? *Really?*

Flustered by his intense stare, Genie flailed around for an intelligent thought—and grasped at the first thing that came to mind. "Beth, do we have time to look around one more time before the auction begins?"

The realtor looked annoyed. "Yes, just be back in fifteen minutes. We start *exactly* at ten."

Pulling a notepad out as she walked, Genie made a beeline to the kitchen.

"Hold up," Jim called. "I'll go with you."

As she opened the door of the large gas range, she glanced up at the tall man beside her. A touch of gray at his temples, a scar across his eyebrow and a few laugh lines around his eyes, but other than that he *still* looked good enough to eat. Urging her inner stalker to slow down, she attempted to act casual and took a deep breath. "The years have been good to you. What brings you back to Summerville?"

"Long story short, I earned a degree from Cornell's Hotel School. Worked for major hotel corporations from New York City to Las Vegas. But I wanted my own place and I missed small towns. And you?"

Momentarily distracted by the ancient behemoth of a refrigerator, she turned and focused on Jim's question. "I'm a graduate of the CIA. I've worked with some top chefs but I want my own kitchen. And I *never ever* want to be a Sous chef again."

Jim's eyebrows flew up. "Seriously?"

The short hairy guy stomped into the kitchen. "Hey, youse two love birds, I hate to interrupt dis Hallmark moment, but I'm here to buy dis here place, not go to a reunion. You guys comin' to dis auction, or not?"

Genie flushed, snapped her notebook shut and followed the troll out of the kitchen into the foyer.

Jim was hot on her heels.

Beth glared at the short hairy man. "I see Tony found you."

Genie swore that if looks could have killed, the realtor would have turned the man to stone.

Beth took a deep breath, and launched into a brisk review. "It's time to begin the auction. Some ground rules: the *reserve* price is two hundred and fifty thousand dollars; bidding *must* be in increments of ten thousand. You *must* have sufficient cash or a cashier's check for a deposit—or the entire amount. *Everything* is due in thirty days. And, the property is sold *as is, no guarantees*. Got it?"

Dick grinned at his wife and gave her the thumbs up sign. "Let the games begin."

"What do I have for an opening bid?"

"Two-hunnert-fifty thou." Tony dug a finger in his ear and pulled out a chunk of earwax.

Genie suppressed a gag and shouted, "Three-hundred thousand."

"Tree-fifty." Tony winked at Dick. "I got a good feeling about dis. Gonna have me a great casino."

Jim stared at Tony. "A casino? Are you out of your mind? This place is a historic treasure. Three-sixty."

Tony smirked, stuffed three sticks of gum into his mouth, and dropped the wrappers on the floor.

Genie shouted, "Three-eighty."

"I got your tree-eighty, little bimbo, and raise it to four-hunnert thou."

Jim's face twisted with disgust. "Why you—"

Genie felt the Inn and her future slipping out of her reach. Her breath came in short puffs. The room began to take on crazy colors and twisted shapes. No. She *had* to have her own kitchen. No more Sous chef. No more crazy bosses with Mount Vesuvius tempers. No. No. No. She *had* to have it, it was hers, Dammit. A crazy idea exploded into Genie's frantic thoughts and out of her lips. She grabbed Jim, pulled his head down to hers and whispered, "I have five-hundred thousand. If you have that, too, we can take this pig."

Jim smiled, straightened up, and said. "Four hundred-ten thousand."

Tony sneered. "Yada, yada, yada. Four-tirty."

Genie clutched Jim's warm hand to her cold one. "Four hundred-fifty thousand."

Tony nearly spat at her. "Five-hunnert thou. Top that, bimbo."

Genie vibrated with rage. "Five fifty."

Disbelief crossed the hairy man's face. He mouthed an obscenity. "Eight hunnert."

Her heart thundered in her chest. How far could the awful man go? Did he really have more cash in hand than she and Jim could amass?

Genie shouted, "Eight-hundred fifty thousand."

The ugly man's face darkened. "Nine-hunnert."

Dear God, this jerk could become owner of her inn. She knew life wasn't fair, but how could such a horrible thing be allowed to happen? She closed her eyes and prayed to Saint Lawrence, Saint Rita *and* Saint Cayetano.

Jim cleared his throat. "One million dollars."

Tony swore a blue streak and stomped out of the inn. Dick followed close on his heels and could be heard by all that he had no part in the biddings or the deal.

The silence in the foyer was deafening.

Beth's blonde bobble head swiveled between Jim and Genie.

"Going once? Going twice? *Sold* to the highest bidder."

CHAPTER THREE

~*~

Jim sat in Sips Coffee Shop, dipped chocolate biscotti into his espresso, and watched the cookie crumble into his cup. Well, *there* was a metaphor for today's event. *What was he thinking?* Why hadn't he stopped the proceedings, taken Genie outside and talked some sense into her? But, no, just like old times, the rush that came with taking crazy risks overtook him—and he gambled big time. He won the property—but now he had to figure out how he would pay for repairs. Where would he get the money for *that?*

Genie put her small hand over his. "A million dollars for your thoughts?"

He gave her a wry grin, pulled the worn medallion out of his pocket and placed it on the table. "I think Saint Aloysius Gonzaga was busy protecting other compulsive gamblers today."

Surprise crossed Genie's face. "I knew you were a big poker player in high school. I had no idea—"

"My parents did a great job of 'helping' me out, covering up for their one and only son, making things right. They had no idea they were enabling me."

"Are you still—?"

"A compulsive gambler?" He rubbed the scar on his eyebrow. "That all came to a crashing halt about ten years ago. I thought—until today."

She covered her mouth with both hands. "I'm so sorry. What did I do to you?"

"Not your fault."

"Yes it *is*. It was my stupid idea, my poor impulse control. And my saints."

He raised a questioning eyebrow.

"I prayed to the patron saints of chefs, impossible dreams, and gamblers."

"Whoa, three against one. Hardly fair."

She held up her palms. "I was desperate. I *had* to have the Inn. I did this to you."

"No, I did it to me. You didn't cause it, you can't cure it and you can't control it. I have a chronic, relapsing disease. Today was a major relapse." *I really need to call my sponsor and find a meeting.*

She placed a tentative hand on his. "But you wanted the Inn, didn't you?"

"Yes—but what I did was *crazy*. I spent every dime I had, plus every one *you* had. Now what do we do?"

She let out a long breath. "We do what we're good at. I'm a well-trained chef. You're an experienced hotel manager."

A small flame of hope flickered in Jim's mind. "Seriously?"

"Yes," she stated and sipped her latte. "Why did you want *this* place?"

"The old girl called to me, begged me to save her." He gave Genie a wistful smile. "Do I sound crazy?"

"You call the Inn 'she,' too?"

"Yes, she's like a grand old dame who's fallen on hard times—and I would love to bring her back to her former glory."

Genie leaped up, ran around the table and hugged him. "I have the same dream. We *can* do it."

He hesitated for a moment, then returned the gesture, his hands unable to resist lingering on her luscious curves just a tad too long. Genie's inviting cleavage made him wish they were somewhere private. He could scarcely breathe and he had to shake his head to dispel naughty images of nuzzling her breasts. "We can do what?"

She sat down again, but clung to his hands. "I've done the research. The Inn should be in the National Park Service

Historic Registry—but it isn't. If we can get her added to the Registry, there are laws and standards about how we make the rehabilitation. We can bring it up to modern codes, but have to use certain treatments—"

"I hate to burst your bubble, but where will we get the money to do all this?" At his age, he wasn't sure he could afford too many more big gambles like this last one.

Her face flushed and her sapphire blue eyes sparkled. "If we can get her added to the Registry, we'll qualify for special low interest loans. *And* for a major tax credit. *And* we have a million dollars in equity."

"Pretty, smart—and you say you can cook? If you can do all that, you *are* a genie."

She released his hands, pulled her shoulders back, and inadvertently gave him a better glimpse of her beautiful breasts. She gave him a scalding look. "Are you *challenging* my cooking, Mr. Rawlings?"

Uh-oh. He never dreamed of Genie having a little temper. He couldn't resist tweaking her. "I'm sure you're a solid cook."

She stood, almost knocking her chair over. "*Solid?* What the hell does that mean? Average? Good enough to make the turkey for Thanksgiving dinner for the family—but not good enough to cook for guests? Tell you what, Mr. Critic, you come to my house for dinner tomorrow night." She threw a business card down on the table. "*My* food makes men go *weak* at the knees."

Hypnotized by the sway of her voluptuous ass as she stalked out of the nearly empty café, Jim bet it wasn't just this saucy woman's cooking that made strong men weak.

~*~

Tony 'the Wolf' Aiolfo sat in his black Cadillac Seville across from the stupid little coffee shop, and drummed his fingers on the steering wheel. It didn't add up. How had those two out-gamed him? He could tell the pair wasn't a real couple. Was he supposed to believe that in the blink of an eye the bimbo with the big tits convinced Ichabod Crane to throw in with her? They had to be shilling for Heade, trying to drive up the price and pick his pockets.

"Cheap and easy," Dick Heade had assured him. "My wife's the realtor. You'll get the place for a song. Trust me." Why had he believed a cop, of all people?

He'd been conned out of the one thing he really wanted in life—his very own casino. Being an enforcer for the Newark family had its benefits, but he never would have the kind of respect that his boss, Vinny, had—not until he had his own setup. His boss hadn't liked the idea at first. Thought Tony was going to cut into his profits. But when he heard it was in a different state, Vinny's eyes lit up. New turf, new business opportunities. He gave Tony his blessings, but told him he had to do it on his own, prove he was a real family member. Then, they'd talk. Well, not a lot of talkin' now. Not after today's clusterfuck.

He really needed a cigarette right now but that damned cancer scare a few months back had him chewing gum like no tomorrow. He pulled out a pack of Chewy Blewy and crammed three pieces into his mouth, grinding his teeth into the spit covered glob with a venomous crunch.

The coffee shop door flew open and the bimbo bolted out like her fat ass was on fire. Well, well, well. Was she running to see Dick Heade? He put the car in gear and decided to sniff out her trail.

He watched the bimbo jump into her Toyota Corolla and pull out of the parking place, driving a little too fast for an innocent person. The woman looked into her rear view mirror and locked gazes with Tony. Her eyes widened and the car veered erratically toward the shoulder, then righted itself.

Inexplicably, the car slowed down to a crawl. He nearly ran up her tailpipe, she was going so slow. What is she up to?

Driving five miles below the speed limit, she crept along the main roads, passing an organic grocery store and high-end wine shop. Stuck to her bumper like a magnet, Tony made no effort to pretend he was just sightseeing. He grinned at her. "Hope yer enjoying the sight of me, sweetie, 'cause I ain't goin' far."

Without warning, she pulled into the police station, began honking her horn and waving frantically at a cop in the parking lot. The cop jogged over to the side of her car and leaned down to talk to the bimbo who turned and pointed at Tony's Cadillac.

Gunning the engine, he took off, tires squealing to high heaven. The bitch. Chewing relentlessly on the gum, Tony sped onto the highway, slowing down only when he saw an upcoming exit for a nearby town. Unfriggin' believable. The bimbo was in cahoots with Dick Heade. First sign of trouble, she ran straight to the SPD.

Clearly they were gaming him. But what's the con? Did they think they could jack the price up so high he'd pay triple what the shit hole was worth? Or did they think he'd come on his knees begging? The only one who belonged on her knees right now was the bitch. He bet she was doing the chief in his office right now, laughing at him and planning her next move. Well, he had a few moves of his own. He couldn't touch the Chief of Police—but he could go after that bimbo and teach her a few lessons. She'd learn to fear the Wolf.

CHAPTER FOUR

~*~

Jim's sponsor answered on the second ring. In recovery for over thirty years, Brady was always there for him. His sponsor knew what this disease was and how it burrowed into a person's brain like an earwig and wouldn't let go. Jim took a deep breath and poured out his story, ending with the thug's plans for converting the Summerville Inn into a casino.

"It was like a knife in my heart when he said that, Brady. I couldn't let him get it. I *had* to take the risk—or lose it forever."

"Playing a long-shot, my friend? Or is this really a new career opportunity for you? *You* are the only person who can decide if this falls into the same category as poker and ponies."

"I'm not selling it. I'm staying in Summerville. I see this as an investment in my future."

"I'm hearing some doubt in your voice, Jim. Why don't you go to a meeting. Today. Only *you* can decide if this is your disease talking to you—or if it's the right thing to do."

Jim's heart sank. He was hoping Brady would wave his magic sponsor's wand, tell him the answer to his question and take away his fears. His brain knew Brady was right, but the little whispers of doubts nagged at him, making him worry that his compulsion might be in charge of his life again. He rubbed the scar on his eyebrow. Not this time. Not while he knew how to get help. "There are no meetings in Summerville."

"Hold on," Brady said. "I'll find you one." A keyboard clicked in the background. "You're in luck. There are three meetings in Rochester. And a bunch in Utica. Not surprised, now there's a new casino there. Poor suckers, they're like moths to the flame."

"Utica's over three hours away. I'll stick with Rochester and stay away from the casino, thank you very much."

Brady laughed. "Good answer." His sponsor gave him the list of times and addresses. Luckily, one would begin in an hour at Rochester General Hospital. "You need to talk, call me day or night. You know the drill."

"I know, I know. It works if I work it—that's why they're called steps." Jim snapped his phone shut and took a deep breath. He had just enough time to get there before the meeting started.

~*~

A man dressed in a dark suit, blue oxford shirt, and red tie called the meeting to order, promptly at seven-thirty. "Hello everyone, I see we have a full house tonight. Welcome to the RGH Gamblers' Anonymous meeting." He pointed to the sign on the table in front of him. "By way of reminder, please remember: Whom you see here, what you hear here, when you leave here, let it *stay* here."

Jim sat next to a rail-thin woman and wondered if she had more than one addiction. He shook his head. He wasn't supposed to judge others. Whatever her reason to be there, they were both in the fellowship.

The man in the suit continued. "This evening we have a guest speaker. Let's begin with the Serenity Prayer."

The stout African American woman to his left smiled.

The group stood and chanted, "God grant me the serenity to accept the things I cannot change, the courage to change the things I can, and the wisdom to know the difference."

"Please be seated. Now we will go around the room and introduce ourselves by first name only. Tell us if this is your first time at GA or your first time at this meeting. I'll begin.

Hello, everyone. My name is Eric and I'm addicted to online poker."

The woman to his left said, "My name is Latoya and I'm addicted to playing the numbers."

They went around the room and at last it was his turn. "Hi, my name is Jim, and I'm addicted to *any* kind of gambling." A wave of knowing laughter broke across the room. "This is not my first GA meeting, but it is my first meeting in Rochester."

A chorus of "Welcome, Jim!" rose in the room.

Then it was time for Latoya to tell her story. "When I was a kid, times were rough and jobs were scarce. My dad ran numbers for the local bookie. We ate better than most other families. I never knew what he did was illegal—until the police came to our house and arrested him." Tears welled up in her eyes. "The bookie got off—but not my dad. My mom worked hard cleaning houses for rich people, but with five kids, she couldn't make ends meet."

As if she was about to get to the meat of things, her fingers toyed with the rim of a Styrofoam cup. "I picked up where Dad left off. I became the numbers runner. I was good at it. Too good. No one ever suspected a twelve-year old in pigtails, with big round eyes. I asked about how the operation ran. The bookie thought it was cute, taught me about the game, and told me how it was better for poor neighborhoods because people could place small bets."

She shook her head and gave a rueful smile. "A real equal opportunity addiction. I started playing the numbers—and didn't get my wake-up call until the police came for me. I was fourteen, charged with chronic delinquency." She stopped, tears rolled down her face and her chest hitched. "I wound up in a juvenile facility. Those older girls—let's just say, *nobody* should have to go through what I experienced."

The skinny woman next to Jim put her hands over her face and began to sob. He guessed she'd had her share of agony, too.

"After I got out," Latoya continued, "I told my mother I was *never* going back there. I went to church, prayed for strength. The pastor saw me and asked me why I was so sad. When I told him my story, he brought me to my first GA meeting. I knew about AA—but I'd never heard of GA. It's been twenty years since I walked out of that juvie hall hellhole. I ain't never been back."

Jim thought back to his first GA meeting. He'd gone there pleading for help, too. Brady had taken him under his wing, led him through his step-work and was there for Jim during each temptation.

Latoya raised three fingers. "For those of you who think the twelve steps are a lot to learn, think about it in three simple steps: Trust God: that's steps one through three. Clean House: steps four through nine. And, Help Others: steps ten through twelve. Thanks for letting me come tonight. And to all of you, keep coming back."

After a hearty round of applause, members of the group shared, one at a time. Jim knew he was in the right place, at the right time—with the right people. He rubbed the medallion in his pocket and thought about the three steps. He trusted God, he was cleaning house—literally and figuratively, and he was helping others by not allowing the mobster to convert the Inn to a casino. He had taken a risk—but it wasn't the same as his old habits. There were no bookies involved, no ponies, and no poker. This time, *Jim* was in charge of his life—not his addiction. He *was* going to make good on his promises to Genie, himself—and the Summerville Inn. After all, didn't the old gal deserve a second chance just like him?

~*~

Genie sat in the back row of a Weight Watchers' meeting and listened to the other women share. It felt as if she'd been attending these meetings all her life, instead of just three years. Despite being in the food industry, she hadn't had a weight problem until she hit thirty-nine and her metabolism screeched to a halt. She had added thirty pounds.

Of all the people in the world, she thought a CIA-educated chef would have known everything there was to know about nutrition. While she knew about food, what she learned was that she had almost zero understanding about why people—herself included—ate too much.

After she'd joined Weight Watchers, the first week's food journal had been an eye-opener. Required to write down not only what she ate but also the time, Genie discovered that she often went too long—almost twelve hours—without eating. Focused on her job and taking care of other people, she often lost track of time. Then she'd be ravenous and eat so fast, she didn't recognize the satiety signals from her stomach and brain until she was stuffed. The hardest thing she'd had to learn was to set time aside to eat *before* she became crazed with hunger. That meant putting herself and her health first, almost an alien thought until she'd started coming to the meetings.

"Genie, would you like to share?"

Startled out of her reverie, she almost levitated off the folding chair. "I was hoping you wouldn't call on me, Wendy."

The group leader shook her head. "No way. You're our poster child for success. Tell our new members what you did this week."

"Well, I used to try to hide under big chef's jackets and pants." She avoided eye contact with the muumuu clad woman in the chair next to hers. "But this week, I had an important event to attend. So I screwed up my courage, braved the thoughts of store clerks looking down their noses at me and went clothes shopping for the first time in over a year. I bought a great looking suit and a gorgeous blouse. Now, I *did* have to tug at the waistband a bit, but I *was* able to zip the skirt."

To murmurs of encouragement, warmth rushed up her neck. "Then, I ran into someone I knew from high school— and he asked me out for a date. So, this week I learned that just because I'm a big girl, doesn't mean I have to hide my body under a burlap sack."

"Awesome. Next week, we expect full details about that date." Wendy grinned and winked at her. "Would anyone else like to share?"

A sudden, unwelcome thought crept into her mind. Maybe she was just kidding herself. Good looking guys like Jim, usually didn't even give her a second look. Why did he? Did Jim *really* like her for her chubby self? Or was he just being nice to her because he wanted the inn?

~*~

If Vinny ever found out Tony had been outbid, the Newark mob boss would ride his underling's ass forever. The family's reputation depended on successful business negotiations. Tony couldn't go back to New Jersey with his tail between his legs. He might as well put a sign on his back that said "Kick me," because the rest of the guys would never let him live it down. He could just hear them saying, "There's that loser who couldn't even manage to buy a shitty, old hotel." No way could he ever let those two idiots, especially the fat bimbo—get the best of him.

Flashlight in hand, he paced the length of the basement and checked the old copper pipes one more time. It was easy to spot the weak places and add a little more stress with his trusty hammer. Over time, water pressure would widen the cracks. He stuffed some gum into his mouth. Soon the Inn would be his.

CHAPTER FIVE
~*~

The next morning, Genie drove past the SPD and parked next to the grocery store. Even though Officer Webster Bond had been a sweetheart after she pulled into the SPD's parking lot, honking frantically, she still felt silly. Web didn't discount her concern, even offered to help her file a report.

But when Tony pulled away, she felt like an idiot. She must have misinterpreted his behavior, that's all. Tony *hadn't* been following her. He just *happened* to be on the same main drag. Summerville was a small town, it was inevitable that you'd run into someone you knew—or in this case, didn't want to know on your daily errands. She took a deep breath and tried to focus on something pleasant—like Jim.

He was different from the other men in her life. The restaurant business demanded so much attention and energy that love, marriage or just dating had to come second. This time she had a chance for some sanity. Not that the Inn wouldn't demand every waking moment of her life over the coming year, but it would be hers—and Jim's. She wanted to make a go of it now in more than one way. Was it possible to combine work and love?

The dinner she would prepare for him had to be special, sensual—seductive. Her nipples hardened at the thought of pouring warm, sugar-free chocolate sauce all over Jim's body, then licking it all off in slow motion. *Whoa girl.* While she was an advocate of the phrase, "Life is short, eat dessert first," there was something to be said for long, slow foreplay. She shook her head, took a deep breath and headed for the seafood counter.

"Hey, Genie. What are you cooking up tonight?" The elderly fishmonger greeted her with a big grin. Sam always set aside the best for her. But, she noted, the lobster tank was empty. That could be a problem.

"Think you can get some lobsters in for me tomorrow?"

"You betcha. How many?"

"No more than two—one-and-a-half pounders."

He quirked an eyebrow at her. "That's it?"

"Oh no, that's just the beginning. A pound of squid, the most tender ones you have. And a half-pound of salmon."

"Ah, that's more like it. Cooking for a big crowd?"

She felt herself blush to the roots of her hair. "No. It's more of an intimate affair—for two."

Sam scrutinized her carefully and whistled. "You're catering to a *different* kind of party. Anyone I know?"

She thought she'd burn up right there, in front of all the trout and cod staring up at her. "He's not from around here."

"Well, you tell him for me that he's is one lucky guy to have *you* cooking for him. I'm jealous."

"Oh, Sam, you'll always be the one that got away."

He waved at her as she turned to head for the produce aisle—and ran her cart right into Beth Heade.

"Oh, my gawd! Twice in one week. What are the chances of that?"

"In this town? The chances are very good." She eyed Beth's cosmetically altered body and wondered how much she'd spent on remodeling her figure. Genie bet she could rehab the entire Inn with the cash the other woman spent on her tits and face.

"So, are you happy with your purchase? No buyer's regrets?"

"No. Why would you ask that?"

"Just wondering. Tony seemed to *really* want that property. Too bad he didn't have enough cash to seal the deal."

What the hell? "Jim and I bought the Inn fair and square. I would think you'd be *orgasmic* with your fee. What'd you get, Beth? Thirty percent? Easy money for fifteen minute's work."

Beth flushed. "I spent a lot of my own money marketing and advertising that place. Not to mention organizing the auction."

Something smells fishy and it isn't the cod. "That guy. Tony? He seemed to think he had an in, like he was going to get the place for a song."

"What are you saying?" The blonde practically vibrated with anger. "I did everything by the book."

"Settle down. I didn't say it was you. He just acted like he was used to getting what he wants—and was really pissed off when he didn't."

Mollified, Beth glanced around the nearly empty aisle. She lowered her voice. "I think he's—" She raised her eyebrows and widened her already over sized eyes.

Genie had no idea what she was getting at. "He's what?"

The realtor looked around again and whispered. "From New Jersey." She bobbled her head several times and frowned, as if to emphasize that was one state *not* to be from under *any* circumstances.

Convinced the blonde had been sipping the cooking sherry in aisle three, Genie said, "Okay. Thanks for the tip. I've got to get going now."

Beth did *not* seem to be in a good state of mind. In fact her comments were downright bizarre. She and Jim had better get a lawyer to review all the paperwork for the purchase of the inn—just in case. Who knew what the realtor might have slipped into the fine print?

~*~

With butterflies dancing the hoochie-koochie in his stomach, Jim stood on the front porch of Genie's house at the appointed hour, clutching a dozen hot-pink roses, his finger poised to press the doorbell. A Halloween witch that appeared to have flown into the siding stuck out of the wall and cobwebs were draped over the light fixture.

Why was he so nervous? It was just dinner. Right? Visions of Genie's teasing cleavage danced before his eyes. No. He wanted it to be more than dinner. A whole *lot* more. He took a deep breath and leaned on the bell.

A moment later, the object of his desire appeared framed by the doorway, fiery hair pulled up in a ponytail, her luscious breasts covered by a huge black apron that read, *Never Trust a Skinny Chef.*

He handed her the flowers. "Trick or treat?"

"I'd say treat. Thanks come on in." She stepped aside to give him room to pass.

He wanted to grab her in the doorway, drag her into the bedroom and take her right then and there. *Down boy. No need to act like a Neanderthal.* He cleared his throat. "Did you get a lot of kids?"

"About two dozen little ones with their parents. After dinner, the teenagers came out in droves. Most of them weren't even in costume. I ran out of candy bars and turned the light off at ten. What about you?"

"The Motel Seven wasn't in the holiday spirit." He grinned. "Just as well, I forgot my costume. The only thing I could have gone as was Adam."

She blushed and said, "*That* would have been interesting." She handed him a glass of champagne. "To celebrate our purchase, I thought we'd begin with a Perrier Jouet. And, since we seem to be in an Indian summer, we're having appetizers on the patio."

She led him through the living room under a cuckoo clock made to look like a green-and-red Swiss chalet. "Interesting timepiece you've got there."

"My father gave it to my mother years ago, on their second date." She opened the sliding glass door. "He wanted her to be reminded every hour of the day that he was cuckoo for her. Corny, hunh?"

He clinked her glass. "To corny love."

She pointed to the small square white dishes on the glass topped patio table. "Tonight's *amuse bouche* is salmon tartare on five-spice crisps."

After he sat, she placed a cloth napkin on his lap. The simple motion aroused him. He shifted in his seat, grateful for the camouflage. He turned to the tasty morsels at hand, closed his eyes and crunched into what appeared to be a large wonton crisp—but with tastes of clove, peppercorn, cinnamon, fennel, and anise dancing on his tongue. Layered in with these flavors were salmon, wasabi, ginger, and a touch of spicy sushi sauce. He moaned, opened his eyes and saw Genie watching him.

He took a sip of champagne. "More please?"

"You may have two more—that's it, or you won't be able to enjoy the rest of the meal."

He savored each bite and realized the chef was not on the patio with him. "Where'd you go?"

"Not to worry." She appeared from another sliding glass door bearing a large platter covered with golden brown rings drizzled with a red sauce and garnished with something green. She placed the dish in front of him. "Sweet-and-spicy calamari, toasted peanuts, and cilantro."

"Can taste buds explode?"

She inclined her head. "We shall see. *Bon appétit.*"

"Won't you join me?"

She sank into a chair opposite from him. "Just for a few moments. I have kitchen duty, you know."

"Yes, and I'm grateful."

She smirked. "We'll see how grateful in a while."

Was that a signal? Was she coming on to him? His heart raced and his pants stirred. *Focus on food, Dammit.* He reached for the calamari. Spicy sweet-and-sour flavors rioted with combined textures of crunchy light tempura batter and tender squid. He licked his fingers. "Dear God, please serve this in heaven."

When Genie laughed, the smile reached all the way up to her sparkling eyes. "You approve?"

"Mmm, yes. Why aren't you married?"

She eyed him and took a sip of bubbly. "You first."

"I was." He grabbed another piece of calamari. "To a hot blonde blackjack dealer." He crunched, savoring the flavors.

"And?"

"What happens in Vegas, stays in Vegas."

"Not fair."

"She left me for a higher roller. Your turn."

She popped a piece of calamari into her mouth and ran her tongue around her lips slowly, getting every little crumb. His pants grew tighter. "Sommelier boyfriend became alcoholic."

"Occupational hazard."

She nodded. "I swore off romance for a while and became best-friends-forevah with every gay guy in New York City. Lots of great shopping stories." She sipped her wine. "Fell like King Kong diving off the Empire State Building for my new executive chef. Man was he hot." She fanned herself.

A flash of jealousy surprised him. "And?"

"Hot, as in temper. As in throwing dishes, pots— anything at hand." She shook her head. "He was Italian; I nicknamed him Mount Vesuvius. I left him and the job the day after he threw an iron skillet, missed me and dented the wall." She dusted her hands off. "That was that. He's the reason I'm here."

Jim reached over and grabbed her hand. Heat pulsed off her palm. "What's his address? I'll send him a thank-you note."

She stood and gave him a Mona Lisa smile. "Save your thanks for when you're done with dinner."

That was *definitely* a come-on. He admired her lovely ass while she sashayed away and looked forward to the next courses.

As dusk fell, they moved into the dining room. She had placed the roses in a vase and set them on the buffet to the side. The table was set for two with fine china and glassware. Everything sparkled in the candlelight. She held a chair out for Jim, and once again placed a napkin on his lap, this time drawing out the ritual a tad longer. She was *killing* him.

She breathed into his ear, sending frissons down his neck. "I hope you like the next course."

Just to have something to hold onto, other than her—he clenched a soup spoon. And a white dish appeared in front of him in the center of which were large lumps of—

"Rich lobster soup with curry." She poured a thick pink liquid around the lumps of shellfish.

The scent of curry rose on the steam grabbing his olfactory lobe, taking his brain to a new plane of existence. "Oh—My—God."

"Some *have* likened my food to a religious experience."

The lobster swam in the smooth soup with a hint of curry while his taste buds danced and sang *hallelujah, hallelujah.* "Any chance I could get this for dessert?"

She took her apron off and sat down. "Not tonight, I have other plans."

The low cut lace top left little to Jim's imagination. Torn between appetites, he wondered if there was an *intermezzo*. He needed to clear his palate—and knew just who he wanted to do it with.

"Are you enjoying your soup?"

"What? Yes, very much." He tore his gaze away from her breasts.

"Mind if we talk a little business?" she asked.

Only if it's monkey business. "Sure." He put his spoon down.

"I think we'd better have a lawyer check out Beth's paperwork."

After she told him about the odd conversation with Beth Heade in the grocery store, he raised one eyebrow. "She said he was from New Jersey?"

"Wearing a look on her face that implied he came out of a sewer. Not that I disagree with that assessment," Genie nodded at him.

"I have some experience with that state." Jim rubbed his eyebrow. "Yes, we should get legal counsel. And we need to draw up some partnership papers, too."

"Good idea." She smiled, stood, and brushed her hand along his as she collected his dish. "Ready for your next course?"

She had *no* idea how ready he was.

Genie disappeared into the kitchen, then stuck her head back into the dining room. "Would you pour the wine for our next course, please?"

He lifted the decanter. The nose on the wine was outstanding. What was it? French? Californian?

She returned with two plates and placed them on the table. "Grilled lamb chops, pomegranate-and-saffron basmati rice."

He closed his eyes and inhaled the aromas of lamb, the rich red fruit, and scented rice. *Heaven. He was in heaven.* "What kind of wine is this?"

"Cabernet—Robert Mondavi Reserve."

He eyed her breasts and sipped his wine. "A perfect pair. Er—pairing."

She covered her mouth with her napkin, but the crinkles around her eyes gave her away.

He savored every bite, gnawing at the bones until it looked as if they'd been dipped in acid. Then he licked his fingers clean. He glanced up and caught her watching him, a smile hovering on her lush red lips. Embarrassed, he wiped his fingers on the napkin. "I couldn't help myself. The best lamb chops... Evah."

"Think you can handle dessert?"

His groin responded before he could open his mouth. "Depends on what we're having."

"A simple one—hot fudge sundae."

He groaned and his erection demanded to be attended to. He slipped off his chair, onto his knees and clasped his hands together. "Please, please, please, may I have dessert?"

"*Now* do you admit that my cooking makes men weak at the knees?"

He crawled to her chair, reached up and pulled her face down to his and slanted his mouth over hers. "Yes," he breathed. "You have made my knees—and other parts of my body weak." He pressed his lips against hers and she responded, opening her mouth. She tasted like pomegranates. He wanted more of her flavors. *Now*.

He ran a hand down her neck and found a hardened nub awaiting his touch through the thin lace. He lowered his head to her breast and sucked at the cloth, pulling her into his mouth until she moaned. Then he moved to the other breast, but pulled the blouse down, exposing a claret-colored nipple the size of a silver dollar. He licked and sucked at that large, lovely rosebud until she clutched at his hair.

"Stop." She panted. "We still have dessert."

"You're my dessert."

"I'm not too *fat* for you?"

He looked up into her eyes, his tongue longing to return to sucking on that big bud. "Skinny women don't turn me on. I love your curves, your hips, your big beautiful ass, your full, delicious breasts and your sweet, succulent nipples. I want to explore every inch of your luscious lovely thighs, right up to your—"

She pushed away from him, stood and took his hand. He tried to pull her back but she shook her head, smiled, and dragged him down a hallway. Illuminated only by candles, her bedroom contained a queen-sized bed, large pillows and red satin sheets. A cooking cart with a chafing dish stood ready to serve.

She turned to him. "Get undressed."

As he ripped his shirt and pants off, she released her hair from her ponytail and peeled out of her lace top and slinky pants. She wore no underwear. He swept his gaze over her large breasts, full hips and the red triangle of hair he wanted to sample next. He stood at complete attention, pointing straight at *her*. He reached for Genie, grazed a breast and she shoved him back onto the bed. "Lie down."

He complied, shivers running up and down his spine.

Hair draping across her face, she stood over him and drizzled warm chocolate sauce on his chest, belly button, hips and erection. Then she dropped dollops of whipped cream in swirls along the same pattern. "Just so you know, this is *all* homemade."

Bending her head over her work, she quickly licked from his neck down to his belly button, and then in a slow, deliberate pace, continued downward. He groaned and grew harder and thicker with each lick.

He grabbed Genie and pulled her onto the bed. "I'm hungry, too."

A dish in each hand, he drew wild patterns with chocolate sauce and whipped cream across her lush curves. After eyeing his handiwork, he licked his lips. "I think I'll start with these two delicious mounds topped with these bright, red cherries. Then, I'll follow the chocolate trail down to here."

He slid a chocolate covered finger into her moist folds, sliding across her center, flicking her until she wriggled and arched her hips upward. He smiled, withdrew his finger and licked it. "Delicious."

Between gritted teeth, she gasped. "Tease."

"Look who's talking. You've been driving me wild all evening." Jim licked his way down the chocolate path. The pool of sweet brown liquid in her navel and below required extra attention to detail, and he lapped up every drop, first licking lazy circles on her soft thighs. She grabbed his head and pushed him to her silky triangle. His tongue probed her saucy folds, then nibbled at her hard nub until she moaned, screamed his name, and clutched his hair.

"I want you inside me."

He crawled on his elbows, maintaining skin contact with each upward movement. He looked deep into her eyes and slid inside her. She rose to meet him at every stroke, urged him onward, and let him know with her touches exactly what she wanted: harder, deeper, stronger thrusts. She shuddered and screamed his name, he couldn't hold on any longer. He came with a shout and fell on top of her.

Genie looked him in the eye. "Ready for the cheese course?"

CHAPTER SIX

~*~

Genie rolled over and felt something warm, long, and hard next to her. "Oh, baby, is that a baguette in your pocket, or are you just glad to see me."

Jim's eyes fluttered.

"I know you're awake. You can't fool me."

Eyes still closed, he smiled and grabbed her close.

She stiffened. Something smelled—wrong, like a pan was burning on the stove. Had she left something on in the heat of the night? No. She was certain she'd shut everything off.

"Jim—get up. *Now*. I smell smoke." At that very moment, the high-pitched sound of the smoke detector startled them into reality.

He bolted upright, flailing around in the sheets. She raced out of the room toward the smell, and into the kitchen. With the mild weather, she'd left the windows open in the kitchen overnight. Now, bright yellow flames beneath clouds of smoke billowed through the screens.

She grabbed a large fire extinguisher and hosed the window with dry chemical in a desperate attempt to slow the orange monster down. Focused on her failing efforts, she jumped when someone grabbed her arm. "Call nine-one-one. Tell them there's a fire, and it's not a kitchen fire."

"We have to leave." He pulled her out of the smoke filled kitchen and slammed the door. "It's not worth losing your life." Somehow, he'd been able to get out of the sheets and into his jeans, shirt and shoes. He held her robe in her hand. "Put this on."

Thick tendrils of smoke oozed under the door. She coughed, looked up and saw the cuckoo clock. Climbing up on a chair, she attempted to get it off the hook—but was suddenly airborne. Jim threw her over his shoulder and carried her naked, kicking, and screaming out of the house.

Sirens sounded in the distance, coming closer.

"I have to get the cuckoo clock," she shouted. "It's the only thing I have left from my parents."

He ran out of the house to the opposite side of the street, where an army of wide-eyed neighbors waited in their nightclothes.

A little boy called out, "Mommy, I can see Miss Genie's butt!"

Fire engines screeched onto her street and the cacophony of trucks, radios, and men shouting distracted the crowd.

Genie buried her face in Jim's neck and sobbed. It wasn't bad enough she was losing her house; her dignity was burning up with it. He set her gently on the ground, sliding her down the front of him to spare her a full frontal nudity moment. Wrapping the silk robe around her, he whispered, "That's one lucky little boy. You have a really nice ass."

She caught herself laughing, then realized she was hysterical. She kept her face pressed against Jim's chest, too afraid to watch, to see if the firefighters could save her home. With the exception of the time when she'd worked in New York City, she had lived in the house most of her life, coming back to touch base and reconnect with reality between bad jobs and bad men.

Her mother had taught her to make her first cake in that house. Her father had sat with her at the kitchen table every night until she went to college, making sure she did her homework, checking each assignment. Her mother's love infused every meal she made and every flavor she tasted in that house and her father's logic had given her the foundation of a good business sense. They hadn't taken a lot of photos, preferring to spend their time and money on Genie's education.

Mom had said, "Each moment is special. Capture the time in your memories, Genie. They won't fade." Other than a few holiday photos and the rare family portrait taken by insistent friends, the damn clock was the most tangible memento she had of her parents' and their romance.

She heard the neighbors cheer and raised her head cautiously. "Is it safe for me to look?"

"Yes." He turned her around to face the house. Wisps of smoke rose skyward into the early morning sun, but the blaze that had threatened to gobble up the house was gone.

A firefighter crossed the street and strode to Genie's side, his face slick with sooty sweat, his hat under his arm. "This your house?"

She wrapped the robe around her like a cocoon. "Yes."

"I'm Chief Von den Broeck. Could you come with me, please?"

Barefoot, Genie gingerly crossed the street, attempting to avoid sharp stones and small rocks. They walked around the side of the house, to the back, where the fire had done the most damage. Shards of glass glinted ahead of her. Jim lifted her up as easily as if she was a feather quilt.

She whispered, "You must work out a lot."

"My daily program consists of twenty lifts of any woman who happens to be nearby."

She kissed his neck. "Thank you. For everything."

He found a safe place and set her down. She turned but her knees buckled at the sight before her. Jim knelt down beside her. "Take a couple of deep breaths and let me know when you're ready to stand."

She nodded, then opened her eyes and allowed him to pull her to her feet. The entire side of the house—what was left of it—was now a smoking blur of charred wood. The wall into her kitchen was gone—as were her cabinets, table, and chairs—everything flammable. The sink lay on the floor, the stainless steel charred and twisted from the strength of the fire. Paint had blistered over the sides of the refrigerator, range, and dishwasher.

Chief Von den Broeck pointed at a gas grill pushed up against the base of the home. "The burn patterns point back to the grill." He bent and, using the tip of a pencil, poked at a loose hose fitting on the Propane canister. "There's where the fire started. You must have left the grill on overnight."

"No," Genie swore. "I'm a professional chef. I never leave anything on—I check everything twice before I go to bed."

The chief looked skeptical. "Maybe you were distracted last night?"

She flushed, certain she must have turned bright red. Before she could protest, Jim spoke. "The lady said no. And, I was right beside her, checking everything two and three times."

Genie scanned the yard. Her gaze snagged on a pile of silver papers. "Jim. Look over there."

Striding through the wet grass, he squatted down for a closer look, then called out to Von den Broeck. "Chief, could you come here for a minute?"

The chief walked over to Jim's side, obstructing Genie's view. Her pulse quickened and she clenched her fists in the silk robe. "What is it?"

The firefighter pulled out his radio and started speaking in low, urgent tones. When finished, he turned to Jim and Genie. "You both need to get out of here."

"What's going on?" Genie demanded. "What did you find?"

Jim was at her side in two long strides. "Gum wrappers—and a throw-away lighter. We have to leave now. This is a crime scene."

~*~

Having chomped through an entire pack of Chewy Blewy, Tony stood in the back of the crowd, eyeing his handiwork with grim satisfaction. Torching the bimbo's house had given him particular pleasure. Not in a pervy, hard-on kind of way. No, he was a professional, used to getting paid for these sorts of jobs. He knew if he wanted something done right, he had to do it himself. Too bad the bimbo and Ichabod Crane woke up in time to get out. In his expert opinion, the house was a total. Fixing up after fire and smoke damage, combined with the mess made by water, would put a major dent in her savings. All he had to do now was wait for the next auction announcement, and he'd get his new casino at a dirt-cheap price.

That'd teach her to mess with the Wolf.

As the neighbors started moving back to their houses, a little boy stopped in front of him and pointed at Tony's hands.

"Mommy, that man has hairy fingers!"

The Wolf snarled at the little puke, turned on his heel, and walked away as fast as he could. Someone should teach that kid some manners. He didn't have time to take care of that today. He shoved another stick of gum in his mouth and tossed the wrapper on the ground.

~*~

Jim sat in his rental car and rubbed Genie's arms, trying to get some color back into her face. Not only had she lost her house and everything in it, but now it was apparent the fire had been set deliberately. "Let's see if the Arson Team will let me into the house, at least to get some clothes for you."

She stared at him, glassy-eyed. "Whatever."

"We need to get you coffee and something to eat."

Genie didn't respond. She just stared at the house, her face a mask of sorrow. He had never lost a house to a fire, but he certainly knew about loss. The day the police called him and told him his parents were dead, killed by a drunk in a head-on collision, he'd felt as if the earth had crumbled out from under his feet. He'd been inconsolable, driven deeper into his compulsive gambling. The day of his parents' funeral, he lost his last five dollars in a slot machine and had to hitch a ride to New York from Atlantic City.

After the funeral, he'd been told he'd inherited his parents' home—but it was mortgaged to the hilt and they owed back taxes on it. The executor—no big surprise—was not Jim, but a lawyer familiar with Jim's habits. At the end of the estate sale, all Jim had left was the Rolex watch his father had put in a safe deposit box. It was the one thing Jim had never, ever pawned to support his gambling habit.

He sighed, patted Genie's hand, and climbed out of the car. "I'll be back in a little bit."

After explaining that the home owner had nothing on under her robe, the uniforms guarding the door got permission from the Arson Investigator to let Jim into the house. One stayed at his side the whole time, watching him pack a suitcase and cataloging what he took. Suspecting he might not have the opportunity to do this again for some time, he stuffed as many clothes as he could into the rolling bag. On his way to the front door, he stopped and made one more request. After a lengthy explanation and a heated discussion, the lead investigator rolled his eyes and nodded.

Jim headed back to the car, opened the trunk, and placed the bag inside. Then he opened the passenger side of the vehicle. "I have something for you."

The look on Genie's face when he handed it to her was thanks enough.

"Cuckoo, cuckoo, cuckoo."

She clutched the clock to her breasts and sobbed.

CHAPTER SEVEN

~*~

Much to Genie's surprise, when she called the insurance company, the agent who answered the phone had already heard about the fire. Then again, Summerville *was* a small town. "I'm so sorry for your loss. We'll have an adjuster out there today. Where can you be reached?"

She held Jim's cell phone to her breast. "Where am I staying?"

"Motel Seven—No. Wait." He snatched the phone out of Genie's hand. "She's staying at the Summerville Inn."

After a long silence, the insurance agent said, "Is this some kind of joke? That place is a dump—has been for years."

"Genie and I just bought that 'dump.' When you have some information about the fire, you can find us there or at this number." He snapped the phone shut.

She stared at Jim, her mouth agape. "Are you out of your mind? We can't stay *there*."

He quirked an eyebrow at her—the one with the scar.

Why did that make her stomach turn to a quivering bowl of Jell-O?

"The Motel Seven is not a suitable setting for a world-class chef. It has no kitchen, not even a hot plate. You belong with the Grande Dame of Summerville." He handed her a pair of jeans and a T-shirt. "Slip into these. We're going to breakfast, then shopping."

The thought of eating made her queasy. "I'm not hungry."

"Well, I am. And you need to eat, like it or not."

As she slid into the jeans under her robe, she glared at him. "Who died and left you in charge of my life?"

He pointed at the smoking house. "Your old life. You have a choice. You can either melt down into a puddle of self-pity—or you can take this as a sign from someone." He pointed upward. "And catch the helicopter ride."

"Helicopter? What the hell are you talking about?"

He leered at her. "You planning to wear that robe to breakfast?"

She glanced down and found half-exposed breasts. "Crap. Hold it over me, so I can put my T-shirt on without giving my little neighbor another show."

He chuckled on the other side of the silk. "I still say little Timmy is a lucky boy—and an excellent observer of fine ass."

She ripped the robe out of his hands. "You—you—" She grabbed his face and pulled his lips to hers, smothering his amusement with an ardent kiss. She broke it off just as abruptly. "You keep that up and I will have to spank you *and* Timmy."

He leaned back against the driver's side window and tapped his index finger on his cheek. "I don't know about Timmy, but that sounds like fun to me." He put the car in gear. "I'm working up an appetite—aren't *you*?"

Avoiding the sight of her lost home, she looked forward. "Let's go see what my future holds."

~*~

Since her driver's license, checks and credit cards had gone up in smoke, they stopped at the bank after a late brunch at Sips Coffee Shop, so Genie could get some cash.

The smiling, gray-haired bank official didn't seem to care that three small children were tearing up deposit slips in the lobby and scribbling on credit applications. He was so focused on a curvaceous Hispanic woman with long black hair and lush lips, that Genie and Jim might as well have been invisible. After what seemed like a lifetime of shrieking children, the woman left the bank with a thick envelope, her brood trailing behind her.

When the flushed man finally tore his eyes off the woman's derrière he seemed startled at the couple's appearance. Mr. Beasley had known Genie most of her life—he had to be in his mid-sixties. She was amused to discover the man was not dead *yet*.

Beasley cleared his throat noisily. "Ah, Miss King. How may I help you today?"

After a brief description of the morning's disaster and her reason for coming to the bank, the talk turned to financing the renovations at the Summerville Inn.

Beasley's expression bordered on that of the subject in Edvard Munch's painting, *The Scream*. "You *bought* that dump?"

Genie glanced at Jim's rigid jaw and put her hand on his arm, hoping to calm him down. "It's not a dump," she said. "It's a fixer-upper."

Jim released a deep breath. "Since we have a million dollars in equity in it, we prefer to call her an investment property."

"Yes, yes, of course." Beasley steepled his fingers. "I'm going to have to see how much credit we can extend you and at what rate. Summerville might give you a grant to rehabilitate the property. The Inn is in an historic district, but I don't recall if it's considered historic property. If you can't prove that it's of historic or cultural significance—then you *might* be able to get money on the basis that you'd be creating employment opportunities and investing in the local community."

Genie pressed a fingertip to the throbbing blood vessel at her temple. Where was the aspirin when she needed it? Oh, yeah. In her burned-out kitchen. "I did research online before I had the building inspected. There *are* historic properties on the same street—but the documentation on the Inn isn't clear."

Beasley stood. "Considering this is an emergency situation, I'll add a home equity line for ten thousand dollars to your existing accounts and will speak with the president of the bank regarding a larger loan for renovations. In the meantime, I suggest you pay a visit to the Summerville Historical Society. I'm sure they'll be happy to assist you."

~*~

Jim led Genie into the Outdoor Gear store and beckoned to a gum-chewing young man in hiking gear wearing an *"Oh-Gee. You're Going To Love Us!"* button. He hoped this kid earned a sales commission because he and Genie were about to make his day—if not his week, or month.

"Yes, sir. How can I help you?"

"We're rehabbing the Summerville Inn."

The sales associate's jaw dropped. "Seriously? That place is a dump."

Jim turned to Genie. "Why does *everyone* call it a dump?" He turned back to the kid. "Please do not refer to her in that manner. She is a Grande Dame fallen on hard times. And until such time as we can get her back on her feet, we will be camping there."

Light dawned. "Yes, sir. Should I get a cart or a flatbed truck?"

"Flatbed—we'll probably need two."

Trailed by the associate, Jim held Genie's hand and led her down the camp kitchen aisle. "What about that stove? Two burners enough? Or do you want two stoves with two burners?"

She dug her nails into his palm. "You don't have to do this."

He winced and released her hand. "Yes, I do. I have a chef and I like to eat."

She shook her head and examined the selection of stoves, then settled on one that would do. Pots, pans, dishes, glassware, and a cooler followed. "That ancient refrigerator might be functional—but just in case, we'd better have one."

"Sleeping bags, pillows, blow-up mattress..." Jim glanced at the kid. "—make that two mattresses."

Genie gave him a puzzled look. "Expecting company?"

"You never know. Once word gets out the Inn is open, people will start coming out in droves." Jim pinned her with a serious look. "Think we need a bear vault to protect our food?"

The associate stopped chewing his cud and stared at him.

She smirked. "Only if you're expecting Tony to show up in the middle of the night."

"You never know." An image of the Neanderthal flashed in his mind. He hoped he'd never see him again. His mouth suddenly sour, Jim turned to the young man. "You have any more of that gum?"

Mr. Oh-Gee! Flashed the pack of gum at him and it reminded him of something—but what? A thought shimmered in his mind, thumbed its nose, at him and danced off into the hinterlands of his forty-two-year-old brain. He shook his head.

Getting old is not for the weak.

~*~

The cash register tape rolled over the counter and down to the floor. Suitably impressed with their purchases, the gum-snapper told Genie everything would be delivered in two days. That meant at least forty-eight hours in the Spartan confines of Motel Seven. *Better than sleeping in a car.*

As they left the store, she caught herself looking over her shoulder—then realized she was looking for someone…Someone hairy. She shuddered. He was gone, had to be. She needed to get her mind off that sleazoid. "Let's go by the post office, so I can tell them to stop delivering mail to my house."

Jim cleared his throat. "Worried a robber will know you're not home?"

She smacked his arm—then laughed in spite of herself. "Yeah, exactly. They'll never notice the back wall's missing from my kitchen. Or the absence of a roof. The smart ones *always* check the mail first."

He held the car door for her. "Think you can stand being in motel without a kitchen for two days?"

"Does your room have a mini-fridge?"

He nodded.

"Good. Let's stop by the grocery store and pick up some chocolate sauce and whipped cream. We can have room service."

He leaned down and gave her a quick kiss. "I like the way you think."

Jim waited for her in the car. She ran into the post office, only to find a line queued out into the lobby. Genie wondered if they were giving something away—then realized it was the first week of November and the early birds were mailing holiday gifts.

She searched the lobby desk for a hold mail form, gave up and went up to the front desk, garnering dirty looks along the way. She didn't care. All she needed was the form. She'd grab one and get out. Genie reached the counter, found the red, white, and blue document, turned around and smacked into something hard.

Envelopes flew into the air, grazed her cheek, then spilled across the floor. Genie squatted and scrabbled at the floor, picking up the large white envelopes and looked for the freaking form she'd dropped in the melee. She was *not* having a good day. In fact it was the crappiest day of her entire life. The only thing that would make it worse was if—

"Oh, my gawd!" Beth Heade shrieked. "I cannot *believe* what you just did." *There. Now it was worse.*

Most of the restless crowd tried to sidestep the scene. An elderly woman leaned on her cane and handed one envelope at a time to Genie—along with a clucking sound of disapproval.

A little boy grabbed a handful and ran toward the lobby, screaming, "I won the lottery!"

Still on her knees, Genie was unable to pursue him.

Beth shouted, "Come *back* here, young man, or I'll haul your butt into federal court."

Jim stood over Genie, holding the giggling child under his arm like a football. "Lose something?"

"My mind, I think I saw it running out the back door."

The little boy's mother extracted him from Jim's clutches. "Thank you. He's *obsessed* with the lottery."

Jim frowned at the little man. "Stay away from the ponies."

The red-headed child stared up at him. "What ponies?"

His mother dragged him out of the post office as he repeated over and over, "What ponies? What ponies?"

Genie allowed herself to be pulled up to her feet. "My hero. Thanks for grabbing that kid."

"You seem to attract little boys." He waggled his eyebrows. "Big ones, too."

Beth harrumphed. "Excuse me for interrupting you two." She jammed an envelope with a partial footprint into Genie's hand. "Take this. I didn't have an address for you, anyway."

Genie stared at the envelope. "Is this your bill?"

"No, silly." Beth fluffed her hair and adjusted her super-sized breasts. "It's an invitation. Now, if you don't mind, I have to get back to work." The blonde winked at a well-muscled construction worker and sashayed out the door.

Genie tucked the hold mail form into her back pocket and opened the envelope.

Dear Fellow Alumna,

Hard to believe it's been 25 years since we last walked the halls of Summerville High. Wouldn't you like to know what's going on with former classmates? The Reunion Committee has worked hard to plan a fabulous, fun-filled three day celebration on the last weekend in June at the historic Summerville Inn.

Come for one day or all three—but register early for the SHS package discount. Bring your spouse or come stag. You won't believe the surprises waiting for you!

RSVP to BethandRich@heade.com

Genie read the invitation twice to be sure she'd hadn't misunderstood it. She handed it to Jim without a word. He scanned the paper then looked up at her, his mouth an O of astonishment.

"Oh, my gawd!" She shrieked in a perfect imitation of Beth. "In six months we're hosting the biggest party in Summerville since 1985—and we didn't even *know* it."

CHAPTER EIGHT

~*~

Housed in the basement of City Hall, the Summerville Historical Society was a large underground warren of filing cabinets and cardboard boxes, all of which were covered with a thick layer of dust. Water oozed from a wall and the smell of mildew hung in the air.

A pale-skinned, elderly woman with a dowager's hump sat at a desk with a nameplate that read, *Miss Harris, Archivist.* She looked up as Jim and Genie approached her desk. "Yes, may I help you?" She spoke in a paper-thin voice.

Her gray hair was pulled back in a French twist and vintage cat-eye rhinestone-studded bifocals perched halfway down her nose. Heavily penciled, upward winged eyebrows gave her a surprised look. A sweater hung on her shoulders, clasped with a chain, each ending with a metal cat's head. Something about her reminded Jim of his grandmother. He wondered if it was the love of cats.

"I was wondering if you could help me research a house—specifically the Summerville Inn. I think it should qualify as an historic property." He handed her a copy of the paperwork from the closing. "We're sort of in a hurry." Not to mention the fact that despite their love for desserts, they couldn't stay in the Motel Seven all day, doing nothing. They needed money for this huge reparation—and where better to start than here?

Miss Harris stared at the paper, as if examining it for authenticity, and looked up at him with a piercing gaze. "Well, this is certainly a surprise. No one has asked me about the Inn for, what is it now? Twenty years." She tapped the paper. "Did you check online before coming here?"

He nodded. "The only places the National Register has listed on line are the Eastman House and the Susan B. Anthony House. And with all due respect to the New York State Office of Parks, Recreation, and Historic Preservation, the Inn is on the same street, in the same historic district as the Crofton-Brown House."

Her eyes widened and a smile creased her wrinkled face. "Well, well, you *have* done your homework. Good for you. Allow me to clarify; the house you refer to was built by an architectural firm of *historic* significance. And it's been functioning as a not-for-profit museum. *Your* job will be to prove to the State of New York that your building is historically or culturally significant."

She turned and clicked away at a keyboard. The computer and her desk were the only areas not covered in dust. "Let me see where the architectural archives are. I have an index of all the major collections. Just give me a minute. Ah. Here we are. Come with me." She stood and motioned for them to follow.

Jim and Genie followed the woman through what seemed like a mile of narrow rows of rusted filing cabinets and mildewed cardboard boxes. He was beginning to wonder how he'd find the way out, when Miss Harris stopped and waved her hand over a row of filing cabinets. "The files you want begin here in 1800 and go to here in 2000. If you find what you need, we can talk about the next steps. Be cautious when you handle the files. Good luck."

Jim picked the files closest to him; Genie headed for the opposite end of the row. He began pulling out the drawers, looking for anything resembling files on the inn, which, according to the title search, had gone through several owners and a variety of names.

Jim glanced at his watch. Thirty minutes of digging to no avail. He looked at Genie and the intense expression on her dust-streaked face told him *not* to ask how she was doing. He wondered how Miss Harris could work in this hobbit's barrow of mildew and gloom. Jim felt a fresh surge of appreciation for the inn's tall windows, wide porch and open vistas.

Genie whooped. "I have it!" She waved a yellowed manila folder. "Schmidt and Stone built it in the early eighteen-thirties in the Greek revival style, which judging by the neighborhood, was all the rage at the time."

Miss Harris suddenly appeared at Jim's elbow. How had she snuck up on him? *Does she have cat's feet?* The older woman put her hand out. "Hand that to me, please. These materials are irreplaceable." She led the little procession back to her desk.

Jim placed his arm around Genie's shoulders. "Great. We'll take the copies home and start filling out the application with the State of New York."

Miss Harris looked up in surprise. "Oh, heavens, no. First you have to complete a form requesting a copy of these materials—then the Board of the Historical Society will review your request."

He frowned. "When does the board meet?"

"Every three months. They just met, so they'll be back together in February." She handed him a pen and a three-page document. "There's also a fifty dollar request fee. Just make your check out to the Summerville Historical Society."

Was this woman for real? Jaw locked, teeth gritted against yet one more roadblock, Jim wondered if maybe this wasn't meant to be. Maybe they should forget about trying to get the historical designation. He had enough on his plate; he didn't need this hassle, too.

Just as he opened his mouth, Genie's viselike grip locked onto his forearm.

She smiled, then placed a one hundred dollar bill on the desk. "Is there *any* way you might be able to expedite this for us?"

What the hell was she doing?

Miss Harris stared at the cash, licked her lips—then stuffed the bill into her blouse. "Give me a few minutes."

As her footsteps faded away in the distance, Jim leaned over and whispered, "Where did you learn to bribe people?"

"Tsk, tsk." She smirked. "Don't you know you should *always* tip the maitre d' for better service?"

~*~

What were the bimbo and Ichabod Crane up to? Tony peeled off another wrapper and stuffed the gum in his mouth. He'd followed them the whole freaking day and still hadn't figured out what their deal was. Breakfast and the bank—that he got. Everyone needed food and cash. The Outdoor Gear store? They went in, stayed forever, but came out empty-handed.

Then, they went into City Hall. Were they filing for a marriage license? Zoning paperwork? He slunk down in his seat and watched the couple stroll past his rental car, completely oblivious to his presence. *Dummies. Why does she have dirt smudged on her cheeks? And what is he smiling about?* After that fire, the two of them should have been pissing their pants. Instead, they both looked as if they hadn't a care in the world.

"La, la, la—*Bimbo*." He spat out the last word. "That hotel is mine. You just don't know it yet."

~*~

Beth Heade stormed into her house, grabbed a bottle from the freezer, and poured herself a tall glass of Russian vodka on the rocks. Just as the first hit of euphoria took over, Dick strolled into the kitchen and cocked an eyebrow at her.

"Is it five o'clock somewhere?"

"You should talk. No, *don't*. I ran into the new owners of the Inn at the post office. Literally. Freaking reunion invitations flew everywhere." She took another slug of liquor. "The place was a zoo."

He smiled. "Good. Won't the new owners be surprised when they find out the Summerville Inn is hosting the class of '85 reunion."

"They know."

His face flushed and his eyes bulged. "How?"

"As usual, you weren't *listening* to me. I said I ran into them at the post office. I gave Genie her invitation."

He was in her face in two steps. "That wasn't the plan."

"Screw your plan."

"I promised Tony I'd make the auction right for him. It was supposed to be his—"

"Why? So you could get your coke free?"

His eyes widened.

She poked at his chest with the tip of her enameled index finger. "You still think I'm just a stupid cheerleader—so dumb that she got knocked up in high school and you *had* to marry her." Tears stung her eyes at the memory of the elopement and its aftermath. "Joke was on both of us. The miscarriage was two months after the wedding."

"That has nothing to do with this."

"It has *everything* to do with how you treat me. I'm an *inconvenience* to you—until there's some sweet real estate deal you or your sleazy pals want in on. Well, this time, I leveled the playing field and gave them notice."

His face turned crimson and veins popped out on the side of his neck. "They'll *never* get it ready in six months. They'll go bankrupt and have to put it back up on the auction block."

"Says *who*?"

Spittle flew out of his mouth as he shouted. "Tony. When he wants something, he gets it. He'll make sure they're buried in debt and *have* to let it go."

She slammed the glass down on the counter and turned on her heel. "You better be careful that thug doesn't bury you first."

CHAPTER NINE
~*~

Genie lifted a pot of coffee off the two-burner cook stove she had placed on top of the non-functioning range in the kitchen. Camping out in the Summerville Inn had *seemed* like a good idea in the beginning of November with a long spell of Indian summer to buoy them along. Holding hands, she and Jim examined every suite and dreamed about how they would renovate them. Sheraton or Hepplewhite furniture would be needed. Matching four-posters, wardrobes, night stands, writing tables, full-length mirrors, and vanities for the huge bathrooms were a must. They spent hours in the Summerville Public Library and the Historical Society, browsing books and researching architectural firms. They asked for references and identified construction companies and artisans who could balance the demands of new codes and regulations with preserving the historic nature of a structure.

Thanks to the home equity line Beasley granted her, they'd been able to get the humongous oil furnace up and running, albeit in a cloud of black smoke and curses from the repairmen. The electric company had reconnected the meter and the water had been turned back on. They had a roof over their heads, heat in the rooms they used, having closed off the heat vents in all but the kitchen and their bedroom to conserve funds, and she heard the faucet dripping behind her because they were putting off getting the plumbing repaired until they had more cash on hand.

She knew she was lucky—she had a home and a good man. The saints *had* heard her prayers. She knew she should be grateful but when December rolled in with a bitter cold snap, it nearly broke her spirit. She still hadn't heard a definitive answer from the bank about the loan—and the application for historic status was sitting on some bureaucrat's desk in Albany.

Cooking on a camp stove had lost its funky charm. The air mattress, although a fun place to create innovative desserts with Jim, had begun to leak and each morning she awoke with her butt on the hard floor. And, if that wasn't bad enough, her bank account was nearly cleaned out, the home equity line of credit was down by half, and the insurance agent wasn't returning her calls.

Jim came into the kitchen dressed in a down coat, boots, heavy gloves, and a hat that looked like it belonged in Siberia. His breath puffed white fog in the air. "The good news is we don't *need* a refrigerator in this weather."

Warming her hands over the camp stove, Genie didn't have the energy to respond.

"The bad news is," he continued, "things that we don't want frozen have turned into rocks." He rolled an egg toward her on the floor. "Set up the ten pins, I think we can bowl for omelets."

Just as she opened her mouth to respond, pitiful caterwauls pierced the cold air. "That wasn't me," Jim said. "Was it you?"

She walked to the kitchen door and opened it. A rail thin black cat strolled in, sat in front of her and howled. Genie contemplated the noisy feline. "You chose poorly."

The cat looked at her with large gooseberry green eyes and yodeled. Jim squatted down and petted the creature. "He feels like a bag of bones. Don't we have some tuna in the pantry?"

Genie cast a guilty glance at the cat. "I was saving it for lunch."

He gave her a wide-eyed look. "C'mon. I think I still have five hundred dollars credit left on one of my cards. Let's splurge. Go out to lunch. Feed the puddy cat."

She sighed. "You're right. I was being selfish." Her stomach rumbled. "Let's do brunch. Eggs, waffles with maple syrup and bacon."

"In bed?"

She punched his arm. "*That* will have to wait."

They watched the cat suck up every drop of fish from the open can.

"What shall we name it?"

Jim touched his index finger to his lip. "How about Hoover? He eats like a vacuum cleaner."

"He is a she."

"Oh."

She threaded her arm through his. "That cat must have been praying someone would take her in. Why don't we name her Hope?"

~*~

Brunch at Sips Coffee Shop was over almost as quickly as it began. One minute her plate was full, the next it was empty. Owner Maggie LaMonica walked by with a pot of coffee and stopped to clear the table.

"Send that back to the kitchen," Genie said with a straight face. "I didn't like it at all."

Maggie lifted the stack of dishes and flatware. "I'll be sure to tell the cook." She stopped and turned. "My short order guy is going on vacation for two weeks. I know you're a CIA-trained chef—and this is *truly* beneath you—but would you consider helping me out for a bit? Just until he gets back?"

Genie bit her lower lip. *Was it that obvious that they were on the brink of financial ruin?*

"Hey, forget I mentioned it." Maggie turned.

Genie swallowed the huge glob of pride stuck in her throat. "Thank you. Yes, I'd *love* to do that. I miss having a real kitchen."

Maggie almost dropped the dishes. "Seriously?"

"Yes—but only if you allow me to experiment and offer some daily specials that are different from your usual ones."

"It's a deal." Maggie pushed the door into the kitchen and called out, "Earl, you'd better watch out. You may not have a job when you get back."

Jim grinned, reached across the table, and grabbed Genie's hand. "That black cat brought us good luck. We'll eat for free for two weeks."

She allowed herself to enjoy a tiny thrill of excitement. Her *own* kitchen. Not a Sous chef. The *executive* chef for Sips Coffee Shop. She closed her eyes and imagined herself in her chef's jacket and pants, whisking up an amazing variety of soups, appetizers, entrees, and desserts—all at reasonable prices.

A woman's voice intruded into her fantasies of butternut squash bisque, goat cheese and leek tart, strawberry crepes, and sweet potato French toast.

"Miss King? Miss Genie King?"

She blinked. A short brunette with large hips made larger by her down coat stood next to the table, her nose bright red from the cold. The woman's voice sounded familiar. "Do I know you?"

"We've only spoken on the phone. I'm Amanda—with your insurance company?" She pulled her purse off her shoulder and put her hand inside. "I heard you were here and I thought I'd give you the news in person."

Genie braced herself. "That can't be good."

The woman sighed. "In cases of suspicious fires, we are *obligated* to examine all possible causes, including the home owner's potential involvement." Amanda paused and looked Genie in the eye. "We hired our own arson investigator."

Dear God. Genie hoped they didn't think *she* set the fire. She and Jim could have died in the blaze. She opened her mouth to protest, but the woman put her hand out like a traffic cop. "I know what you're thinking. But it's standard protocol. After extensive research, our arson investigator ruled you out as a suspect."

Her breath came out in a long whoosh. Genie hadn't even realized she'd been holding it almost the whole time the woman had been talking. Amanda continued. "I regret to inform you that the adjuster has determined that your house is not salvageable."

Jim squeezed her hand. Hot tears welled up in her eyes and she felt her lower lip tremble.

"Between the fire, the water damage, and the subsequent temperature drops, it was totaled. Minus the land, the company has decided to pay you the value of your damaged property." She handed Genie an envelope. "I'm sorry. I wish we could have saved your home."

Genie watched the woman leave the restaurant through blurry eyes. *Dammit. It just wasn't fair. How much was a person supposed to take?*

She withdrew the papers from the envelope, looked down and gasped.

Jim leaped to his feet. "What is it? You look as if you're going to faint."

Without a word, she handed him the check.

He ran his fingers back and forth across the numbers.

Genie leaped out of her seat and began jumping up and down. "Call the architect. Get Restoration Hardware on the line. We can start the renovations!"

Jim grabbed her and swung her around, knocking into empty tables and chairs. He stopped dancing. "There's something we have to do first for our lucky charm."

Breathless, she could barely speak. "What's that?"

"We can buy Hope a *lot* of cat food with five hundred thousand dollars."

~*~

Richard Heade could scarcely believe his eyes when he read the insurance company's report to the Fire Investigation Team. Not only had Genie King been absolved of any wrong doing, but they paid her a ridiculous amount of money for the house. Who knew the dump was worth that much? Tony Aiolfo had been certain that torching her home would push her over the edge and force her into selling the inn. He'd even returned to New Jersey to await the call from Beth offering him the Inn at a fire sale price.

Instead of falling into a pile of manure and drowning, those idiots had come out smelling like the New York State flower—all thanks to the crook's not-so-well-laid plans. Pacing his office, Rich rearranged his trophies, and then straightened framed photographs of himself with various dignitaries.

What was he going to tell Tony the Wolf?

CHAPTER TEN

~*~

Genie shouted through the serving window. "Order up."

"I'm coming, I'm coming." Maggie hustled into the kitchen after seating yet another out-of-town couple. "You know, all I wanted was for you to fill in for two weeks. I never expected you to stay on after Earl went AWOL and turn this place into a celebrity food show."

Genie put a hand on her hip. "You mad at me?"

Maggie grinned. "Hell, no! We've gotten rave reviews from local papers, and now I suspect that Mr. and Mrs. Incognito out there, just might be food critics for a New York City newspaper."

Jim looked up from chopping vegetables. "Does this mean we can hire another kitchen assistant? This woman is *killing* me."

Genie shook a spatula at him. "Back to work, slacker."

He bowed at the waist and lowered his voice in an imitation of Boris Karloff. "Yes, mistress, as you wish, mistress."

She laughed and turned back to speak to Maggie, only to find Webster Bond in her place, looking serious. "Can we talk?"

"Sure." She motioned Jim over to her side. "Whatever you say to me, he should hear, too."

Web pulled out a notepad and a pen. "I'm on the Fire Investigation Team. It's been three months and we still have some unanswered questions. Both the Fire Department's Arson Investigator and the insurance company agreed that it was an intentional blaze. The cigarette lighter had no prints and the propane tank was expertly set up—so it was someone who had experience." He frowned. "We have the wrappers you found. One of them had a piece of chewed gum in it—but we can't match the DNA to anyone in state or FBI databases. And we can't test everyone who's in Summerville to see if we get a match."

Jim grimaced. "Don't you hate it when ethics stand in the way of getting the job done?"

Web nodded. "So, our job is to narrow down the suspect pool to the most likely offenders."

Genie tapped her spatula on her palm. "Don't you have a list of convicted arsonists? Couldn't you look at them?"

"We've already started. A large number of them had to be eliminated because they have alibis. Incarcerated or dead firebugs aren't very helpful."

"There's something about the gum wrappers that's been bugging me." Jim shook his head. "It's like it's right in front of me and I can't see it."

"Genie, do you recall the day you pulled into the SPD and honked your horn at me?" Web asked.

"Yeah. I felt like an idiot for doing that."

"Didn't you say someone was following you?"

She flushed. "My overactive imagination. I thought the guy we outbid for the Inn was tailing me—"

Jim shouted, "That hairy guy, Tony, was chewing gum at the auction. Wads and wads of it, kept throwing the wrappers on the floor. I remember thinking what a pig he was."

"You *really* think he would burn my house down because he lost the auction? He could have killed us!"

"I've seen people murdered for their shoes," Web said. "If this guy felt like he'd been screwed out of something he wanted, that's a powerful motivator."

Genie recalled the gleam of hatred she'd seen in her rearview mirror that day. *Yes, that thug is capable of arson—and murder.*

Web looked up from his notes. "Did either of you happen to catch his last name?"

Genie shook her head. "No, but your boss seemed to know him. Kept slapping him on the back and telling him what a great casino it would make."

It was Web's turn to look surprised. "My boss?"

"Yeah. The Chief of Police, Richard Heade. He was at the auction the whole time."

Lips tight, Web snapped his notebook closed and gazed off into the distance. At last, he spoke. "Thanks. I'll see what I can find out from him—if anything."

~*~

It was all Tony Aiolfo could do not to leap through the phone and strangle Heade. Stupid sonuvabitch. No wonder they called him Dickhead.

"So, instead of putting the Inn back up for auction, they're going ahead with renovations?"

"Like I said, Tony, there was nothing I could do. I can always control the outcome of the SPD investigation—but how the hell was I to know the insurance company would hire their own investigator? They usually only do that when the property's worth over half a million. Who knew they'd haul in the big guns for a fucking shack? And now that the reports been filed in a million different places, there's nothing I can—"

Dickhead's whine had all the charm of a droning buzz saw.

Tony shoved three sticks of gum into his mouth. The old adage was true: If you wanted a job done right, you had to do it yourself. "I'll be back next Wednesday. Make your big-titted wife do somethin' useful for a change and find me a place to lay low, so I can keep an eye on the Inn."

He heard Dickhead's sharp intake of breath—but nothing more. "Glad you unnerstand who's in charge here."

~*~

Midnight, exactly one week after Web interviewed them at Sips, Jim walked through the door of the inn, ass dragging as bad as his feet. The construction crew had swept up the sawdust and debris and left the work site in good condition. He felt something brush his legs. "Hi there, Hope. Are you hungry?"

She stared at him with gleaming eyes. "Meowrp."

"I take it that's a yes." He rummaged in the pantry for a can of pureed turkey and placed it in her dish. She lunged at the wet food and hoovered the plate clean. He ran his hands down her back and sides. "You're putting on a little weight, my dear." Maybe they were overfeeding her.

Genie came in through the back door, hands filled with bags of food she'd prepared for the workmen.

"You're spoiling the guys," he told her. "They'll never work for anyone else after this."

She loaded the bags into the new brushed chrome refrigerator. "Who says loyalty can't be bought?"

"Did you happen to notice that Hope is getting fat?" He pointed at the creature in question, currently licking her paws and grooming her face. "I think we should cut down her food."

Genie reached over and patted the cat's head, then felt down to Hope's belly. She stood up, a smile wreathing her face. "She's not fat. She's pregnant."

"But she stays inside—"

The woman who still made him weak at the knees, with or without food, gave him an amused look. "She arrived in December—in the middle of that terrible cold snap. It's now the end of January. So, she must have been pregnant when she landed at our door."

"Poor Hope." Jim lifted the cat into his arms. "I hope your baby daddy isn't out catting around on you." She head butted his arm and purred loudly.

"I can't wait to hit our lovely new bed with the *real* mattress," Genie groaned. "I'm beat and I know *you're* exhausted. The lunch crowd will be clamoring at us tomorrow." She yawned and stretched. "Before we go up, we'd better find a cardboard box and put some blankets in it for Hope."

"There's a box in the foyer. It will be just the thing."

Jim set the cat down and flipped on the light switches as he headed toward the lobby of the inn, pausing to admire the work that had been completed. The mahogany surface of the refinished registration desk gleamed a welcome beacon. The floor, too, had been refinished; the windows, once cracked and broken, had been replaced. He knew the crew was moving room by room, repairing and renovating the space in preparation for decorator approved furnishings.

As soon as the insurance check cleared, he placed the order for thirty rooms of identical Hepplewhite replicas and coordinating décor items with one of the top manufacturers in the country. Out of habit, he reached into his pocket and rubbed the medallion in silent thanks to *all* the saints who had helped Genie and him get the old gal back up on her feet.

He searched the dark corners for the cardboard box he'd seen earlier that morning, and after some digging around, found it. Whistling a happy tune, he picked it up and heard something rattle inside. *Crap. Had the guys used this for trash already?* He opened the lid.

Inside was a wad of crumpled gum wrappers.

~*~

Tony sat back, turned on the TV and surfed for the porno channel. *Nuthin' like a little footage of naked broads to help a guy relax after a hard day's work.* He snickered. Dat bimbo and Ichabod Crane were gonna have their hands full when they found his latest surprise. He clicked away at the remote—

channel after channel of nuthin' to watch. Where the fuck was the triple X channel?

He'd told Heade's big-titted wife to order *all* the cable channels—but each time he clicked on the *Adult Entertainment* icon, a message flashed on the TV screen, informing him he didn't have that service.

In a fury, he hurled the remote control device across the room and decided Mrs. Tits would pay for the hole in the wall. *Stupid bitch.*

Now he'd have to find a different way to entertain himself.

CHAPTER ELEVEN

~*~

Genie cradled Hope to her chest, rubbing the cat's ears while Jim spoke to Web. "I'm telling you, the work crew sweeps this place clean every day before they leave." Jim nodded at her as he spoke into the cell phone. "They're bonded for life to Genie through her cooking...Yes, we're up. We won't be going to bed anytime soon. See you when you get here. Thanks."

Hope jumped down and slipped through the basement door.

Genie washed her hands and patted them dry. "Is Web on the way?"

"Yeah. He said he'd bring crime techs with him to collect the wrappers."

She shuddered. "I can't believe that creep had the nerve to come into our home. He must have found the key we left for the construction workers and came in after they left." Her eyes suddenly wide, she locked gazes with Jim. "What if he sets a fire here, too?"

Though his heart took a major leap into his throat, Jim tried to stay calm. "The crew put the sprinkler system in last week. I'll take a good look around the Inn, go room by room. You stay here and let Web in."

"Jim, I'm afraid. We barely got out with our lives last time, what if—"

He grabbed her, held her tight, and kissed the top of her head. "We're one step ahead of him. I'm sure he didn't think we'd find his spoor."

He handed her the cell phone, then lifted one of the kitchen fire extinguishers. Thirty suites, thirty areas to hide a smoldering flame that could rage out of control. Trying not to panic, he began the search on the third floor.

~*~

Genie clutched the phone and paced back and forth in the kitchen, hoping Web would get there soon with a crew from the SPD. When she heard the front door bell, she almost wept with relief. She raced down the hallway, across the large foyer and threw the door open.

The Neanderthal in a suit stood on the darkened front porch with a gun pointed right at her chest. "Hullo dere, little bimbo. Remember me?"

She wanted to scream for help but her voice froze in her throat.

"Ain't you gonna invite me in?"

Mute, she stepped away from the door—and hit the re-dial button on the phone.

"Turn around. There's a good little bimbo. I gotta make sure you ain't packin'."

As he ran a beefy hand under her blouse then down her front and between her legs, she bit back a shudder. Her skin felt as if it was crawling with bugs.

"Turn around to face me."

What should she do with the phone?

She pressed the speaker button and handed it to him. "It's for you."

"Summerville Police Department, nine-one-one."

She screamed, "Help me, there's a man with a gun—"

Tony backhanded her and the lights went out.

~*~

Jim stopped his search of suite 302. Was that Genie? He stepped out of his shoes and raced out onto the balcony hallway to peer over the balustrade. A body was crumpled on the floor with the thug standing over it.

It was Genie. She was down. *Is she alive?* Pulse pounding, his breath coming in short puffs, he patted his pocket. *She had the phone.*

While he watched from above, trying to decide what to do next, the creep pulled her hands over her head and dragged her out of sight across the newly finished floor.

Where are the police? He couldn't just stand there like a statue. He had to do *something.*

He wanted to run to her, but was afraid that if he moved too quickly, the crook would hear him and maybe hurt her worse. He dared not take the elevator. *Too noisy.* It took all he had to tiptoe down the hall and test one step at a time, one flight at a time, avoiding squeaking floorboards. By the time he arrived at the first floor, he was dripping in sweat and the fire extinguisher in his hand felt like it weighed a hundred pounds. He stood still and listened hard.

"Stupid little bimbo. Tink you can take this place from Tony the Wolf?"

The thug was in the kitchen.

Someone mumbled.

"Don't talk back to me." The distinct sound of a slap shattered the air.

Genie whimpered, then fell silent.

"I'm asking you again. Where's Ichabod Crane?"

"He went to the police department—took your gum wrappers with him."

"So it's just you and me, little bimbo. You and me are gonna party."

"We're on to you." Her voice was defiant. "Your DNA was all over that gum at my house."

"So, what? It ain't in no police database. I'm no dummy." Tony guffawed. "Enough small talk. Lemme see those tits."

Jim slipped around the corner—and froze.

With both arms bound behind her, Genie sat in a kitchen chair with her blouse torn open. The creep's hands were on her breasts. She looked up. Her eyes widened—and Tony wheeled just in time for his chin to meet the butt end of the kitchen extinguisher.

The Neanderthal wobbled—but didn't fall.

Just as Tony pointed his weapon at Jim, Genie lifted her leg in a sweep, connecting with the thug's crotch.

He dropped the gun, went down like a tree, grabbed himself and shrieked, "You bitch!"

Jim grabbed the gun and trained it on the creep.

In the distance, the reassuring sounds of sirens came ever closer.

~*~

"You have the right to remain silent. Anything you say can and will be used against you in a court of law—"

"Stupid pig." Tony smirked the whole time Officer Bond read him his rights. "Your boss will have me out in two heartbeats."

"I called Chief Heade on my way over, to see if he wanted to join us." Bond shook his head. "Said he didn't know you. Only met you that one time at the auction. Told me to treat you like any other criminal."

Tony glared at the uniform, not believing his ears. "I'll have your badge."

"I don't think so. You're going to give us a nice DNA sample and we'll tie you to arson and attempted murder—in addition to burglary, and now, attempted rape."

Tony shouted, "Vinny DeCapo will have your *head*."

Standing to the side of the room, the bimbo's boyfriend asked, "Did you say Vinny *DeCapo*?"

"Yeah, jerk-off," Tony snarled. "You heard me right."

The jerk-off boyfriend started laughing.

"What's so funny?"

"Vinny and I are old gambling buddies from Atlantic City. I pulled him out of the ocean one time. He couldn't swim. And he almost drowned. He gave me his medallion." He held up what looked like a gold coin. "He told me, if I ever needed a favor, to just call him. I think I'll do that right now."

Suddenly, Tony wished he was someplace far, far away.

~*~

A cat yowled from the basement.

Releasing herself from Jim's arm, Genie straightened up, pulled her blouse together, and wiped the tears off her face before calling out, "Kitty, kitty?"

She flipped the light switch and opened the door, expecting to see Hope on the top step. Instead, she heard water rushing in the background. She whirled on Tony who was being led out of the kitchen by Officer Bond. "What did you *do?*"

The creep snickered. "Just a little housewarming present for you and Ichabod Crane."

She ran down the stairs. The sound of rushing water grew stronger. Water covered the bottom step. *Where was Hope?* Tears filled her eyes. That black cat was their good luck charm and she loved her. *Where was she?* "Hope? Here kitty, kitty."

"Meowrp?"

Water lapped at the next step—the one she stood on. She yelled up the stairs. "Jim, find the main water cut off."

Footsteps pounded overhead and the gush of the water slowed down to a trickle, then just a drip-drip-drip.

"Hope?"

"Don't go in the water," Jim shouted. "You could be electrocuted."

In the gloom of the dimly lit basement, Genie strained to see beyond the steps. Boxes they had left down there floated on the water, along with newspapers and other detritus.

"Kitty, kitty?" Her voice choked. If that creep hurt her cat, she'd—

"Meowrp?"

She looked down. Floating in front of her was Hope's litter pan—with the proud new mother and three black-and-white kittens.

Epilogue

~*~

The ballroom of the Summerville Inn shimmered with candles; the air was filled with the scent of white lilacs, the first of the spring from the English gardens surrounding the property. A string quartet played classical tunes and the crowd chattered happily. Genie smiled at Jim and gave his hand a tight squeeze. Everything was set for the big event. Not that it had been easy over the last four months.

Between dealing with the insurance company—*again*—cleaning up the water damage, fixing the pipes that Tony had damaged, and removing the sodden trash out of the basement, they had hardly had time to relax and enjoy the reparations and decorating of the upper floors. At last, each suite was completely outfitted in the neoclassical lines of Hepplewhite-style furniture, the best bedding, marble baths, and thick white towels.

Hope and her kittens, Faith, Charity and Love, had inspected each suite and deemed them all perfect.

Maggie LaMonica found a new cook for Sips Coffee Shop—another refugee from New York City and the pressure cooker world of *haute cuisine*. Genie had stayed on at Sips to get the new chef settled in—and to release Jim from his duties as kitchen assistant. He lost no time getting the front desk up and running.

She turned back to the crowded ballroom. She could not believe the turnout. It was beyond her *wildest* expectations. The food critics and journalists had gone over the top with the coverage. When the stories hit the wires about the CIA-trained chef, the Cornell School of Hotel Administration graduate, and their struggles with a low-level New Jersey mobster to return the Summerville Inn to her former glory, people sent cards, letters—and checks. With these generous donations, Jim and Genie started the not-for-profit Summerville Inn Foundation for the express purpose of providing scholarships to deserving students to attend culinary or hotel management school.

After the bureaucrats in Albany were inundated with e-mails and letters of support from the town citizens for the Summerville Inn to be declared an historic property, the pencil pushers *finally* approved the application on the grounds the Inn would be creating employment opportunities as well as investing in the local community.

Despite his protests all the way to jail, Tony 'the Wolf' Aiolfo was never able to make his allegations against Chief Richard Heade stick. The Wolf made bail, failed to appear for court—and never was seen again. Officer Bond had told Jim that when he asked Vinny DeCapo if he knew where the thug was, the head of the New Jersey mob had shrugged, said he had no idea where the arsonist went and he smiled while he answered.

Jim leaned over to whisper in her ear, "This will be *excellent* practice for the new staff for the Class of '85 Reunion. Are you ready?"

She took a deep breath and nodded.

He motioned to the musicians to begin the wedding march. Everyone stood and applauded as Jim and Genie walked hand-in-hand down the aisle, toward the justice of the peace and into their new life with the Summerville Inn.

Release Your Inner Wild Woman:
Kiss of the Silver Wolf
—✶—

�֎

Prologue:
The Hunt

HE LEANED DOWN on his front paws, relieved the kinks in his back, and shook out his thick coat. Beneath the cold air, a hint of spring tantalized his senses. Under the moist leaves, between the tree roots, alongside the chortling streams, the sleeping earth mother stretched her legs and wiggled her toes, too.

He gazed at the pearl white moon as she rose on the horizon, full and iridescent in the February sky. Only a few days left to enjoy this part of his life.

Time for a run. He began to trot, then broke into a long easy gait, loping around the perimeter of his territory, through trees and winter-bare brush. He picked his way across a snow-melt-swollen stream, past massive rock formations and darkened houses, enjoying the feel of his muscles as they kept pace with his pounding heart. *This is what it feels to be alive!*

Too soon, he reached the asphalt and the end of his fun. Panting, he turned away from the road and walked at a slow easy pace, back to the pack's meeting place. *Time to speak to the Old One about the future.* Midnight runs no longer suppressed his primal feelings, the visceral urge he felt when the full moon rose.

Each month, the call to mate was stronger—irresistible as the pull of the moon on the oceans—and on him. The females in the pack were off limits, bonded forever to their soul mates. Besides, their scents didn't arouse him. No, the one he wanted was far away, almost an unattainable being. The moment he saw her smoky-eyed image, he knew she was,

The One. Often, when he was alone at night, he gave into his dark urges and fantasized about holding her and making her his own. But in the morning, he was still alone, his dream-mate a dust mote on a sunbeam. He shook his head to clear his thoughts and stepped into the apple orchard.

Half-hidden in shadows beneath the moonlight dappled trees, the Old One nodded his head, a knowing glint in his bright orange eyes.

The younger male trotted over to him and bowed his head. Half a dozen adolescents tumbled over and around the Old One, bit his gray ears, and nipped his toes. When the smaller ones looked up and saw the younger male, they yipped, hobbled over to him, and threaded between his legs. The Old One's mouth opened in a grin, and his tongue lolled.

Okay, here comes the Uncle routine. The younger male fell to the ground, rolled on his back, and the six pups leaped on his belly. He chuffed and pawed at them, cuffing each one lightly. He enjoyed this role, but what he really wanted was his *own* pups to play with. After a few minutes, he gave a great sigh and flipped onto his belly. The little ones seemed to sense his change in mood and hobbled off to play with sticks.

He locked gazes with the Old One. *When will I have my own mate? It's not enough for me to watch the little ones play.*

The Old One winked and nodded. *My job is to preserve the pack, to keep our people alive. I have chosen your mate. You know who she is. You have my oath.*

The younger male shook his head. *You didn't answer my question. When? When do I get my mate and become Pack Leader?*

The Old One leaped to his feet, glared at the younger one, and growled a deep throaty roar that belied his age. *You dare to question me? Me? The one who saved you? Is that how you show your gratitude?*

The younger male put his ears down and lowered his head, his nose touching the ground. *Forgive me. I'm--I'm so lonely. My heart aches for a loving mate and my own pups. Every moon the urge gets stronger, the hunger greater.*

The Old One came closer, grabbed the back of the younger male's neck with his teeth. The large signet ring on his iron necklace clanked as he gave the upstart a small shake. *The time is coming near. I promise. You will—*

The unmistakable crack of a rifle sounded in the distance.

The Old One's mate barked out orders to the other females. *Grab the pups. Get them home. Hurry, hurry.*

The younger male found a straggler hobbling along as fast as his legs permitted. He lifted him by the scruff of the neck. *C'mon, little one. I've got you. You're safe now.*

A second shot rang out closer by.

The little one whimpered and shuddered in his grip. *Please don't let the hunters kill me, Uncle Zack. Please?*

~*~

"I told you to hold your fire!" Special Agent Eliana Solomon stood by the abandoned mine and drummed her fingers on the butt of her Sig Sauer.

"Sorry, Sir—Ma'am…I thought I saw a wolf in my night scope." The newbie looked downward as she glared at him.

"This isn't a hunting trip with your buddies. It's an active operation and I'm in command. One more shot and I'm taking your rifle away from you. Got it?"

He gulped, clutched his weapon, and nodded. "Yes, Ma'am."

She had asked for experienced soldiers; instead they sent a bunch of green boys. She understood the Middle East took precedence, but didn't the Army get the concept of domestic terrorists?

The mission of Project Aladdin was to find Jinns, the portals where they came through from a parallel dimension and to shut them down. Contrary to popular TV images of a pretty girl in a bottle, the jinn, or genies, were *not* nice. Powerful shape shifters, they hated humans and wanted to take over the world. If a terrorist ever found a way to conjure and command a jinni, the world would never know what hit it.

Despite her obsession and round the clock investigations, she'd been unable to make any progress. With her evaluation coming at the end of the month, she had to find *something*. Otherwise, she'd be exiled to a desk and spend the rest of her professional life analyzing emails. She shuddered at the thought of death by tedium and twisted the heavy signet ring on her left hand.

Strange energy signatures had been seen on satellite images of this area and identified as jinn. The abandoned mine was the logical place for a portal—but so far, the scout they'd lowered down into the shaft hadn't reported anything. She glanced at her watch. In fact, he'd been silent for twenty minutes. He was supposed to be reporting in on the quarter hour.

Mouth dry, she keyed her radio. "What's going on down there?"

Static.

"Hello. Can you read me?"

A long burst of static was followed by garbled voices. A man screamed.

She wheeled on the pale-faced young corporal holding a rope. "Get him out of there!"

He leaned back and grunted, red-faced with exertion. "Something's wrong, Ma'am!"

She raced behind him, screaming at the stricken-looking young men huddling together. "Get over here. Help us get him out."

Three of them put their backs into the effort, finally bringing the scout up into view. Limp-limbed, the young man's head lolled back, his camouflage uniform covered in blood. They hauled him onto the ground and rolled him over.

A soldier held a flashlight as Eliana pulled out a handkerchief and wiped his face off. Something was on his forehead. She dabbed at it and stopped. The words burned into the man's forehead told her all she needed to know. She stood on shaky legs.

Bug eyed, the corporal turned to her. "What is it? What's it mean?"

She chose her words with care. "It's Hebrew. It says: GET OUT."

She flexed her fist and rubbed the heavy signet ring inscribed with pentacles and letters from an ancient language. She was going to need help from a source that *some* people said didn't even exist.

CHAPTER ONE
~*~
Say No Eulogies

Charlene Johnson stood ramrod stiff in the over-heated, wreath-filled Serenity Parlor of Charles and Sons' funeral home—half-numb with grief and shock from the sudden loss of her parents. *I just need to get through the next two hours without falling apart. One foot in front of the other.* A mélange of lilies, wet wool, body odor, and a hint of alcohol pressed against her nose as if it were a hot, wet rag. Despite the March winds and bitter cold rain lashing the building, she longed to go for a long run, stretch her legs, breathe fresh air, and ease the tightness binding her chest.

What happened? What made her father drive into that concrete buttress? Was he trying to avoid something? A heart attack? Bad brakes? What? And why wouldn't the police answer her questions?

Despite making all the arrangements for the visiting hours and funeral, she still couldn't believe her parents were gone, killed in a single-car accident on an empty road, on a bone-dry night, by the light of the March moon.

A crowd of colleagues, co-workers, and friends, waiting to pay their respects, queued out the door, but Charlene had never felt so alone. A gangly, skinny outcast in high school, she'd been best known for her speed as a long-distance runner and her preference for practice runs at night. Even now, she still felt different, separate from her peers at her metropolitan university. Although she'd dated a lot of guys, and even had a serious relationship with one for a year, her family stayed her only *real* source of unconditional love.

Her gaze snagged on the memory table laden with a satin stainless steel urn and photos of her parents. In one, Mom held her in the crook of her arm. Dad looked over her Mom's shoulder, smiling broadly. In another, her grinning parents stood behind her and Joey, her older brother. Someone in the funeral home had artistically arranged candid shots of her father at work in the Johns Hopkins genetics lab, and her mother in her nursing scrubs between the family portraits. A fresh wave of grief washed over her.

She had to be strong for Joey. He was all the family she had left.

A classical arrangement played in the background, not quite covering the crowd's whispers and murmurs. "Tragic! So young…cause of accident?"

She winced and mentally thanked her parents for their memorial service plans. Practical to the end, they had ordered cremations and no eulogies. She would have never been able to deal with a viewing. Not after what she'd seen in the morgue. She shuddered at the memory. No amount of post-mortem grooming and cosmetics would have covered—*No. Don't go there. Don't think about the medical examiner's odd questions. She had to focus on the here and now.*

"Thank you for coming, Dr. Hoffman." She shook the stooped, gray-haired man's soft hand.

"Fred was a wonderful guy. I'll miss his quirky sense of humor. We'll be a boring bunch of nerds without him around."

"You believed in his research. That meant a lot to him."

Hoffman nodded and looked down at the floor. "He was passionate, obsessed with a cure for Joey."

A sudden vision of the medications, needles, and syringes she found in her brother's room after the accident flashed into Charlene's mind. *Did her father use experimental drugs on Joey?* She opened her mouth to ask Hoffman about it, but closed it, instead. She hadn't been home much for the last year and a half, much less Joey's caregiver. *What choice did she have but to continue to use the medicine her parents had left for her brother? What right did she have to criticize her parents? She was always too busy with her life, her studies, her research, her career to ask how they were doing. She'd been self-centered and myopic. Now they were gone and she'd never get to talk to them again.* Tears welled up in her eyes and she choked up.

Hoffman pressed his business card into her palm and snapped Charlene back into the present. "If there's anything I can do for you, call me."

She could only nod. Vision blurred, she searched a nearby table for a box of tissues. When she turned back to the line, an old man in a threadbare black suit, snow-white shirt, and a thin black tie shuffled up to Charlene and grasped her hand with his callus-hardened one. As she stared at geometric patterns on the large signet ring on the elder's hand, the scent of apple pie laced with cinnamon wafted over her. For a moment, her shoulders lost their tension and she smiled. *Her mother loves—loved—apple pie.*

Taut skin, the color of beef jerky and deep creases in his forehead and cheeks gave the man the appearance of a puppet when he spoke. Only his ice-blue eyes and thick gray hair appeared to be human. "You don't know me, but we're kin."

Apprehension tickled the back of her neck. *Kin?* Charlene mentally compared his face with her mother's photo albums and came up empty. "I'm sorry, I don't recognize you. Your name is…?"

"Jethro Carter. This is my wife, Rebekkah."

An elderly woman with iron-gray hair pulled back into an impeccable bun stepped up to Charlene, gave her a slow once-over with piercing blue eyes, and nodded. "You're a bit taller and your hair's a little redder, but you're hers, alright. You have her eyes."

"Thank you." When Charlene extended her hand, the old woman pulled her close and sniffed her neck.

Rebekkah stepped back. Tears shimmered in her eyes. "You even smell like her."

What was that about?

The old woman glanced at Jethro and he nodded. Rebekkah reached into her pocket and retrieved a dark metal bracelet. "This was your mother's. She would have wanted you to have it." She slid the oddly heavy bangle onto Charlene's wrist. "Wear it always."

A fresh wave of grief hit, and Charlene could barely speak. "Thank you."

Jethro cleared his throat. "And this is Zachariah Abingdon."

Charlene expected to see someone the same age as Jethro and Rebekkah. She caught a whiff of soap and some unrecognizable musky spice and jumped, startled to find him standing at her elbow.

The younger man flipped shocks of silver hair away from his piercing blue eyes. A trail of heat blazed in her face, and ignited a fire in her core. He gazed down at her, an amused hint of a smile playing on his full, sensuous lips. "Call me Zack."

When he spoke, she felt as if he had reached out and caressed her cheek. He took her hand, and a surge of energy jolted her. *Did he feel that?* Dry-mouthed, she squeaked, "Are we related?"

He smiled, showing beautiful white teeth. "Not that I know of. Is that a problem?"

Heat rushed up her neck, and she felt a blush blooming on her face. She looked down at his large hand still clasping hers. She didn't want to let go. "No. Not at all."

Jethro cleared his throat again, and Zack grinned at her, a sly look in his eyes as he slid his fingers away. She glanced down, half-expecting to see a visible red glow where his touch lingered on her skin in a trail of heat.

"We should let other people speak with you." Jethro pressed an envelope into her hand. "There are no orphans among our people. You and Joey need to come home. We can help you take care of him in Eden."

Goose bumps ran up her spine. *How did he know about her brother? Eden. Her mother had warned her about that place. Who exactly are these people?* She stared at the odd trio in their old-fashioned garb as they moved toward the memory table and whispered to each other. She couldn't make out the words, but the tone sounded pleased.

Pleased at what? She examined her new bangle. Feathery-scripted *J*s twined across the surface. *Joanna.*

As she puzzled over the dark metal, a dumpling of a woman lunged at Charlene and pulled her into a bear hug. The brassy-blonde reeked of cheap perfume, and her nose bore the signs of time spent with a bottle.

"I'm so sorry. This is such a tragedy."

Charlene remembered meeting the woman at Joey's school. She'd overheard her whispering to another parent, making a joke at her brother's expense: *"Doesn't he remind you of Lon Chaney when he played Wolfman?"* The gossip's son attended school with Joey. Charlene liked her son, Todd. But the mother was a pain in the neck. *What was her name? Did it begin with an N? M?* "How's Todd?"

"Oh, isn't that *just* like you and your parents? Even in your hour of need, you ask about my son." The woman clutched her hand in a sweaty grip and pulled her closer. Her voice dropped to a hoarse whisper, and the smell of alcohol layered over the cloud of cologne. "Will you be putting Joey in a home?"

Charlene slipped her hand out of the woman's grasp. "Why would I do that?"

"Well, dear, the school is *very* expensive," Todd's mother continued in a condescending tone. "Trust me, I know. Now that your parents are gone, I don't know how *you'll* be able to afford it."

"Thanks for your concern." She remembered the woman's name. "I assure you, Mrs. Morton, I have no intention of taking my brother out of our home."

The woman huffed and moved to the memory table on unsteady feet.

Charlene scanned the crowd. Zack caught her gaze, and winked at her and turned away. A metal chain dangled out of his back pocket, much like one a biker would wear. *He's a bad boy.* Her heart jittered. She forced herself to take a deep breath and chided herself for her instant and powerful attraction. Her brain chemicals were in hyper drive, nothing more. She recalled her mother's warnings. He was from Eden. He *couldn't* be good for her.

CHAPTER TWO

~*~

Death's Hostage

Shortly after the last mourner shook her aching hand, Charlene sat on the edge of her seat in her family lawyer's office and spoke between gritted teeth. "What do you mean, there's no money?"

Will Rutler handed her a sheet of paper. "Here's the medical examiner's final report. Cause of death: Suicide."

"I don't understand. They were happy, in love—"

"The police interviewed Dr. Hoffman and reviewed your father's lab notes. Your dad was having trouble at work, depressed over his lack of progress in his research on Gorlin-Chaudry-Moss Syndrome."

She shook her head. "No. I don't believe it. He was a scientist. He knew breakthroughs take time."

Rutler looked down at his yellow legal pad and underlined something with his Montblanc pen. "The National Institutes of Health wouldn't renew his grant—questions about the direction of his research."

Her mind whirred with reasons to disbelieve the family lawyer and financial manager. She sensed another shoe mid-air. "What are you hiding from me, Mr. Rutler?"

He looked pained. "I think you have no choice but to place your brother in a group home."

She leaped to her feet and the dark, book-lined room seemed to whirl and close in on her. "No. I won't do that. It's *my* job to take care of him. I have to do this myself."

"Your father changed the policy less than a year ago, increasing the payoff to a million dollars in the event of his death." He paused. "But, the insurance company won't pay for a suicide."

"I don't believe he killed himself—and what? Murdered my mother, too? Never. He loved her, would have given his life for her—" As soon as the words were out of her mouth, the weight of it all—the loss, the grief, the unknown— crashed onto her. She slumped into the red leather chair and buried her face in her hands. "What am I going to do?"

"Your mother had a modest insurance policy, fifty-thousand dollars. That will take care of the funeral, their credit card debt, and you and Joey for a while." He slid a sheaf of papers across the desk to her. "Sign these, so I can take care of the bills."

She gazed at the papers, and his voice became a murmur in the background to her thoughts. Rutler wasn't being unkindly. It was his job—she knew that. He was trying to be helpful. He'd known her parents for over twenty years, even been to dinner with them on many occasions. They'd been more than business acquaintances. They'd been *friends*. How could he believe her father would commit suicide and murder her mother?

"Charlene?"

She looked up and saw him gazing at her with a concerned expression.

"Sell the house. Put Joey in a state-supported group home. Finish your doctorate. You're only twenty-four. You have your whole life ahead of you."

"What kind of life will I have if I disown my brother? I'll find a way, Mr. Rutler—even if I have to quit my PhD program and work three jobs. I will never, *ever* place my brother in a home."

She stood. He opened his mouth to speak and she put her palm out. "I want a copy of the Medical Examiner's report, and I want copies of all the photographs."

"You shouldn't do that to yourself. It's too—too gruesome."

She took a deep, shaky breath. "I'm a neurobiologist, Mr. Rutler. I spend my days and many nights dealing with blood and brains, stuff that makes most people queasy."

He pursed his lips and shook his head.

"I need to see with my own eyes. I need to know what happened. I need *closure*. Please do as I ask."

~*~

A month later, Charlene pulled into her gravel driveway with Joey in the converted minivan. She glanced in the rearview mirror, and smiled at her brother. "You need a shave and a haircut, Joey. Time to get my clippers out." She made a buzzing sound, and he laughed and signed, "Moon, moon, moon." How he *loved* the moon.

A dark sedan with tinted windows parked at the curb. Will Rutler climbed out of the car, his forehead creased with a frown. "I've been trying to reach you, but your phone's been disconnected."

"I just switched to a cell phone. It's cheaper. I was going to call you." Charlene gave him the number as she struggled to move the heavy wheelchair off the lift, her bracelet clanking against the chrome. Baltimore roasted in a surprise late April heat wave and sweat poured into her eyes.

Rutler strode to her side, his expensive citrus-scented cologne preceding him. "How are you? How's Joey?"

She mopped her brother's brow with a handkerchief. "We're okay. I got a job at Joey's school, and they trained me to be a bus driver. Between that, my school loans, and his scholarship for students with disabilities, I'm making ends meet." She eyed Rutler. "But you didn't come by to make small talk. What's up?"

"I have bad news and good news."

Her mouth went dry.

"You have the medical examiner's report? The photos?"

He nodded and held up a bulky manila envelope.

She reached for it, but he pulled it away. "Not just yet."

"*Now* what?"

"Your Aunt Jessie died. That's the bad news. You inherited her farm. That's the good news."

"My mother's older sister? I never met her, but Mom said she tried to get Aunt Jessie out of that place." *Eden. The little town her mother ran away from.* "They used to be close." *Why didn't she come to the visiting hours?*

Rutler waved his hand in a sweeping gesture. "You can leave all this behind and become an apple farmer."

"Yeah. Right. Just my style. This city girl who knows zip about gardening, much less farming, is not about to set foot in Eden to grow apples." *Besides, her mother warned her: Stay away from Eden. Nothing good happened there. Secrets within secrets within secrets, she said. Stay away.*

Rutler frowned. "What do you want me to do?"

A surge of guilty relief at the prospect of paying off their bills washed over her. "Sell it. Get whatever you can. Maybe I'll be able to finish my PhD after all." She put her hand out. "I'll take the envelope now."

He hesitated a moment, then placed it in her palm. "Think twice before you open this. There are some things you're better off not seeing—or knowing."

As he pulled away from the curb, the weight of the envelope felt heavier. She turned it over, looked at the seal of the Office of the Chief Medical Examiner, and felt her resolve waver.

One foot in front of the other. Joey needed to be taken care of first.

"Okay, Joey, time for dinner, a little TV, then bedtime. And don't you worry. We're staying right here in Baltimore."

No matter what she found out, no matter what she saw in that envelope, absolutely nothing and no one would ever convince her to uproot Joey and move to Eden.

CHAPTER THREE
~*~
The Hunger

Zachariah Abingdon closed the book of Kipling stories and sighed. *The Mark of the Beast* had been another disappointment. Half the horror authors in the world hadn't a clue, he thought. Kipling got the bite right. But he was wrong about reversing the effect. Once bitten hard enough to draw blood, there was no going back. He laughed at the idea, stood, and growled at the stiffness in his back, an annoying reminder of his experience at the hands of drunken hunters. Breathalyzers should be required on rifles and shotguns. *Might save a few more lives than just my sorry hide. Probably would have saved Jessie, too.*

No. Her death—her murder—had been different. The Other People had stalked her like prey, cornered her alone near the highway, close to the perimeter of the pack's territory—despite the No Trespassing signs posted all along the roads. More than one of those monsters had brutalized her. When he found what was left of her on his early morning run, he barely recognized her. The stench of the enemy's blood mixed with her clean copper scent gave him grim satisfaction that she had put up a good fight and managed to injure one or more of them.

Sorrow squeezed at his chest. His friend, lost in a heinous act of revenge. Somehow, he had to right that wrong, find justice, peace, and protection from THEM, The Other People. That's all the pack wanted. The Jinn's revenge came with a price too high, the loss of a good woman, a friend, and his future mate's aunt. When would it end? Never, unless something was done, something *final*. Otherwise, his intended mate could be the next victim.

"Charlene." Speaking her name out loud made his skin ripple and his cock harden. He wanted—no—needed a mate. The call—strong and constant—urged him to settle down and have his own family with Charlene.

Even engulfed in grief at the loss of her parents, she'd been beautiful. The connection between them had been instantaneous, unmistakable. He'd wanted to take her right there in the middle of the funeral home, in front of everyone. She had wanted him, too. He had smelled her desire, felt the heat of her body flare when they touched. Thinking about her made every fiber of his body ache.

He closed his eyes and recalled her strong female scent, discernible even through the stifling odors of the funeral home. She threw off a heady blend of roses mixed with musk and the promise of passion. Her smoky blue eyes were hollow with grief, but clearly capable of joy. He'd wanted to run his fingers through her strawberry blonde hair, kiss her crushed berry lips, then her soft white neck, and her large breasts—poorly disguised beneath a demure dress. Thinking about her made him harder. Not satisfied by memories alone, he growled in frustration. *When would he have her?*

Just a few months ago, when Jessie had been alive, he'd visited the farmhouse, seen the family photos on the mantelpiece, and he knew the Old One was right. Charlene *was* The One. Jessie had been so proud of Charlene. What had she said? "She looks like Grace Kelly." He had to agree. With that long, swan-like neck, upturned nose, and big blue eyes, she *was* a princess—and royalty in Eden.

When Charlene heard the news of her aunt's death, he was confident she'd answer the call: *Come home to Eden, to your people. Assume your rightful place in the pack.* He smiled, anticipating the good news. Surely the Old One must have heard something by now. Tired of chasing his own tail, he decided to motor over to Jethro's General Store and talk to the Old One.

~*~

"What do you mean, she said no?" The hair on Zack's neck bristled and an unbidden growl roared out of his throat. He paced back and forth, and dust flew into the air.

"She told her lawyer to sell the farm. She won't take Joey out of his school."

Zack pounded his fist on the wrought iron railing. "What kind of woman does that to her pack?"

Jethro sighed. "She doesn't know."

He stopped short and faced the Old One. "Doesn't know?" He sagged against the porch in disbelief. "How could she *not* know?"

The Old One shook his head. "Her Momma was head-strong. Wouldn't stay here, ran off after—Oblis died. Didn't stay with our kind, she married a—a *human*. Charlene thinks her brother has some rare genetic disorder. Her human father was working on a cure—until he died."

Zack gaped at the old man. "You never told me this before. I've been here five long years. Waiting for the perfect mate, my one and only. You told me it was her. Charlene. Now you're telling me she doesn't even know her *birthright*? How could you lie to me like this?"

"I didn't lie to you. What does it matter that she wasn't born a full-blooded werewolf?" Jethro fixed him with a hard stare.

"But—"

"What *matters* is loyalty to family, and that girl has it in spades. Not sure I can say the same for you."

"You said—"

"Who found your half-dead body when you were shot?"

Unable to maintain eye contact, Zack looked down. "You did."

"Who gave you his own blood to bring you back to life?"

"You did."

"Who gave you a family, a pack to belong to after yours was wiped out?"

"You did," he whispered.

"Who swore to do anything—anything, because I saved your life and the pack took you in?"

Zack looked up, and saw the blue eyes of the old man deepen into green glowing orbs with sparks of orange. "I did."

"She's my kin, and your destiny." Jethro pointed at a spot on the porch. "Wait here."

Zack fumed, paced the porch, and ran his hands along the metal railing. How much *more* time was he going to waste on this mating game?

The Old One returned with a package. "You need to know about her, and her upbringing. Rebekkah found this when she cleaned out Jessie's house." Jethro handed the shoebox to the younger man and said in a gruff voice, "I'll get her here. But then, it's *your* job to persuade her to choose the family. The pack."

Zack stared at the box and wondered what secrets Jessie had kept from him. Jessie. Her murder *had* to be avenged. "What of the Other People? You told me yourself you knew they were responsible. When will we go after THEM?"

Jethro shook his head. "Even if we had more able-bodied males left in our pack, we can't go into the old mine. Their powers are too strong in there. We wouldn't get out. The best possibility we have against them is on *our* territory."

Zack opened his mouth to protest, but Jethro held up his left fist. The pentacle on the copper and iron signet ring flashed in the afternoon sunlight.

"You know the law. Retribution belongs to the alpha male. I may be old, but I'm not dead yet. I promise you, when the time is right, I will take my revenge on the ones who savaged my daughter. They *will* suffer."

~*~

Jethro stood at the front door of Charlene's house, and wondered if it was too late to knock. Lights burned in the back of the house. *She must be awake.* He hesitated, took a deep breath, and tapped. No response. He knocked again, harder this time, feeling the urgency of his mission with every rap of his knuckles on the wood door.

Charlene stood by the window, her strawberry blonde hair long and loose. He sucked in his breath and growled low in his throat. *Joanna, you rejected us, but she won't. She can't.*

The young woman stepped away from the window and peered through the peephole. "Who is it?"

"Jethro. I need to talk to you."

She opened the door a crack. "At midnight?"

"I drove straight through. Just got here."

A pause. "Can't this wait until tomorrow?"

He bit back a snarl of frustration. "No, this is an urgent matter."

"Where's Rebekkah?"

"Home. Can I come in? *Please?*"

She opened the door and stepped back. "If you must, but please keep your voice down. Joey's asleep." She led him to the kitchen. Books with photographs of brains lay open on the wood and tile table. A mug stood half-empty next to a pad and pen. "Coffee?"

He glanced around the room. White blinds at the windows. Modern white refrigerator and matching appliances. Grief speared him. He never had the opportunity to explain, to apologize to Joanna. To beg her forgiveness. Now it was too late.

"No, but I'll take some water. It's been a long drive."

She handed him a glass, sat down, and stared at him, her pupils large.

A whiff of fear hit him and made him feel sad. *His own kin, afraid of him. What had Joanna told her?* He'd have to handle her with care. He didn't want to spook her. He emptied the glass in one long gulp and licked his lips. "I see you're wearing her bracelet."

"Yes." Charlene ran her fingers across the engraved letters. "It makes me feel connected to my mother. I haven't taken it off since Rebekkah gave it to me."

He heaved a sigh of relief. "I'm glad it gives you a measure of comfort." *She would need it more in the days to come.* "Did you read the letter I gave you?"

"Yes." Her brow furrowed, and her gray blue eyes deepened a shade. "But it made no sense."

"I didn't want to ask you at the funeral—your pain was so fresh." He spoke in a low voice, trying to choose his words with care. "Did you see your parents before they were cremated?" The look of horror that flashed across Charlene's face told Jethro she had. He paused. "We need to talk about what you saw."

She jumped up, knocked the kitchen chair into the white counter, and slid her back along the wall. She stared at him— her eyes wide, her breaths shallow and ragged. Fear poured off of her in waves.

She's going to pass out.

"Charlene, please take some deep breaths." He stood and took a step closer to her. "I can help you."

She put her palm out. "No. Don't come any closer." She took a deep shuddering breath. "I'm just…upset. The accident photos were worse than I ever imagined. I thought I could handle it. But, it was…it was—" She turned her back to him and fresh waves of fear mixed with grief radiated from her.

Her palpable pain seared through him. *If only she would let him help her.*

His beautiful, stubborn granddaughter whirled around and spoke in a hoarse whisper. "What do you *want* from me?"

"Your brother, Joey, he has a—a problem seen among certain types of individuals—"

She cut him off mid-sentence. "He has a disease. A *medical* condition." Charlene passed a hand over her red-rimmed eyes, and scrubbed her face. "A rare genetic disorder called Gorlin-Chaudry-Moss Syndrome. Passed on through the mother. Joey has it worse than most others. My father died before he could find a cure."

Jethro sighed. Her rational mind would struggle with the reality of their nature. There was no way he'd convince her tonight. There were no medical tests that would conclude: *Werewolf.*

She sank back down into the kitchen chair and tapped the textbook. "I think there's a connection between neurochemistry and Joey's condition. If I can find a way to repair the altered brain chemistry, I could reverse some of his extreme spasms and neurological tics." She gave him a teary smile. For a split second she looked so much like Joanna, he thought his heart would break. "At least that's what I plan to do my dissertation on."

He cleared his throat, half afraid he'd start crying, too. "Blood will tell, Charlene. We've seen a lot of this in Eden. Among our pa—people." Jethro bit his tongue. He'd almost said pack. He put his wrinkled hand on top of hers. "Come home. We understand better than anyone else. Let us help you. We're family."

"I know you mean well." Charlene pulled her hand away and looked him straight in the eye. "I can do this on my own. Joey is happy here. I appreciate your offer. But I have no interest in running an apple farm."

He pulled a stack of photos out of his coat pocket and spread them across her papers and books. "Take a look at what you're missing." Trees covered in light pink blossoms filled one photo, a gray and white-trimmed farmhouse appeared in another, and in one whimsical shot, a huge red pig stared up at the camera.

Charlene smiled. "The pig's pretty cute. He looks like he's smiling."

"Name's Trotter. Jessie loved that porker. Said he was a human in a pig's body."

"A pet pig?" She lifted the photo for a closer look. "I've read they're smart. Never thought of one as a pet."

"She left you the farm *and* the pig." Jethro stood, weariness creeping into his old bones. "We'll take care of everything for you until you come home."

She stood, and he smelled her anger. "For the *last* time, I'm not moving to Eden. I have work to do." She glanced at the clock and sighed. "It's late. I can give you a pillow and blankets for the couch..."

"No. That's not necessary. I'll be on my way." He paused on the threshold and handed her one last snapshot, this one of Zack smiling and petting the pig. "You *will* come, Charlene. In time, you will come." He reached out to hug her, but she drew back. He nodded. *So be it.*

Exhausted, Jethro climbed into his mud-splattered old truck and leaned back in the seat. The moon journeyed across the sky, not quite half-full. He had time before the Change, but would it be enough to convince the girl to come home? He shook his head. *A stubborn streak runs deep in that one, just like Joanna.* He hated to do it, but she left him no choice. Tomorrow Jethro would call in the note for the second mortgage on Charlene's home, the one Jessie had fronted for him so he could pay for Joey's special school.

~*~

Two months after Jethro's midnight visit, Charlene opened the mailbox and gasped at the avalanche of envelopes. She'd been trying to pay the bills, scrimping and saving on food, turning off lights, working as many hours as she could between trying to keep up with her studies—all to no avail.

Every letter was a demand for payment of an overdue bill. Worst of all, this time the third and final red paper notice from the lender said: the second mortgage on her home was due, in full, immediately. Tears blurred the words. All she could read was FORECLOSURE. Her parents had ransomed their home—not once—but twice to take care of their son and Charlene.

She had tried her hardest to do it all herself, like her parents. Now, crushed under the weight of financial burdens, she couldn't do it anymore. She couldn't keep a roof over Joey's head, much less keep him in school. *Where would they go? What would she do?*

Unbidden, Jethro's words came to her. "There are no orphans among our people. You and Joey need to come home. We can help you take care of him in Eden."

She collapsed in the chair, put her head down on her arms, and sobbed. She had no choice but to go to the last place on earth her mother would have wanted her children to be—*Eden.*

CHAPTER FOUR

~*~

Help Wanted

A murmur of voices sliding between blue grass music reached Charlene through the store's screen door, background for a late July afternoon. She caught some of the words in the conversation: "rain coming," "big crop," and "new gal." The air did smell of an impending storm, the trees were laden with fruit, and she had no doubt about the identity of the new gal under discussion.

Perched on the top step of the wrap-around porch of Jethro's General Store, Charlene sipped a cola, skimmed the tiny local newspaper, and swatted at flies. Joey slept in his wheelchair in the shade in front of the store window, while Trotter rolled in a puddle at the bottom of the steps—oozing the distinctive odors of wet porker and mud. Head cocked toward the chatter in an attempt to tune in the rest of the conversation, she turned the paper over. Surrounded by a thick black border, the advertisement sat in the middle of the back page, in the midst of offers for apples, pigs, guns, and pick-up trucks.

Part-time school bus driver wanted for special needs children. Call 555-555-5555. Ask for Zack.

Her heart somersaulted. *Is it the same Zack?* Maybe not, since in this part of the world, everyone seemed to have a biblical name. She hadn't seen him since her parents' funeral. A month ago, when she arrived in the little town of Eden, population 4,000—if you included pigs—her minivan crammed with everything the creditors didn't want, her entire focus had been on getting settled. Aside from the one time a pack of stray dogs woke her with their howls at the full moon, she'd found nothing to support her mother's dire warnings. Everyone knew everyone else—and their business. *What secrets could this little town possibly hide?*

True to his word, Jethro made sure she'd received help from the moment she told him she was moving to Eden. A spotless house with a wraparound porch and decorative wrought iron railing contained a specially outfitted room for Joey. Her brother surprised her with a quick acclimation to his new home. Joey laughed and clapped the moment the big red Duroc sniffed him the first time. Based on his near constant presence and frequent nuzzling, she could tell the well-fed pig enjoyed Joey's company, too.

She stood, stretched, and padded inside the store. She smiled and nodded at Rebekkah and two other elderly ladies, chatting over mugs of coffee. The women looked as if they'd be more comfortable in a horse-drawn buggy than in a pickup truck. The only thing that seemed to be a *real* secret in this town was a modern style of clothing. Had they never seen a fashion magazine? How about a television commercial? Come to think of it, where *were* the satellite dishes that dotted most American landscapes? And what was up with all the wrought iron? Every house seemed to have metal railings and matching mailboxes. First, she'd ask Jethro about the job—then televisions and mailboxes.

"Hey, Jethro, you know anything about this ad?"

The old man paused in his sweeping and gave her an assessing look with ice-blue eyes. "What's that, Miss Charlene?"

"It's a notice for a school bus driver." She pointed at the newspaper. "Have you heard anything?"

The chatter stopped, and the women stared at Charlene. Rebekkah reached across the table and turned the radio off.

The better to hear you, my dear.

Jethro passed a hand over his thick gray hair, gripped the wooden broom, and leaned toward her. "Why do you want to know?"

She glanced down at the floor and blushed. "Keeping up with the farm is a full-time job, but I'm broke and need a part-time job on top of it to survive." She gave a rueful chuckle. "It's not like there are any biology labs around here looking for help dissecting dogs."

A collective gasp caught her off guard. She glanced at the women's tense faces. Rebekkah looked as if she was about to faint. *Did she say something wrong?*

"Them special needs kids can be tough." Jethro turned his head and coughed. "You might wanna think it over a bit. Fall's coming. Your Aunt Jessie's apple trees are big producers. She did okay."

"Thanks to you, the trees were sprayed, the apples are growing, and kids are lined up to help pick in the fall. If I get the job, there'll be plenty of hours left in the day to sell apples."

"Suit yourself."

Avoiding eye contact, she played with her bracelet. "Is this the same Zack I met at the funeral?"

The tension in the room seemed to melt away. One whispered, "Isn't that adorable?" Rebekkah smiled and the other women giggled.

Heat rose in Charlene's cheeks. *What's so funny?*

The old man gave the coffee-klatch a hard stare, turned back to Charlene, and nodded. "That's him alright. When you see Zack, you tell him Jethro said to remember his promise."

~*~

Charlene sat in the sweltering bus depot office and debated the wisdom of applying for the job. She glanced around the room lined with file cabinets and the desk stacked high with books—Kipling, Poe, Koontz, King—nothing she'd *ever* read. She sniffed and willed the hairs on the back of her neck to lie down. Supernatural tales defied the rational world, the *real* world. *The truth wasn't out there. The truth was in laboratories waiting for scientists to make discoveries.*

Clean and untainted by perfumed soaps, Zack looked and smelled just as good as the first time she met him. Other guys covered themselves with cologne and aftershave in a feeble effort to smell manly. Not Zack. She could nuzzle and lick this man all over—*Stop that! Where did that come from? You're here to interview for a job—not a date.*

Dressed in a gray uniform shirt that had a "Jericho Bus Company" patch on the right side, Zack flipped his silver hair away from those amazing blue eyes. The heavy cotton uniform shirt strained across his broad chest, and biceps bulged out from under the short sleeves. He rocked his chair back on its legs and read her brief resume while he chewed on his lower lip.

His luscious lower lip. Whoa. One foot in front of the other, girl. She fanned her face with her hand, and looked around for a window—*anything* that would cool her down.

"Charlene J. Johnson. School bus driver in Baltimore. Halfway through your doctorate in neurosciences." He thumped the chair down on the floor, and his voice became gruff. "What the hell you wanna do this for? Is this some kind of science project for you? An experiment?"

"No, it's not like that at all. God, no, I love kids. I wanted to find a cure for my brother's disease, but after my parents died…" Grief and loneliness welled up in her chest and throat, catching at her words. "My life—things—fell apart. Here I am. Broke and living in Eden on my Aunt Jessie's farm. With her pig." She took a deep breath, looked down, and willed herself not to cry. *I'll never get a job this way.*

"Does your brother like Trotter?"

She looked up in surprise, and flicked the tears off her cheeks. "What?"

"My big red friend, Trotter. Does he like him?" He smiled, and two canines that were just a tad longer than normal appeared.

The photo of Zack and Trotter came back to her. "He loves him. And, if I'm not mistaken, Trotter loves my brother, Joey, too. Almost as much as the porker loves rolling in mud puddles."

Zack snorted. Then Charlene realized he was laughing. And found herself giggling. When they stopped snorting and giggling, she said, "I almost forgot, Jethro said to tell you to 'remember your promise'."

A slow, sexy smile crossed Zack's face. He rubbed his hand across the back of his neck, and frissons of excitement rippled up her back, raced across her neck and scalp, almost as if he were touching her.

He tapped her resume with one long index finger, and placed his other hand on his chin. "Your Aunt Jessie and I were good friends. She told me a lot about your mama, showed me pictures of her. And you. Like Miz Rebekkah said, you have her eyes. But I think you have her smile, too. Jessie said she was full of piss and vinegar. Left Eden and never came back."

"I never met my aunt. Now I wish I had."

A palpable silence filled the air, broken only by a fly's angry buzz as it bounced against the sun-filled window.

Zack frowned, and his eyes glinted green. "What was your dad's name?"

"Fred. Fred Johnson. He was a genetics researcher. My parents met at Hopkins when my mother was a student nurse."

Zack nodded, a faraway look in his green—no blue— eyes. He stopped rocking, pulled the chair up, and put his elbows on the desk. "What's your middle name?"

Whatever does he want to know that for? This is one heckuva strange interview.

"Jessie. After my aunt."

"Okay, you got yourself a job." He rummaged around on the desk, found some papers, and handed them to her. "Fill these out. School starts next week. You're gonna need to learn the route in a hurry. Be here tomorrow, seven in the morning. Don't be late. I've got to get you up to speed. And wear this."

He pulled a long dress made out of the same material as his shirt from a drawer, and extended it to Charlene. *Ugh. Please don't take photos of me in this dress.* As she took the old-fashioned jumper, his hand touched hers and heat blazed up her arm. Startled, she locked eyes with him. Sounds ceased, the room faded, and time froze.

Did he feel the same jolt of adrenaline from his ears down to his toes?

After an eternity of an unbreakable gaze, he swept her body with a long, assessing look. His eyes lingered on her breasts, while his tongue trailed a leisurely circuit across his luscious lips. She wanted to know if they were as succulent and soft as they looked. *She wondered if he was a good kisser.* Charlene's nipples hardened and strained against the thin material of her blouse. An image of his mouth on her breasts, nuzzling, licking, and sucking, leapt into her mind—rendering her weak-kneed and breathless with lust.

The phone shrilled once and broke the spell.

Zack shook his head, and said in a husky voice, "You'll probably need to let it out in some places, and take it in others. The last driver had a different um—figure."

She forced herself to focus, stay in the present. "Why'd she leave?"

He put a baseball cap on his head and pulled the bill down, covering the upper half of his handsome face and those slanting, intriguing eyes. He shrugged. "It just didn't work out."

CHAPTER FIVE
~*~
Driver's Education

The next morning she beat Zack to work, ten minutes before she was due. Her heart fluttered when she spotted him in the distance. She'd spent the entire night in a state of sensual arousal, her hands roaming her body, stoking the coals of excitement, but failing to satisfy her deepest needs. When she awoke, she looked at the other pillow on her king-sized feather bed, half-convinced her dream of being mounted and ridden by Zack to orgasm after orgasm was real.

She'd always had a powerful sex drive, surprising many of the men she'd dated. One particularly inept lover, initially full of braggadocio about his sexual prowess, called her a nymphomaniac when she demanded more. In the months after her parents' deaths, she'd been too exhausted to even *think* about sex. With each passing moon, she'd felt no sexual desire—until now.

Despite all her sexual experimentation and one serious relationship, she had never hungered for a man like this. She stood next to her car and watched Zack's fluid motions as he climbed out of his dusty pick-up truck and hid something behind his back. A rush of heat filled the core of her body, and she practically vibrated with anticipation. If she got through this day without tearing his clothes off, it would be a *miracle.*

He called out to her across the parking lot. "I like a punctual worker. Who's looking after your brother?"

"Rebekkah." Charlene had been surprised by the older woman's immediate and positive response to her request for help.

Zack loped to her side in long, fluid strides. With a flourish, he produced a bouquet of daisies from behind his back. "Congratulations on your first day of work."

Momentarily taken aback, she could only say, "Thank you," in a squeaky voice. *Wasn't that sweet of him?* She clutched the bouquet in her still shaking hands.

Zack pointed to a bright yellow school bus equipped with a lift. "There's your ride."

The vehicle was larger than she'd expected. The one she'd driven in Baltimore had been a little bus. Zack opened the folding door. Inside were a dozen dark metal bench seats with heavy padding, all with seatbelts. She noted space for two wheelchairs, and straps to secure them in place.

She whistled. "Pretty state of the art for a small town." She ran her hand over the steering wheel. "Looks like new."

He cocked his head, grinned and licked his lips, sending tremors through her thighs. "We may be country, but we know what's *needed.*" His voice became husky on the last word, and he raised an eyebrow.

Did his eyes just change to green with orange sparks? She blinked. Looked again. They were the same startling shade of blue.

"So, what do you say?" He patted the driver's seat. "Let's take this baby out on the road. You're driving."

"Aren't you going to show me how it works? It's different from the one I used to operate."

"Experience is the best teacher. Key's in the ignition." He threw himself onto the bench seat behind the driver's, gave her a lop-sided smile, and winked.

Was he flirting with her? The unshakeable thought that he might be as attracted to her as she was to him made her heart stutter. Stirrings in the core of her body undulated from her stomach down to her inner thighs—and all points between.

She slid into the driver's seat, snapped on her seatbelt, clutched the steering wheel, and attempted to cage her wild urges. *No sex. Work. One foot in front of the other.*

By dint of great effort and many gear-grinding, gut-wrenching minutes later, Charlene managed to get her rebellious body and the uncooperative bus under control. Sweat trickled into her eyes, down her back, and between her breasts as she jounced up and down the dusty hills.

"Follow this road, then make a left at the first intersection," Zack directed. A manly smell tickled at her nose and teased her. It was almost hypnotic.

"I'll introduce you to the mothers on the route," he said as he fiddled with the label in the neck of her dress. "They're gonna love you."

She warmed at his light touch and feathers of desire stroked her spine. Each pothole and rock caused bounce added to her state of arousal. *Good God, I'm going to have an orgasm if he doesn't stop that. Focus, Charlene, focus. You're going to run off the road.*

A dented aluminum mailbox perched on a wrought iron pedestal half-covered in clematis marked her first stop.

"Just stop here and honk," Zack said.

Charlene leaned on the horn and waited. A few minutes later, a worn-out looking woman came down the dirt driveway. Half a dozen kids trailed after her—all tow-haired, blue-eyed girls in matching dresses.

Charlene opened the door, and the woman climbed up the steps.

"Zack! Who's the new gal on the route?" The woman pushed strands of dishwater blonde hair off her face and shushed her little ones.

"Miz Jones, this here is Charlene Jessie Carter."

"Just call me Charlene."

The middle-aged woman eyed her up and down and turned to Zack. "Which is it? Jessie or Charlene?"

"She's Jessie's niece. Joanna's girl."

"Ahhh. Well, then, welcome to Eden." Mrs. Jones smiled, showed gleaming white teeth, and bowed her head. "Learning the route?"

"Yep, I have a feeling she'll do just fine." Zack gave Mrs. Jones a two-finger salute on the brim of his gray baseball cap.

As she drove away from the Jones brood Charlene asked, "Where's the little boy I'm supposed to pick up?"

"Oh, it's a big job, bringing him down to the bus stop. Don't worry. Come Monday, he'll be out here, waiting for you."

"And the girls? How do they get to school?"

"They go in earlier than the special needs kids, on a bigger bus."

Each stop was the same. Each woman had a brood of blonde-haired, blue-eyed girls in matching dresses. Zack would say, this here's Charlene Jessie Carter." She'd say, "Call me Charlene." And he'd add, "Jessie's niece. Joanna's girl." At each stop, the mother gave her an odd little bow of the head. *What was that about?*

As she drove, Zack reached over her shoulder to show her where to go, and brushed her cheek with his hand. She felt the heat rise in her face—not to mention elsewhere. She struggled to focus on driving and not on the disturbing reactions her body had to this man and his touch. "Tell me, have you lived here all your life?"

"Nah, I'm a newcomer. Only been here five years. From a couple towns over the mountains. Jethro took me in when I fell on hard times and sort of adopted me."

She glanced in the rear-view mirror. "A little old to be adopted, aren't you?"

The corner of his mouth quirked. "How old do you think I am?"

She shrugged. "Thirty?"

Laugh lines crinkled around his eyes. "Close enough."

"While we're on age, I *have* to ask—how old *is* Jethro? He seems ancient. Is he in charge of everything? I can't figure him out."

Real laughter now. "Three days older than dirt would be about right, I'd say. Town elder and all that, but his power— let's just say he's not as strong as he used to be. Jethro knows Eden needs new blood."

"Speaking of new…why aren't there any satellite dishes on anyone's homes? I haven't seen a single television."

He chuffed, almost to himself. "This area has bad reception, lots of problems with electrical things. Folks in Eden tell me it's because of the old mining camp and all the underground tunnels. I'll show you when we go past it on the route. You don't want a break down there. Even radios don't work near that place."

"Does the school have computers?"

A hard laugh, almost a bark. "Yes, the Regional School has real live computers and cable television. That area doesn't have the same problems we have in Eden. We're not in the dark ages— we just have our own way of life. Not bad. Different. Simpler. Haven't you ever wanted your life to be less complicated? People to be more direct?"

She flushed and knew her cheeks had to be apple-candy red. "I'm not sure I'm ready to handle that. I'm a city girl, you know."

"Yeah, I noticed that about you right off." He played with a strand of hair that had escaped from her ponytail. "But I won't hold it against you. I'm hoping to *seduce* you to our way of life."

Yes, he was definitely flirting with her. It had been months since a man had touched her, and she hungered for more. A vision of him in her bed, as Charlene nipped at his ears, neck, and other tasty places distracted her from driving. *Whoa! Slow down!* Her tame side chided her inner wild woman. *You hardly know this guy.* She shook her head and focused on asking more questions, instead of smelling his scent.

"I can't help but notice, it looks like every house has a wrought iron railing and the mailboxes are all identical. Why is that?"

Zack's eyes darted away from her gaze in the rear view mirror. "Protection—" he paused, seemed to be trying to find the right words, "—from the, um, elements."

"One more question," she paused, almost afraid to ask. "What is up with these old time clothes? Why do all the women dress like they're in some weird cult?"

Gazes locked, she waited. His blue eyes shifted to green, and he took a deep breath.

"The women here are modest. They don't like to send the wrong messages to—Other People."

She opened her mouth to ask who "the other people" were and stopped, suddenly aware that her questions sounded like criticisms of the residents of Eden and their way of life. How would she like it if someone did that to her? Better get back to a safe topic—work. "I know what time I take the kids to school, but when do I pick them up? Is it three, like other places?"

"Yes, but some of the boys get additional after school therapy and you may have to wait for them. It's a good habit to get all the kids home before dark. Otherwise their parents worry and start calling me. Got it?"

She nodded. "What if the bus breaks down? My cell phone is useless here. There's no service."

"Use the radio. Sometimes in the hollows and by the old mining camp, the reception is poor, but once you're up on a ridge, it works." He massaged her shoulders and neck. "Don't worry...you'll be fine." The tension she'd held in all day melted away under his strong fingers. She closed her eyes and took slow deep breaths.

With each stroke, her pulse increased, her breath came faster—in short, shallow puffs, and her breasts strained against her clothing. *She felt as if she was in heat!* A little moan escaped. "Keep that up and I'll be a puddle!"

Much to her frustration, he stopped kneading, laughed, and patted her shoulder. "It's time for you to do the route on your own. Tomorrow morning. A dry run."

~*~

Early the next day, she drove off, and he waved at her as she left the bus depot. *If he doesn't ask me out soon, I'm going to have to do it myself. He's driving me crazy! Those eyes. Those lips. Those biceps. That cute little butt.*

She shook her head to clear her hormone charged thoughts, glanced down at the list clutched in her hand, and repeated the kids' names out loud: "Joab, Jehud, Julius, Josiah, Justus, and Jared." Add Joey to the list and they'd be lucky seven. *What is up with all these J names?*

Mrs. Jones stood by the mailbox. "I hope you like apple pie. It's hot out of the oven."

She smiled and Charlene noticed she had long canines, too— like Zack. *Odd.* "Thanks! Can you tell I'm a little nervous?"

"Don't worry. You'll do fine." She smiled, walked down the steps of the bus, and waved good-bye.

By the end of the morning, Charlene had two apple pies, two apple cakes, twelve jars of applesauce, and a tray of candied apples. She returned to the bus depot and found Zack in the parking lot, grinning, and holding another bunch of daisies.

Charlene shook her index finger at him. "You knew this would happen, didn't you?"

He handed her the posy. "Just our down-home welcome."

"Unless you help me eat this food, I'll gain back all the weight I lost after my parents died." She looked at the stacks of apple products and the flowers. An unfamiliar feeling of contentment rose in her chest. Was this happiness? For the first time in ages, she felt optimistic about the future, about connecting with her family's roots, and about the presence of an exciting, virile man in her life.

Any doubts she had about staying in Eden evaporated in an apple and cinnamon scented cloud. She felt a sense of ease that had eluded her most of her life. The town had welcomed her with open arms. She belonged here. "How am I supposed to get all this home?"

He leaned in close to her, flipped an errant lock of hair away from her face, and drew a finger down her cheek. His low voice thrummed in her chest. "I think I can give you a hand—or two—and maybe a little something more."

CHAPTER SIX

~*~

The Feast

When Zack climbed down from his battered pick-up, Trotter circled around his legs, alternating between playful pushes with his snout and leaning against him.

"He really likes you," Charlene said.

Zack rubbed the red porker's ears. "Trotter's my buddy."

"I'd say he's a pretty good judge of character." Charlene latched the screen door against Trotter's prehensile nose. "No. You stay out there." He grunted and flopped down on the porch. She placed the last carton of baked goods on the table, picked up a note from Rebekkah, and turned to Zack. "That's odd. She took Joey over to her house for the night."

They were alone.

Her voice came out in a husky tone. "Guess it's just you and me. Would you like some apple pie? Or cake? I seem to have enough for two—or two-hundred."

Zack gave her a long, lazy smile that made her breath catch and said, "I was hoping for a taste of something else."

Heat raced up her neck and face, and she could barely whisper, "Applesauce?"

He put his arms around her waist, pulled her snugly against his chest, and brushed her lips with his. "You," he breathed. "I want to taste you."

She ran her tongue along his luscious lower lip. "Like that?"

He growled and pressed her up against a wall.

Deep within, she felt a primal stirring, an almost animal urge to throw him down to the floor, and tear at his clothes. Her rational self wondered what she-beast he had awakened, but her inner wild woman said, *Shut up and enjoy the ride!* Charlene pawed at his shirt, the buttons eluding her fevered grasp. Frustrated and crazed with lust, she yelped, "Take the damn shirt off!"

He stepped away from her, grinned, and began to undo the buttons at a leisurely pace. "Am I going too slowly for you?"

"Yes!" She yanked the gray jumper over her head, tore her bra off, and stepped out of her panties. She was nearly panting with exertion and arousal. "I want you naked. Now."

His shirt flew across the room, followed by his pants, the chain on his back pocket jangling as it hit the floor. No underwear impeded her view of his impressive erection. She couldn't take her eyes off his long, thick penis pointed straight at her like a dowsing rod.

He took a step toward her, and she put her hand out like a traffic cop. He stopped. "What's wrong?"

She gave him an expression of mock concern. "That thing could keep me from sitting down for a week."

He was at her side in a flash. He nuzzled her neck and nipped her earlobe. "Let's make it two weeks."

A wave of desire crashed over her. She gasped and arched her back, pushing her breasts onto his hard chest. Her mind lost its ability to form words. She closed her eyes and gave in to the free fall of lust.

His hands roamed her body, rubbing her breasts, making her nipples harden and hurt with desire. "Are you sure? Maybe we should wait. Get to know each other better. Go for dinner and a movie? What do you say?"

Breathless, she reached down, fondled the tip of his penis, his slickness belying his patter. Still holding on, she began to walk backward. "C'mon big boy, I've got plans for you."

They erupted in laughter when she bumped into her four-poster bed and he fell on top of her. He ran his fingers through her hair, releasing the long blonde strands from what was left of the ponytail. She closed her eyes and melted under the light touch of his fingers. When his tongue grazed her nipples, she gasped.

"You like that?" He continued to lick his way down to the center of her belly, and she arched her back—each kiss, each lick and nibble filling her with urgency. By the time he traced lazy circles around the sensitive skin just below her silky triangle, she could barely breathe.

"Now, please," she begged him. "Now!"

Without warning, he flipped her over on her stomach, pulled her hips up in the air, and molded himself to her body. His thighs pressed against her buttocks—his erection urgent between her legs.

"Up on your hands and knees," he growled.

Breathless and half-dazed with desire, she complied, and sighed when he entered her aching, wet folds, filling her. He wrapped his arms around her, one long fingered hand finding her throbbing clitoris, the other pulling at her nipple. She moaned and he began to plunge harder, deeper, longer strokes.

He nipped at her shoulders, clutched her waist, and thrust faster, releasing musky scents of sweat and sex. Just as she screamed in orgasm, pain shot though her shoulder, and he howled.

She fell flat on her face, struggled to roll over, and stared at him. "Did you just bite me?"

He looked abashed. "A love nip. No blood drawn. Honest. Sorry, I got a little carried away."

She scooted backward on the bed, surprised by the bite and confused by her unexpected arousal from it. "You do this often?"

He knelt at her feet and gave her a mischievous grin. "I could ask you the same question, couldn't I?"

She reached over, lifted his chin, and said, "Hoisted by my own petard—or perhaps by your petard? I have to tell you, you brought out my wild side." She patted the bed. "Come sit next to me so I can play with your petard."

He crawled on his hands and knees, rubbing her legs, belly, and breasts in slow, tantalizing strokes. She trembled as his hands slid between her legs. "You know I'm the one for you. You quiver when I touch you. When I'm inside you, our souls meld and I'm complete. We're meant to be together. Let me show you how much I need you, Charlene."

With him inside her, her loneliness fled—a distant memory. Was this what she'd been yearning for all her life? Was this man her home? Tonight, she didn't want to think. She wanted to live in the moment and enjoy the sensations she felt with Zack. She sighed, opened her arms, and released her wild woman once again.

~*~

Later that night, sexually sated, Charlene sat alone at the kitchen table, sipping tea, and eating apple pie. Zack had left an hour before, to give her time to rest—and to think. What the hell had come over her? She'd *never* had sex without insisting on the man using a condom before tonight. She closed her eyes, saw him naked, and a fresh wave of arousal warmed her center. *Hot, hot, hot.* Her brain went out to lunch every time she thought about him. That's why.

She ordered herself to focus on the leather-bound family Bible she'd discovered on a table in the front parlor—along with a beautifully illuminated Koran in English. *Did Rebekkah leave these here?* She wiped her fingers on a napkin and flipped through the Koran, examining the bookmarked and heavily underlined chapters and verses—

"The Cattle—*And they make the jinn associates with Allah, while He created them, and they falsely attribute to Him sons and daughters without knowledge; glory be to Him, and highly exalted is He above what they ascribe.*"

"The Ant—*And his hosts of the jinn and the men and the birds were gathered to him, and they were formed into groups.*"

"The Jinn—*And that some of us are those who submit, and some of us are the deviators; so whoever submits, these aim at the right way: And as to the deviators, they are fuel of hell.*"

"The Saba—*And (We made) the wind (subservient) to Sulaiman, which made a month's journey in the morning and a month's journey in the evening, and We made a fountain of molten copper to flow out for him, and of the jinn there were those who worked before him by the command of his Lord; and whoever turned aside from Our command from among them, We made him taste of the punishment of burning.*"

The only name she recognized was Sulaiman—King Solomon. *What the heck did this stuff have to do with the people of Eden?*

She placed the Koran back on the table and gently turned the onionskin pages of the Bible—careful not to get food on them. A hand-written family tree was inside the front cover in beautiful calligraphy. She sat up straighter when she read her mother's name.

"Joanna Abigail, daughter of Jethro and Rebekkah Carter. Joey, son of Oblis and Joanna Abigail Carter. Charlene, daughter of Fred Johnson and Joanna Abigail Carter." Her brother had a different father? No. That couldn't be. Fred adored Joey. Worked tirelessly to find a cure for him. Her head spun trying to connect the pieces. *If true, this would mean Jethro's my grandfather. Why didn't he tell her? And he's Joey's grandfather. None of this makes sense.* The clocked chimed twelve times. *Too late to call now.* The next time she saw Jethro, she'd make him explain—especially the part about Joey.

After she found the medicine in Joey's room, along with directions on how to give it, she had tried to get more before she left Baltimore. But the pharmacists just gave her strange looks and told her they'd never heard of the drug. Joey seemed to be fine—or was she kidding herself? What if he died?

Her mother called him her Sweet Joey, and told Charlene he'd been born with a thick pelt of baby hair that never went away—despite the doctor's assurances. When she was a little girl, she asked her mother why her older brother couldn't talk. Mom said it was his disease, and her Daddy was going to find a cure for it.

Grief welled up in her chest—captured her heart in its iron fist, and wrenched sobs out of Charlene's most guarded memories. Overcome by sorrow and terrified by the knowledge that she teetered on the edge of an abyss of secrets within secrets within secrets, she clutched the Bible in her arms and wept.

Unbidden, her mind returned to the night at the morgue. Her mother, neck broken, but face intact. Her fingers and nails covered in blood. Her father, eyes bloodied, face shredded with what appeared to be claw and bite marks— *Stop going there! Forget the medical examiner's questions about her mother's nails--and teeth. He must have been watching too many horror movies. Shame on him, he was supposed be a scientist. The marks were from the accident. Nothing more. Her mother was not some kind of mutant.*

CHAPTER SEVEN

~*~

The Route

"Good morning, Mrs. Jones!" Charlene called out her first greeting of the day. Joey sat behind her in his wheelchair, clapping and signing, "Good morning! School!" over and over again.

"Morning, Miss Charlene!" Mrs. Jones led a boy in denim overalls down the rocky driveway. He took halting steps, and his hands flopped as he walked. An oversized baseball cap shadowed Joab's face.

Charlene stood to assist her, but the mother insisted on getting the child onto the bus by herself.

Small hands, covered with fine light-colored hair pushed the brim of his hat back from his face. He impaled Charlene with his smile. "Bus," he signed.

She stifled a gasp. "He looks like Joey."

Mrs. Jones smiled. "Now how'd you know that was Joab's nickname?"

Charlene shook her head. "No, my brother Joey—right here—he looks like Joab."

Mrs. Jones gaze followed Charlene's pointed finger. "Well, I'll be! They do look like brothers, don't they?" A firm hand gripped her forearm, and Charlene looked up into Mrs. Jones' green-blue eyes.

"The boys—they're real hard-of-hearing or—like Joab—completely deaf. They need their routine; otherwise they get upset. Be sure to get them home before sundown. Okay?"

"Yes, ma'am." She blinked. Mrs. Jones eyes were crystal blue again, not a hint of green in them. "I'll see you this afternoon."

She signed "Hello, good morning!" to each child as he climbed onto the bus with halting steps. Each mother thanked Charlene, said they'd see her in the afternoon, reminded her to "get the boys home before dark," and waved good-bye. The shock of seeing her brother in each one of them punched her in the belly.

They weren't really boys, but grown men with severe disabilities like her brother. An image of the Koran and the old family bible came to mind. She had to talk to Jethro, find out what it all meant—but damn that old man. When he stared at her with those ice blue eyes, it was almost as if he could see right through her. She'd have to work up the nerve to confront him.

Secrets within secrets, within secrets.

One of her charges grunted, interrupting her disturbing thoughts. She glanced in the rearview mirror and Justus? Joab? Smiled, waved at her and signed: "Joey is my friend." *They're really children. All innocent and sweet, like Joey.*

~*~

The summer heat lingered and then autumn blazed through the orchards, with trees bursting into red, orange, and gold flames. During the month of August, Charlene eased into a routine of driving in the morning, coming home to crate apples, then running out to pick up the kids in the late afternoon. Doing business under her aunt's company name, *Janie Appleseed*, she had boxes of apples in her cellar and orders from wholesalers piling up on her kitchen table. It was exhausting, back-breaking work. Every now and again, she wished someone would take care of her—but she couldn't give voice to that thought. *One foot in front of the other.*

Each night, Zack came to her house after she'd fed Joey and put him to bed, and they would share a meal—and something more. Much as she wanted to be with him, part of her was afraid to take the next big step and accept his proposal. She valued her independence. Would she lose her identity if they married?

One evening, he arrived at her house and told her that Joab needed his school books, they'd been left on the bus.

He handed her book bag. "I'll stay here with Joey, while you run them over to his house."

Upon her return, she opened the door and inhaled the mouth-watering aromas of sizzling meat and herbs. By candlelight, the simple dining room was transformed into a romantic hide-away. Everywhere she looked, there were daisies and candles. A white lace tablecloth covered the table and in the center was a large vase of red roses.

Her hands flew to her mouth.

"Madam," he pulled a chair out and bowed. "Please be seated."

"What's going on?"

"I thought the city girl might need a fix. So tonight, you are dining Chez Zack. I am your chef, your server, and your dishwasher. Your wish is my command."

Tears sprang to her eyes. "How did you know?"

"I have my ways." He poured a glass of wine for each of them. "Now, relax and enjoy your first course, a little apple and walnut salad on a bed of fresh field greens with a hint of balsamic vinaigrette." He placed the plate in front of her, sat down, and lifted his wine glass. "To you, to me—to us."

She raised her glass in kind. "To you, for making this a magical evening."

"We've only started. I have a wonderful ending in mind."

That night, his nips were harder, and caught up in the throes of passion, she found herself biting his shoulder, too. Embarrassed, she stopped, only to have him beg for more.

"Don't you see? We're meant to be together. I think about you every morning, when I wake up and before I go to sleep at night. I dream about you. I love you. Be my mate!"

After he left, she stood in front of her full-length mirror, assessing the tiny bruises on her neck and shoulders. She glanced down and gasped at the now luxuriant curls where once a light silky triangle had been. A layer of blonde hair grew down her inner thighs. And a faint shimmer of golden fuzz shone all over her body. *What's happening to me?* She grimaced and then stared at her teeth. *That can't be. No. I've had too much wine. Time for bed.*

As Charlene drove out to pick up her charges from school the next afternoon, she caught sight of herself in the rearview mirror and stared.

Who's that woman? She seems familiar, but her face is fuller, tanner, and healthier looking than it's been in years. Was she happy at last? Yes, and Zack was a big part of her newfound joy in life. Six months ago, if someone had told her she would be thinking about marrying and settling down in Eden, Kentucky, she would have laughed. *Funny what love can do to a girl. Love and fantastic sex.*

The school librarian, Shoshannah, came out with the teachers' aides and waved Charlene over. "I heard Zack is courting you."

Heat blazed in her cheeks. "Can't keep any secrets here, can I?" Charlene wondered if they knew how often she had sex with him, too.

"Here in Eden, we have the *original* grapevine! The whole town is buzzing. When are you going to let him know?"

"Know what?"

"Don't play games with me. He asked you to be his mate, didn't he?"

Charlene felt her mouth open and close like a fish out of water. *Were people listening when they made love?* "How did you know that?"

"*Everyone* knows he wants you to marry him." Shoshannah's pretty face scrunched up in a frown. "Honey, he's the most eligible bachelor in town."

"It seems like he's the only bachelor in town."

The librarian cleared her throat. "We—we lost a lot of our young men to genetic diseases."

Charlene felt heat rise in her face at her poor choice of words.

"We're depending on you to do the right thing. Make him an honest man. How long do you think you can string him along?"

Time to change the subject. "Oh my! Look how dark the sky is! I have to get the boys home."

A short time later, as Charlene negotiated a sharp turn in a hollow, miles away from her first drop-off, she drove into a green fog and almost hit a large pack of black dogs crossing the road into the woods. She jammed on the brakes, the bus fishtailed, and the world went dark.

~*~

She awoke to the sound of someone banging on the door of the bus.

"Ma'am? Are you okay in there? Ma'am?"

Her head pounded and something trickled down her face. She touched her temple and looked at her hand in the light of the setting sun. Blood covered her fingertips. Still in a daze, Charlene twisted in her seat and stared at the dark haired woman in the black suit through the still-closed door of the bus. *Where did she come from?* "Who are you?"

"I'm an agent with Homeland Security. Would you like me to call for an ambulance?"

Charlene turned to check on the boys. Joey's chair sat on its side, the security straps ripped off, useless. The other boys, safely seat-belted, whimpered, whined, and cried. A long, low, agonized howl erupted.

"Joey! The boys! Oh my God!" Charlene stood. Her head throbbed, and her vision blurred. She groped at the back of her seat to stand, and made her way to Joey. "Are you okay?"

As she rolled him over, she sucked in her breath. Her eyes had to be playing tricks. *I must have a concussion. Yes, that's it.* She had *never* seen her brother this hairy. Long canines jutted out from his mouth, and his eyes were deep orange. He pulled his lips back, growled at her, and lunged for her face with claw-like fingers.

She jerked back and screamed.

"Ma'am, I'm going for help." Footsteps crunched away on the gravel.

Help? No she had to handle the situation by herself. No one could see him this way. "Joey, it's me, Charlene!"

Recognition glimmered, and he signed, "Moon, moon, moon!"

Tears blurred her vision. "Yes, it's a full moon. And I've got you."

At last, she was able to slide him back into his chair, despite her sudden fear that he might revert to the creature she *thought* she saw. The sunlight faded, and Charlene felt the full force of all the warnings: *Get them home before dark!* Moving as fast as she dared, she checked each frightened boy with caution. She was terrified at the changes she observed—fuzzier faces, shinier teeth, longer nails—but was determined to get them home to their families safe and sound.

A screeching sound pierced her ears. She turned. A soldier wearing green camouflage was attempting to pry the door open.

"Stop!" She pulled the lever and opened the door. "I've got everything under control."

The agent stepped in front of the men, looking skeptical. "Are you sure? Looks like you could use some medical attention."

"No, I'm fine." Charlene tried to smile. "Just banged up a bit."

The woman peered into the bus and seemed to be staring right at Joey. "What about everyone else?"

Charlene reached down, picked up Joab's oversized baseball cap, and placed it on her brother's head, pulling the bill down to hide his face. "All good, thanks. But I *really* have to get them home. They have special needs."

The agent nodded, seeming to be satisfied. She reached into her pocket and extracted a card. "You see anything odd out here, call me."

Charlene read the card: *Special Agent Eliana Solomon, Department of Homeland Security, Science and Technology Directorate.* "All I saw was a green fog and a pack of black dogs in the road. I swerved to avoid hitting them. Looked like they were heading into those woods."

Solomon's eyebrows shot up. She shouted orders to the men standing alongside the road. Weapons at the ready, they began a cautious entry into the forest.

Charlene gave a sigh of relief and plopped into the driver's seat. After multiple grinding attempts, the bus started and she maneuvered it out of the bushes and back onto the road. The radio began to work when she made it to the top of a ridge.

"You're late. The parents are frantic."

"The boys are okay. A little shaken up, but the only one hurt is me." She told him about the pack of black dogs.

Zack began to curse.

"Please don't be angry with me. The windshield is smashed, but the bus is drivable. Tell everyone, the boys are on their way."

"I'm not angry—I'm worried. Drive as quickly as you can. When you're done, go straight home." His voice was urgent. "Don't go back to the bus depot. It's not safe for you to be out tonight. I'll be at your house when you get there."

"No. Please *don't* come. Not tonight. We need to talk when I can think straight." Before he could insist, she snapped the radio off. The last thing she wanted was for Zack to see Joey like—this. She was on her own

Joab's mother stood at the side of the road, waving at the bus. Charlene pulled up, opened the door, and called to his mother. "Something's wrong with the boys, we need to move fast."

The woman jumped up the steps, looked at Charlene's forehead and gasped. "What happened?"

"Not now. Long story. I have to get these other kids home."

An hour later, the full moon crested the horizon as Charlene pulled the bus into her driveway. Wild-eyed, Joey whimpered, huffed, and rocked back and forth in his wheelchair. She'd never seen him this agitated before. Maybe he wanted the pig. She whistled and clapped, but the normally social Trotter failed to appear.

Stay calm. One foot in front of the other. Focus on getting Joey into the house. Over and over again she heard Mrs. Morton's voice, *"Doesn't he remind you of Lon Chaney when he played Wolfman?"* Then the medical examiner's astonished voice rose up in her head, joining Mrs. Morton's high whine, *"I've only seen this sort of thing in books about cryptozoology. Always thought it was the stuff of fiction and crazy people. Was you mother on any medications to control her um—condition?"*

She covered her ears and whispered, "There's a logical explanation for this. He must be starving. That's why he's so agitated." *Stay calm. Act normal.* "Are you hungry Joey?"

His eyes gleamed orange, and he growled.

"I take that as a yes. Let me see what we have." She pulled a container of raw hamburgers out of the refrigerator. "Dinner will be ready in a jiffy."

At the sight of the box, Joey clawed the air and bared his teeth.

Shaken, she placed the entire package on the table within his reach and stepped back. She turned and plugged her ears with her fingers to cover the snapping sounds and snarling. At last, when the noises ceased, she glanced back over her shoulder. Joey slept with a smile on his furry face. Careful not to wake him, she rolled her brother into his room, covered him with a blanket, and locked the door.

Charlene stuffed her fist into her mouth to stifle her rising hysteria, and ran into the bathroom. She flipped on the overhead light, and the world came to a halt. She gasped at her own slanting green eyes filled with sparks of orange. She pulled off her jumper, determined to jump into the shower and scrub away the dreadful events of the day, and recoiled at the image of her hairy arms and legs in the full-length mirror. The little room whirled around her.

"I'm hallucinating." She barely recognized her own voice, a low husky growl. She turned the light off and stood with her back to the door so she could think. *Think, Dammit! Use the scientific method. One step at a time.* When did these changes become noticeable? Was it the night Zack made her dinner? "The food. There must have been something in the food."

Then, as if her mother stood in the dark space with her, Charlene heard her words. "Secrets within secrets, within secrets."

Terrible memories sucked her back in time, back to her home in Baltimore. Her mother growing hairier, locked in her bedroom at 'that time of the month', the muffled sounds of howling, the syringes for her mother's 'migraines'. The shame and fear her beloved mother was some kind of side-show freak, mutant, insane or worse. She recalled her race away from the unknown, her rush into the embrace of hard science, and the loss of it all to an out-of-control car. Unbidden, images of the syringes she found in Joey's room after the accident came to mind.

Leave Eden. Go back to Baltimore, back to the life of science. She pulled herself up on the sink. That was the only thing she could do. *Take Joey away from this place—get him some help.* She touched the doorknob and stopped. *Joey. What should she do about him? She couldn't take him tonight—not like that. She couldn't abandon him. What was this place doing to him? To her? If she left, where would she go?*

Jethro's words floated up in her mind. *"Blood will tell, Charlene."* Jethro. What was he hiding from her?

Anger boiled up in her chest, filling her with fresh energy. *Enough of this mumbo-jumbo.* She pulled her shoulders up straight, stood, and splashed cold water on her face. She stared at herself in the mirror. "I'm good at research. There is a *scientific* explanation for this and I'm going to find it."

CHAPTER EIGHT
~*~
Secrets

After a sleepless night, Charlene fed, dressed and rushed the now back-to-his-usual-self Joey onto the bus. She raced to Jethro and Rebekkah's house after daybreak—before her resolve wavered. After storming up the front porch steps, she pounded on the oak door.

"Jethro," she shouted. "Get out here. Now!"

Moments later, she heard heavy footsteps, then the old man stood in the open entry, still in his nightshirt, wide-eyed and wrinkled from sleep. Rebekkah peeked from behind Jethro, her normally impeccable bun gone, her iron gray hair draped in shiny waves over her shoulders.

"What's wrong? Is Joey sick?" Jethro craned his neck to see beyond Charlene.

She put her fists on her hips. "I don't know. You tell me. He ate two pounds of raw beef last night and nearly snapped my fingers off. You think that's normal?" She held out the holy books. "What are these doing at my house? What do they mean?"

Jethro sucked in his breath, his eyes flared green, and he took a step back.

Charlene moved in, matching him step for step. "What's happening to Joey? And, who the hell is Oblis?"

"You want answers?" Jethro spat out. He turned and pointed at his wife. "Ask Rebekkah. It's her Koran, her Bible. Don't know why she had to go and do that."

Thin-lipped, ashen-colored, the old woman refused to make eye contact with Charlene, instead staring at the floor as she spoke in a near whisper. "It was the right thing to do. She needed to know—about…about *him*, and THEM."

Jethro stomped into the kitchen, cursing under his breath.

She stomped in right behind him. "Who is Oblis?"

He kept his back to her, grabbed a coffee pot, and began to fill it with water.

Charlene reached out and placed her hand on his shoulder.

The old man turned and stared at her, a stricken look on his face. "Please. You don't want to know. Just knowing about them puts you in grave danger."

She refused to look away, stared deeper into those color-shifting eyes. "Rebekkah thinks I need to know. If Fred Johnson wasn't Joey's father, then who the hell *was?*"

Jethro's voice fell to a harsh whisper. "A sexual predator. He crawled out of a hole in the ground, slithered into town, and took our girls' innocence."

"How did he get away with it?"

"He went after our girls at night. Got them alone, told them he'd kill them if they cried out. Raped them and vanished."

"The police didn't help?"

He snorted. "State Police couldn't track him." Jethro looked off into the distance. "He was a disappearing, reappearing snake." He shook his head. "A terrible, evil piece of work he was."

Her lips trembled, but she forced herself to speak. "Was? Where is he *now?*"

He clenched his fists, and the black signet ring stood out in stark contrast to his white knuckles. "Dead and gone."

Charlene wrapped her arms around herself, afraid to ask the next question, but unable to stop. "What happened? I need to know the truth—Grandfather."

He flexed his left hand, made a fist, and adjusted the ring. "I caught him with your mother. I killed him."

Charlene's stomach dropped, and she grasped a counter to steady herself. "The boys--Joab, Jehud, Julius, Josiah, Justus, Jared, Joey—all his?"

Now weary looking, he nodded. "He left the girls—all of them barely eighteen. The families kept it secret—until the babies were born, all the same, all marked by this—this *creature*. I never had the chance to tell your mother why—why I did what I did." Tears filled his eyes. "She ran away. I couldn't find her—not until she contacted your Aunt Jessie. She was pregnant with you and wouldn't speak to me. She thought I wanted to kill Joey, too. I would have never harmed my grandchild—no matter *what* his father was."

He passed a shaky hand over his face, and Charlene's heart twisted.

"She blamed herself. Thought she should have known better than to say hello to a stranger. But he had this *power*. He whispered in her ear and led her to the woods. When I realized she was missing, I tracked them and saw him with her. I went mad, killed him with my bare hands." The old man broke down and sobbed. "Oh, my poor baby. My poor child."

"Our child."

Charlene looked up.

Rebekkah stood in the kitchen doorway, a haunted look on her pale face. Her voice shook. "My daughter. My beautiful daughter. How she suffered from her guilt and shame. And none of it—*none of it* was her fault."

"Grandmother?"

"Yes, dear. I'm your grandmother. And that old fool *is* your grandfather."

Charlene shook her head. "Why didn't you just tell me at the funeral?"

Rebekkah gave her a sad look. "Would you have believed us?"

She had no answer.

"You had no history, no knowledge of your family."
Rebekkah shook her head. "Your mother didn't trust us to
tell her the truth. Why would you? We had to *show* you the
truth of who we are and how we live our lives. Does that
make sense to you?"

"Yes, but—Joey, the boys—I don't understand what
happened to them last night. And where did that pack of
black dogs come from?"

Jethro's eyes widened. He shook his head, his voice
gruff. "That's enough for today. Go. Take care of Joey. Go to
work. But know that we love you, are here for you. Blood will
tell, Charlene. We are your blood and you *belong* here with us
in Eden. We will care for you and protect you. Don't forget
that—Ever."

~*~

The mothers on the route called soft greetings and gave
Charlene sideways glances. The boys seemed more subdued,
less exuberant than most mornings. It was as if a gray veil had
fallen across the normally sunny skies of Eden. Charlene
wondered if it was because she knew their secret or if it was
because they knew that she knew. *But how could they?*

She parked the bus in the side lot at the Regional School
and made her way into the library. Shoshannah glanced up at
her from the reference desk, did a double take, and took
Charlene by the arm into her private office.

"Honey, you look terrible. What's going on?"

"Oh, that good, huh? No wonder the mothers have been
giving me strange looks."

"I have never seen you looking so poorly. You always
have a smile on your pretty face and your eyes light up when
you say hello. You look like you lost your best friend." She
gasped. "Tell me you didn't break up with Zack."

Startled at the idea, Charlene shook her head. "This is
about my grandparents—and Oblis."

Shoshannah's lips curled and she snarled, "Don't ever say that name again!" Tears glimmered in her bright blue-green eyes. Her voice fell to a whisper. "I'm sorry. Please don't speak that monster's name."

Painful understanding hit Charlene like a body blow. "Oh, Shoshannah."

"I was just a young girl. After—after he was done—he left me for dead out in a field, my throat slashed." She pointed to a scar on her neck, and her metal bracelets jangled. "Your grandfather—he found me—saved my life."

"I'm so sorry. I didn't—"

"How could you? We tried to forget that terrible chapter in our community's life, but..." She dabbed at her eyes with a tissue and sighed. "The monster took away our innocence— but we survived. He didn't, thanks to *your* grandfather."

Charlene spoke almost in a whisper. "My grandfather is a *hero*."

"Yes. Yes he is."

"And the children—no one cast them out?"

"The children can be, shall we say, *aggressive* at times, but there are no orphans among our people. Don't you ever forget that, Charlene. No orphans."

Still trying to process everything, Charlene closed her eyes and thought about her mother and father, her brother, all alone in Baltimore, disconnected from this loving clan of relatives. Her grandparents were good, not evil. *What would have made Joanna so afraid of her own family?*

Shoshannah's now chipper voice broke into Charlene's thoughts. "So, what brings you to my lair?"

"The Internet. I need to do some research. Is that okay?"

A bell rang and children's voices clamored in the distance. "Oh, look at the time. I'm supposed to be on first lunch duty today." Shoshannah motioned for Charlene to sit at the desk. "Use my computer. There's paper in the printer. Help yourself to whatever you need."

She had the office, the computer, and her scientific research skills. She also had a sinking feeling she was on the verge of discovering her mother's secrets and her own worst fears.

CHAPTER NINE

~*~

Secrets within Secrets

Despite recalling her father's near daily explanations of his research, Charlene decided to do some digging beyond her memories of his work. Gorlin-Chaudry-Moss Syndrome was similar to—but in no way explanatory for the events of the previous evening. An extremely rare genetic disorder, children with this condition were often deaf, hirsute, and developmentally delayed. In addition, bone plates closed prematurely, causing shortened or uneven limbs, hence the gait problems she'd seen in the boys. The disorder was possibly an 'autosomally recessive trait'. She twisted a strand of hair. That meant the mothers would have to be carriers, too. But *only* the offspring of Oblis exhibited these characteristics. And not one scientific article offered *any* explanation for the changes she observed in her brother overnight.

On a whim, she clicked on the website for the Johns Hopkins Genetics Lab. And found nothing related to her father and his research.

Her stomach fell in a long swooping glide and her heart thudded in her throat. Where was his name? His list of publications? All the grants he'd garnered? What the hell was going on?

She decided to call Dr. Hoffman. After all, he told her, *"If there's anything I can do for you, call me."* What he could do for her was tell her why her father had been erased from their institutional memory as easily as she'd erased the cookies and web addresses from the Internet browser on Shoshannah's computer.

When she finally reached the lab by phone, an underling said the esteemed lab director might be around, but 'deeply regretted' that he 'truly needed' to know who was calling. When she identified herself, a quick intake of breath told her that her father's name wasn't *completely* forgotten. Hoffman came on the line shortly after the gasp.

"Charlene, my dear, how *are* you?"

"How long did it take for you to wipe out every trace of my father's work at your lab? A day? Two?"

"Oh, come now, my dear girl. It's not like that." His voice fell to a whisper. "Let me close my door." She heard a door slam and he returned to the line. "Your father was chasing after a non-existent disorder. That's why the NIH wouldn't renew his grant. Good God, Charlene, we've only just begun to understand the *magnitude* of his delusions."

"Delusions? My father wasn't mentally ill."

"He was obsessed, obsessed with a cure for your brother, so much so that he went off in bizarre tangents, into *cryptozoology* for God's sake! Do you know how that looks to funding sources? We were the laughing stock of the NIH Rare Gene Disease Program. If he hadn't died in the car crash, we would have been forced to fire him. And he *knew* it."

She took a deep breath and exhaled slowly in a futile attempt to stop the alarm bells in her head, the ones that were taking her back to the medical examiner and the trip to the morgue to identify her parents. "Did you say cryptozoology?"

His voice now fell into a low whisper, "Yes. He was looking into cases of lycanthropy and harassing the psychiatrists for the medical records of the few lunatics they saw here who claimed they were werewolves." He paused. "People were *talking*. My funding agencies were beginning to ask some very *difficult* questions. A fraud investigation would have destroyed the lab and many fine researchers' lives. You *do* understand, don't you?"

A chill fell on the once cozy librarian's office.

"No. I *don't* understand, Dr. Hoffman. Please. I would like a detailed explanation. Tell me *exactly* what you mean."

"I couldn't cover up for him any longer, my dear. He *refused* to go to the Employee Assistance Program, see someone to stop this bizarre behavior. I had no choice. I *had* to tell your mother what he'd been up to, ask her to get him professional help." He sighed. "Naturally, she was upset and defended him. Said I was out to get him. Jealous of his brilliance. When I explained the exact nature of his—his *werewolf* investigations--she was shocked into silence. Thanked me for my concern. Said she'd speak with him." His voice broke. "Next thing I knew, they were both dead. A week after the funeral, a Special Agent from the Department of Homeland Security showed up with a warrant and demanded we turn over all his records."

Charlene flashed on the bus accident and the dark-haired woman. "What was the agent's name? Why did Homeland Security want my father's notes?"

"Solomon. Like the king. I have no idea what use his crackpot research could have been to them. I was happy to give her everything we could find and to take all mention of his work off our website." He stopped speaking.

"Dr. Hoffman?"

"Oh, my dear, I've said too much. I'm sorry. I really must go." He hung up and the dial tone buzzed in her ear like a million angry flies.

She placed the receiver into the cradle and stared at it for a very long time, not really seeing the phone, the desk, or the office.

One part of her was convinced Hoffman's concern was all self-serving, his unctuous sympathy a ruse to cover his overweening ego and agenda to promote the genetics lab. The other part felt a twinge of guilt for even thinking that about the man. He'd been her father's boss for years. Dad never complained about him. Not once. If they had been at odds, she would have overhead something, right? Then again, she hadn't been living at home for the past two years.

Exactly *when* did her father's obsession drive him away from scientific explanations and into supernatural ones? How long had it been going on? Her mother would have *never* encouraged him to search for a cure for a disease that her brother *did not have*. That would have been a waste of time, money, *and* career suicide.

What possessed her father to think this tangent was a *viable* research path? Her mother was a nurse, not prone to flights of fancy. In fact, she'd discouraged Charlene from her occasional forays as a child into any supernatural reading, calling it 'irrational, superstitious garbage'. Knowing her mother's animosity toward all things outside the scientific realm, how *would* her mother have dealt with her father's bizarre quest? Had Hoffman's call to her mother provoked a fight between her parents—*and* the subsequent car crash?

And what was Homeland Security looking for, first in her father's notes and now in Eden? What the hell was going on? She pulled the woman's card out of her pocket and stared at the phone number. *Should she call Special Agent Solomon? Would the woman tell her the truth?* She put the card away. Not now. Not until she had more information.

Jethro—Grandfather, said Joanna contacted Jessie when she was pregnant with me. Was she *really* trying to reconnect with her sister? Or was it an attempt to discover if she carried that elusive recessive gene? Eden wasn't the only place with secrets—but it seemed like a good bet that these other secrets started here. *Secrets within secrets within secrets.* Joanna stayed in touch with Jessie. And Jessie was friends with—

She leaped to her feet. The *only* person she hadn't pressed for more information was the one she'd been *sleeping* with. If she hadn't been blinded with lust, she would have been on her game—poking at him with her scientific reasoning, asking hard questions. Instead, when she asked about his past, he dazzled her with his smile, neatly sidestepping any real replies. He *had* to know more than he had told her. One way or another, she was going to get some genuine responses out of Zack.

~*~

She found the charmer rocking on her front porch when she arrived home with Joey. He held a large bouquet of red roses and a bottle of wine. When their eyes met, his eyes filled with concern. Zack joined her at the bottom of the ramp and placed his hands on her arm.

"Let me help you."

She shook his hand away. "I'm fine, thank you. I can take care of my brother."

Joey's face lit up when he saw the man and he signed, "Zack, Zack, Hi, Zack, Zack. Hi, hi, hi."

Charlene wanted to cry and laugh at the same time. *Is Joey keeping secrets, too?*

She fed Joey, then Zack assisted her in bathing him without saying a word. As soon as Joey's head touched the pillow, he began to snore. She wished she could sleep like that. Unworried and innocent—Safe.

She pulled Joey's door closed and walked toward the kitchen, Zack trailing behind her.

He reached out, grabbed her arm, and pulled her around to face him. "You have a hell of a bruise. Let me put something on it for you." He touched her forehead and pulled back at her wince. "I know you had a bad night last night—and a rough day."

"Really? Now how would you know that? The grapevine buzzing its way to you? Jethro maybe? What about Shoshannah? Did she give you a shout and tell you all about my visit with her?" She glared at him. "You're the only one around here without a J name. Does that mean something? That is, you and Oblis."

The color drained out of his face. "I am *nothing* like that viper."

"You *seem* to be a nice man. You are *great* in bed, I'll grant you that. But, I have to wonder why the bum's rush? How could you *really* be in love with me? You barely know me. Or was fabulous sex just a way to keep me from asking hard questions about my aunt and my mother? Hell, for all I know you're working for Homeland Security."

His brow creased and he sounded genuinely baffled. "What are you talking about?"

"I've seen no dogs in Eden until the accident. Not one. Then, I almost run down a pack of them near the old mining camp. Next thing I know, a special agent from Homeland Security is racing into the woods after a bunch of black dogs." She took a shaky breath. "*And*, the same agent seized my father's research records from Hopkins."

Zack pulled her close, and she struggled to wriggle out of his hug. He held her tighter and whispered, "I can't tell you what Homeland Security is investigating. Honest. But I can tell you that I will always be here for you. No matter how much you try to push me away."

When placed into the context of this house, this day, and this moment, the intensity of her emotions and the reports of her father's bizarre research collided. She sagged into Zack's arms and sobbed, grieving anew for her parents, for their lost hopes, and for her father's desperate course of action when science failed him. The pathetic delusions of a man driven to delve into the supernatural world of lycanthropy and werewolves.

Zack rocked her like a child, patted her back, shushed her and finally lifted her up and carried her into the bedroom. Distraught, worried he wanted sex, she smacked at his hands and pushed him away when he began to undress her.

"No. It's not like that," he soothed. "Let me take care of you."

She took great sucking breaths between sobs as he carefully removed her clothes, then covered her with a quilt. He stepped away from the bedside. She rolled over, closed her eyes, and tried to get control of herself. No luck. The torrent of emotions held in for so long ran wild. She beat at her pillow. Why, why, why had her father done this? Had he no idea what would happen next?

Zack returned, lifted her up again, and took her into the bathroom. He assisted her into the claw foot bathtub filled with bubbles. With a large, soft sponge, he gently bathed her from head to toe. Then, he scrubbed her back and rubbed her scalp until her breathing slowed to a slow, steady rate, and her sobs died to occasional hiccups.

When she tried to speak—to ask questions, he would only say, "Shhh, relax. This is your night off. I'm in charge."

When she stood, he lifted her out of the tub, and toweled her off with a huge fluffy terry cloth robe she didn't recognize. Then, he brushed her hair until her scalp tingled, and she felt a glow of warmth trickle down to her fingers and toes. At last, satisfied with his labors, he led her to the bed, plumped up the pillows, tucked her under the covers, and told her to stay there.

A short while later, he returned with a tray of food and two glasses of wine. She wondered where the meal came from, but the thought disappeared when he pulled up a chair next to the bed and began to feed her. Between sips and bites, she tried to speak. But he would only say, "Shhh, you need to rest. Tomorrow, you'll have answers to most of your questions."

He turned down the lights, and as she felt herself drifting off, he leaned down, gave her aching forehead a feathery kiss, and breathed, "I love you. I have loved you since the first time Jessie showed me your picture. And now that I have the real you, here with me in Eden, I am even more in love with you. You are my soul mate. Please sleep on this request: Marry me. Be my mate for life."

Limp limbed and befuddled, she watched with heavy eyes as he opened her window, backed out of the room, and left the door slightly ajar, leaving a sliver of light to comfort her. She sighed, rolled over, and fell deep into sleep.

A strange thumping sound woke her. She sat up in bed, heart racing—and stared into glowing eyes at the foot of the bed. She gasped, a scream caught in her throat.

I must be dreaming. It looked as if the creature shimmered and coalesced into the form of a large silver wolf. The animal jumped down to the floor, walked over to the side of her bed, and nuzzled her hand.

She recoiled. Then, thinking it was a dream she reached out and touched a solid nose. She walked her fingers up his head and began to stroke his ears and neck with care. The wolf was real, as real as the dark metal chain collar he wore.

Wide awake, heart in her throat, Charlene dropped her hand, scooted back up the bed, and took a deep shaky breath. "Where did you come from?"

The iridescent wolf gazed at her for what seemed like a very long time. He cocked his head to one side, then went to the door and nosed it open. He looked back at her, his eyes glowing.

Puzzled, she sat upright and clenched the sheet in her fists. "Am I supposed to follow you?"

He shook his head.

"Wait here?"

He nodded twice and trotted out the door.

Super intelligent wolves? Not possible. She must be asleep. She pinched herself—hard. "Ouch!"

Just as she yelped, the wolf walked back into the room with one red rose in his mouth. He put his paws on the bed next to Charlene, and placed the flower on her lap.

Tears filled her eyes. He stared up at her, his eyes shimmering from green to gold. *If he was going to hurt her, he'd had ample opportunity.* At last, she threw her fears aside and wrapped her arms around his neck. His fur was so soft, but beneath that velvet, she felt the iron of his collar and the vigor of his strong muscles. A familiar scent enveloped her— soap and a musky spice. The tingles of her skin told her this was no ordinary wolf *and* that he was without a doubt *very* male.

She lifted her head, put her nose to his, and gazed into now sea green eyes. "What—who are you?"

He shook his head, loped over to the open bedroom window, and bounded out.

Red rose clutched in her hand, she flopped back onto her pillow, and her mind raced until she was dizzy. What just happened? What and who was that beautiful creature? Where had he come from? Other than the mysterious pack of black dogs, when had she last seen a dog, much less a wolf, in Eden? *Never.* There were no dogs—or wolves—in Eden. Yet sometimes, she heard *something* howling at the moon. *Where were all the dogs?*

CHAPTER TEN
~*~
Dead Letters

The next morning, still puzzling over the curious incident of the wolf in the night, Charlene shuffled out to the kitchen to make coffee and found a freshly brewed pot and a dozen apple cinnamon muffins, still warm from the oven. A note propped up against a mug said, "I have Joey and I'm driving the route. I'll take Joey to Rebekkah after school. You need to get some rest and do some reading. Love, Zack."

She smiled and placed the now limp red rose from the night before next to the note. "Maybe I *will* keep him."

She pulled out the kitchen chair to sit down and found a shoebox with her name on the lid. She opened it, and saw stacks of envelopes addressed to her Aunt Jessie, postmarked from Baltimore, Maryland. Her breath whooshed out.

Was she really ready for this?

She plopped into the chair and fanned the letters out with shaking hands. She began with the oldest one.

"Dear Jessie—

I miss Eden so much. I can't tell you how lonely I've been. I've been trying to decide what to do about the baby. Here in Baltimore, there are options—but I can't bring myself to do any of them. Please don't tell Father I've decided to keep the baby, raise it myself. I found a job as a nurse's aide. I'll write when I can.

Love, Joanna"

She thought of her mother—pregnant, young, alone, afraid to go home, terrified of her father. Charlene wondered what she would have done.

"Dear Jessie—
I've met a nice man. His name is Fred Johnson. He wants to marry me, doesn't care that I'm pregnant.
Can you believe that? He's working on a doctorate in genetics. I think I will marry him. He is very kind. He would never hurt me or my baby.
Love, Joanna."

Tears blurred Charlene's vision. Her mother married Fred because he was kind. Not because she fell madly in love with him. But they loved each other. Didn't they?

"Dear Jessie—
Fred and I were married in a courthouse in Baltimore. We have a nice little apartment near Hopkins and our neighbors are all students too. The baby is due any day now.
Love, Joanna
PS: I'm looking forward to your visit."

Jessie had gone to Baltimore?

"Dear Jessie—
It was so good to see you. And so nice you arrived right after Joey was born. If you hadn't been here to help, I think I would have lost my mind! The doctor kept reassuring me that my 'pregnancy related hair and skin condition' would go away after I delivered. If they only *knew*! Thank you for telling Fred that Joey's problems run in our family. He is convinced that he will find a cure for whatever it is. Isn't he a dear sweet man?
Love, Joanna"

Charlene flipped through the years, and found the news of her birth.

"Dear Jessie—I wish you could be here to meet your niece. She is *PERFECT*. Not a single thing wrong. I cannot bring myself to give her a J name as a first name. I know it's our family tradition, but thanks to Fred, she has a fresh start in life, untainted by Eden and our 'condition.' I've decided to name her Charlene Jessie Johnson.

Isn't that pretty? Here's a photo of your beautiful, perfect, perfect, perfect niece.

Love, Joanna

PS: I hope this pregnancy mask goes away soon. It reminds me too much of you-know-what."

Smiling, she pulled the snapshot out of the envelope. A perfect infant peered up at the camera from her mother's arms. Joanna had long, luxuriant shiny blonde hair and a symmetrical brown discoloration across her cheeks, the pregnancy mask. *What did she mean by 'you-know-what?'*

The letters were filled with chitchat about daily life in Baltimore. The tone was always upbeat, and each missive extolled Charlene's brilliance and perfection. Why was her mother so hung up on her being "perfect, perfect, perfect?"

"Dear Jessie—I cannot thank you enough for the loan. I *promise* we will pay it all off. The school is so good for Joey. He's happy there and now we can give Charlene the opportunities and attention she needs, too. She's so smart. She loves her science classes. I think she's going to be a scientist like her father.

Thank you, thank you, thank you.

Love, Joanna"

Now she knew where the money came for Joey's school. That horrid Mrs. Morton was right. It *was* expensive, more than her parents could afford on two incomes. Money was tight, but they made sure she had ballet lessons, summer camp, and never had to work while she was in college. The year she entered her doctoral program and moved out of the house, the letters began to take a darker turn.

"Dear Jessie—

I miss my darling Charlene. As long as she lived here, I could focus on her, on her perfection. When it was that time of the month, I took the injections to control my urges, to protect her from the knowledge of what her mother really was. But now the moon calls to me, and I want to run, run, run. It is getting harder to resist. Poor Fred tries to understand, but how can he? Do you think you could come visit?

I miss you, and some nights, I confess, I miss the family and Eden, too. Sometimes I think I made a mistake by running away. But then I remember my perfect daughter.

Love, Joanna"

So Joanna had misgivings about Eden, after all. But why keep warning Charlene away from the town, when she herself was homesick and lonely?

"Dear Jessie—

Joey's urges have become difficult to control. He's gotten so big, so strong, and so *aggressive*, the sedatives don't hold him now. Fred was able to bring some experimental genetic treatments home from the lab. But Joey doesn't have Gorlin-Chaudry-Moss Syndrome. The charade has worked for over twenty years, but how long will I be able to keep the truth away from Fred? What do the other mothers do with the boys Oblis sired? How do they control them when the moon is full? Call me. Please. I am desperate. I fear Joey will hurt someone.

Love, Joanna."

Charlene had to re-read the letter three times.

"Joey doesn't *have* Gorlin-Chaudry-Moss Syndrome?" She blinked once, twice. No, there it was in her mother's own writing. "Oblis." "The other mothers." "When the moon is full." The words ricocheted around in her head, and she thought of the night of the accident, the boys' distress, and Joey's snapping teeth.

She set the letters down and wandered back to the parlor. The photos of Joanna, Jessie, Jethro, and Rebekkah stared back at her—their gazes now heavy with meaning. She looked at each of them, and tried to piece the story together.

Joanna was raped by a predator—Oblis—who carried a mutant gene of some sort. Jethro killed Oblis—but terrified his daughter so much she ran away. Jessie kept in regular touch with Joanna—and colluded with her to fool poor Fred into thinking the family carried Gorlin-Chaudry-Moss Syndrome. But it wasn't Joanna's genes that caused Joey's condition. The mutant gene Oblis carried caused Joey's problems. Joanna's final letter to Jessie, was angry, desperate.

"Dear Jessie—Fred has gone and done something foolish. His boss called to tell me that his NIH funding is being pulled because he has gone off the deep end. Fred has been harassing psychiatrists to give him their patient records for cases of people who think they're *werewolves*. I can't believe he's doing this, risking his funding and *our* lives. Why couldn't he have just stayed with genetic diseases? I can't do anything about Joey or me, but I'll be damned if I'll let him ruin Charlene's life. I have to stop him.

Love, Joanna"

Fred's love for Joanna and obsession with finding a cure for Joey led him to the *last* place Joanna wanted him to look. When Hoffman called Joanna, she became terrified all would be exposed and her 'perfect' daughter's life would be ruined.

Charlene picked up Joanna's photo as a pretty woman in the bloom of her youth.

Her mother a werewolf? She scoffed out loud. *Not possible. Look at her. She'd been beautiful. Perfect.* She closed her eyes, thought back to happy times in high school—and flashed back to her mother and father fighting.

It had been in the middle of the night and she'd gotten up to go to the bathroom.

Her mother's voice had been uncharacteristically whiny. "I really *need* that medicine, Fred."

"The moon won't be full for another week."

"*No.* I *need* it now." Her mother was crying. "Please, please, *please.*"

"You're becoming addicted, Joanna. If I give it to you now, you'll never be off the damn drug."

"You bastard!" The distinct sound of a hand slapping a cheek had rung out in the house. A gasp. "Fred. I'm sorry, I don't know what came over me."

A door had slammed.

Charlene had crept back to bed, pulled the quilt over her head, and cried herself to sleep.

She opened her eyes as the realization overwhelmed her. The signs had all been there, but she'd never had the family history to put them into context. Not until now.

She stared at the perfect picture of her mother. *Perfect, perfect, perfect.* Not.

"What happened, Mom? Where were you going that night?"

The police placed the accident on I-83, heading south, at about midnight. Why were they out at that hour? Were they heading to the genetics lab two exits away? Had her mother convinced her father to destroy his werewolf research? Who was she hiding it from? Why bother? Hoffman knew and was planning to fire her father soon.

"You wanted to protect me. You confronted Fred at a full moon."

Her mother must have been furious. Did she forget to take her medications—or did she skip them on purpose? Without medications, when the full moon of March came to collect her due, did Joanna change like Joey and the boys on the bus? Knowing how frightened she'd been, Charlene could only imagine Fred's reaction. In her rage, had her mother attacked her mate, clawing and biting him? Maybe the car *had* gone out of control. Or maybe Dad had felt he had no choice but to drive straight into a concrete buttress. Each, in their own way, fought to protect the next generation—her—from knowing the family secrets. And in the end, they both lost. Because, as Jethro said over and over, "Blood will tell."

An unbidden thought bubbled up in her mind. *What had her mother looked like in her werewolf form?* She sat down hard in an armchair, her mother's photo clutched in her hand. The fact that she found herself accepting the *possibility* of such a creature, and that she even *wondered* what her mother looked like when she changed overwhelmed her.

She took deep cleansing breaths and tried to think of rational explanations for all the strange experiences she'd had before coming to Eden. Her mother's monthly migraines, her brother's fixation with the moon, her *own* urges to go on long distance runs on nights when the moon was full. And, now, here in Eden, all the other weird events, even the visitation by the strange silver wolf. She stood up and walked back to the bedroom.

Next to the bed on the floor, she found a few strands of silver-white hair. The same color as Zack's. The animal's eyes had been the same as his, too. She whispered to herself, "I'm either going crazy—or I'm in love with a werewolf."

How could she leave Eden now? She found her family, her home—and a man who made her feel complete. Her soul mate. There must be another solution. Her mother and father had chosen a path that led to death. What should she do? Her mother struggled for decades to protect her perfect daughter—and died to keep the secret.

Now that she knew, Charlene had to choose. But what should she do? Be *disloyal* to her mother and all the sacrifices she made for her? Or accept her hidden birthright and *destroy* the last vestiges of her mother's perfect human child? Was it all or nothing? Or was there a way to have a 'mixed marriage', like her parents, and live in *both* worlds?

CHAPTER ELEVEN
~*~

Secrets Within Secrets, Within Secrets

Zack pulled the bus, now empty of all riders except Joey, into Charlene's driveway. His beloved stood on the porch in a cobalt blue dress that accentuated her smoky blue eyes. Her berry red lips looked as if they were waiting for his kiss. His heart sped up, and his pants tightened at the thought of rubbing his hands across her breasts and hardened nipples. *Later, he would make love to her and lick her all over.*

Not making eye contact, Charlene looked distracted and played with her bracelet. She approached the bus after it stopped, and climbed aboard.

"Hi there, Joey!" She signed and spoke at the same time. "Did you have good day?"

"Moon, moon, moon," he signed. "Big moon."

Strands hair fell into her eyes when she nodded, and she brushed them away. "Yes, there is a full moon tonight, but you'll be in bed—before it rises." She lowered the lift. "Now, let's get you an early dinner, so Zack and I can have a private conversation."

Joey's evening rituals took on a soothing quality for Zack, even as questions bubbled up in his mind.

Charlene spoke very little to Zack directly, instead keeping her focus on Joey for the next hour. When she met his gaze, her eyes slid away from his, as if she was afraid of what she might see.

He wondered if he repelled her now that he had revealed his true identity to her. Had it been too soon? Part of him wanted to drag the truth out of her, but his other, fearful self was relieved at her silence.

Too soon dinner was over, Joey bathed and in bed, and she led him by the hand out onto the porch. "It was *you*. You came to me last night."

"Yes, I wanted you to see who I really was."

Her smoky blue eyes changed, grew darker. "You— you're a man—and a wolf?"

His breath gushed out. "Yes."

Her lower lip trembled—she looked as if she might cry. The love of his life took a deep breath. "Are there others?"

He took both of her hands into his and gazed deep into her eyes. "I think you know the answer to that question."

"My father?"

He shook his head. "One hundred percent human."

Her nails dug into his palm. "My mother?"

He nodded.

"So that makes me—a half-breed." She shook her head. "A genetic condition—just not one most people can talk about."

Zack worried as he watched doubt and fear chase each other across her face.

Would she stay? Or would she run away?

She yanked her hands away and his worst fear—losing Charlene—clutched his heart and soul. Instead, she threw her arms around his neck and hugged him, nearly choking him. Zack's dread of her being disgusted by him evaporated in a rush of lust. His hands found her breasts and stroked her nipples.

She moaned. "I want to be with you *always*."

"It's not just about you and me—it's about our family, the pack," he growled. "Jethro's ready to let me take charge. The pack can only survive with a new pair of leaders. All the men—except your grandfather—have died young from years of inbreeding. That's why they need us so desperately. And we need them, too."

"What do I need to do?"

He stopped nuzzling her neck and stepped back. "I have to bite you hard enough to draw blood. If I do that, you can *never* be fully human again. There's no going back."

A pained look crossed her face and tears welled up in her eyes. "My mother gave up her life to protect me, to keep me human. I want to be with you always, but—"

Zack took a deep shuddering breath, moaned, and pulled away. "Your mother was right to protect you, to be afraid for you. Once you make the change, you won't be able to resist the call of the moon. You'll be persecuted and hunted. Your mother knew."

"When I'm with you here, in this place, the world is brighter, fuller and happier." She put his hand between her legs and whispered, her voice husky. "You do *this* to me." She was wet and trembled at his touch.

His heart jumped erratically in his chest. He tore himself away from her and stepped back—afraid he wouldn't be able to stop once started.

"Without you and me, the pack will die out. You and I can make babies, Charlene—healthy ones. But you must choose to become one of us."

"Healthy werewolf babies, Zack? Or babies like Joey?"

He snarled. "No. That—that—evil creature—that predator caused Joey's disease, and all the others. I left your mother's letters for you so you would know—from her, not just from me. He wasn't like us. He was one of *those people*—" He bit back the rest. He wanted to tell her, but Jethro had forbidden him from speaking their name for fear of conjuring one up.

The fading sunlight danced across her face and set her blonde hair glowing to gold. A bewildered look creased her beautiful face. "What are you talking about?"

Zack turned on his heel and stamped toward the bus. "I have to see Jethro. Now."

"I don't understand," she called after him. "What was he?"

He had to see the Old One, bring him here, force him to tell Charlene the truth about Oblis and his evil clan of jinn. She needed to know that a genie could live for thousands of years—and that the blood feud between the clans began when King Solomon favored the loyal and obedient werewolves over the disloyal and disobedient genies.

~*~

Charlene watched the bus until it was a yellow dot in the distance. Was he angry with her? Had she driven him away with her questions? She loved him with all her heart, but couldn't make this momentous decision. Not yet. She needed time to process everything, to get her head around her mother's history and her possible future. Even though it was early evening, she was exhausted. Charlene climbed into bed and fell into a fitful sleep.

In a dream, she saw herself married to Zack, pregnant with werewolf babies—and they were trying to claw their way out of her. She doubled over in agony, looked down, and her fingers turned into claws. She screamed and woke up with cold sweat dripping down her back and between her breasts. She took a deep cleansing breath, got up, and opened the window. The full moon peeked over the horizon, enticing her to come for a run, like in the old days when her parents were alive and her life was a protective cocoon.

A man whispered. "Come to me."

She looked around. "Zack? Where are you?"

"Come to the woods, come to me. I *need* you."

The whispers thrilled her, setting a fire in her loins that only Zack could quench. She lost all other thoughts, could only think about how to get to him soon.

"Come to the woods. Leave your bracelet at home. I have a new one for you. Come to me."

"Yes," she whispered as she dropped the bangle on the kitchen table and grabbed the keys to the minivan. "I'm on my way."

~*~

Zack found Jethro on his front porch, whittling a piece of wood.

"We have to tell her about THEM. Now."

The Old One looked up at Zack, his eyes flecked with sparks of orange, as they did at the start of each full moon before the Change. "The more she knows, the more likely they'll come after her."

"You told me you kept the cause of Jessie's death quiet, to keep the pack from panicking—because of Oblis and his clan." The younger man paced the porch. "Charlene's asking questions, is worried about having healthy babies, about joining the pack. She's afraid she'll have a baby like Joey. She needs to know the truth. From you."

The Old One ran his finger over the stick. "As long as she wears the bracelet and doesn't know the names of the evil ones, she's safe."

Zack snatched the piece of wood out of Jethro's hands. "Have you heard nothing I've said? She won't marry me until she hears the truth. And I can't force her to become one of us. She has to choose on her own."

The elder's eyes sparked orange. Jethro bared his teeth at Zack. "It's too much for her—she can't handle the truth."

"*She* can't? Or *you* can't handle telling her the truth. Let her decide what she can handle. She's not a child, she's a woman."

"Those Other People are shape-shifters and powerful."

"All the more reason for her to know, so she can be on guard."

"It will sound like a fairy tale to her human ears."

"You MUST tell her."

A faraway look came into the Old One's eyes as he gazed into the distance. "Our pack goes back to the time of the great King who had dominion over all creatures. He enslaved the Jinn, forced them to build his temple. He commanded all creatures—including werewolves. But because of our great loyalty, we earned the right to one of his rings. She's still new to our ways. How will she understand our history and all that means to us *now*?"

"Your granddaughter will hear the truth in your words. You once told me she had more loyalty to her family than I did. You *must* tell her."

The Old One stood slowly and shook his head. "This is a fool's errand, you'll see." He called out to his mate. "We're going to Charlene's. I'll be back before the Change."

Hair loose, blue eyes flecked with gold and her face more youthful looking as the Change approached, Rebekkah appeared in the doorway. "About time, you told her."

Zack realized she'd heard the whole argument.

She pulled the door behind her. "I'm coming with you."

With the full moon rising, a sense of urgency seized Zack and he rushed them into Jethro's pickup truck. "I'm driving."

He flew down the dirt roads, hitting potholes and tearing around corners. The brakes screeched as he slammed them on in front of Charlene's house. The front door was wide open and the minivan was gone.

He leaped out of the vehicle and took the porch steps two at a time. "Charlene? Where are you?"

Jethro and Rebekkah came up the stairs behind him.

Zack turned. "She's not here. Where the hell is she?"

Rebekkah peeked into Joey's room and returned to the kitchen, a stunned look on her face. "She left her brother alone. She would never do that."

Silence fell over the little group as Jethro pointed at the kitchen table. Her iron bracelet lay in the center. "She's unprotected. This is what Oblis did to her mother. He whispered her into the woods." He began to wail, "What have I done? What have I done?"

Jethro's face crumpled and he clutched the side of his head. He fell to the floor. Rebekkah cried out and grabbed at his hand.

Zack went down on his knees. "What should I do?"

Speech slurred, Jethro reached up a shaking hand and pulled the iron chain off his neck. On it hung the large signet ring inscribed with pentacles and Hebrew letters.

"Take the Ring of Solomon," he gasped. "Save her."

~*~

Charlene climbed out of the minivan and stared at the woods near the old mining camp. "How did I get here?" She shook her head and turned to get back in the car and hightail it home.

"Charlene!"

"Zack?" She searched the moon-dappled forest for signs of her lover. "Where are you?"

He stepped out from behind a large tree, his silver hair a strange hue of green from the mist that surrounded him. "I'm so glad you're here. Come closer, I want to hold you in my arms."

She took a few steps toward him and stopped. "What are you doing here?"

He grinned. "I wanted to make love to you here in the woods, under the full moon."

Something was off. His teeth were even his canines a regular length. She began to back up and heard a low rumbling. Five black dogs stood between her and the minivan. One growled and nipped at her hand. She cried in pain.

"Come over here and the dogs won't hurt you."

She hesitated and one bared his teeth at her and snarled. She picked her leaden feet up, one at a time, her mind trying to make sense of the dogs and Zack's strange behavior.

"Closer."

She shuffled up to him.

"Take off your nightdress. I want to see you naked in the moonlight."

Trembling with fear and cold, she lifted the flannel gown over her head.

Zack trailed his fingers down her neck, across her breasts, and rubbed at her nipples. Unbidden, a rush of erotic images of him taking her from every side, her mouth on his hard cock, his fingers in her moistness, stroking her, forced their way into her mind.

He whispered, "Oh, yes, we are going to have a very good time." Zack slid his fingers down her belly, played with her silky triangle.

Heaviness filled her limbs, lassitude took over her body, and she leaned back against the tree for support.

"You are so beautiful. Even more beautiful than your mother was when my dearly departed father, Oblis, took her."

Her eyes flew open and Zack shifted and shimmered, morphing into a creature with a forked tongue and scaled skin. Life flowed back into her lungs and she began to scream.

~*~

Zack pulled up behind Charlene's minivan and killed the headlights. *Where was she?* He looked in the rearview mirror. His hair was more silvered, longer, thicker. His eyes glowed orange, his shirt strained across his chest, and silver fur stuck out between the buttons. He was running out of time, already changing. He climbed out of the truck and heard a gut-wrenching scream.

"Charlene! I'm coming—" His voice turned into a howl as heat filled him and frissons of pleasure and pain undulated from his toes to his head. The sounds of his clothing ripping came to him as if from a distance. He fell to all fours, heard her scream again, and raced into the forest, searching for her, hoping it wasn't too late.

He found the man-sized lizard in a swirling mist of green standing over her, laughing and taunting her with what he was going to do to her. Black dogs, too many to count, held her wrists and ankles in their teeth, growling and snarling. She was white-faced and bleeding profusely. He had no time to waste.

Jaws snapping, Zack jumped on the creature's back and sank his teeth into his neck. The evil one arched his back, threw Zack off, and turned to face him. The black dogs whined, but didn't release their prey.

"Zack, oh thank God, it's *really* you," Charlene cried out.

Claws extended, the shape-shifting deviator jinn came at Zack, hissing and screaming in a strange language. Then in clear English, the creature shouted, "Not even Solomon's daughter and her soldiers could capture me. You think a *dog* can hurt me?"

The snake man swiped at Zack and grabbed a handful of his fur. Zack yelped in pain, then lowered his chest to the ground, a deep growl morphing into a snarl as he hunkered down and prepared to leap.

The reptile snickered and danced before him, a whirling dervish of death and destruction as Charlene lay pinned to the ground by the jinni's companions. The night sounds of the forest ceased. Zack's nostrils twitched at the dank smell of the genie and the clean copper scent of Charlene's blood. He thought of his friend, Jessie, and how she must have been tortured in the same manner by this evil being. His paws gripped at the moist ground, and a rush of energy coursed through his legs into all of his muscles—as if the earth mother reached up to give him additional strength against this creature from another world.

Snarling, Zack jumped on the capering tormentor's chest and hit him squarely on the face with the Ring of Solomon. There was a deafening bang, a blinding flash of light, a puff of green smoke, and the world went black.

~*~

Zak didn't know how long he was out. He blinked his eyes and when he could see again, the jinni was gone, along with the dogs.

Running to Charlene's side, he found her barely conscious and pale—as pale as the moon.

She smiled. "You're here."

He couldn't speak, could only try to communicate with his eyes, his paws, and tongue. He licked her terrible wounds and whined.

"It's bad, isn't it?" she asked.

Zak nodded.

"I'm dying." Not a question.

He whimpered.

"If you bite me, will I live?"

Zack nuzzled and licked her neck.

The light was going out of her eyes. *Please choose, please choose*, he urged mentally.

Charlene whispered, "I choose life. You and the Pack— bite me."

Worried that it might be too late, he placed his teeth on her neck, and drew blood. *Nothing.* He pushed at her with his nose. Her head flopped to the other side, lifeless.

The love of his life, his one and only soul mate was still and cold. He staggered away from her body, threw his head back and gave a long mournful howl. All was lost. Jessie, Jethro, and now Charlene were dead. The pack was going to die out. He had failed. Zack thought his heart was going to break. He howled again, and again—until his throat was hoarse. He paused to take a deep shuddering breath.

A female howled back.

He turned.

Resplendent in thick golden fur, her smoky blue eyes flecked with emerald green, Charlene trotted over to him and nuzzled his ear. *"I can hear your thoughts."*

"Charlene," he breathed. *"You're so beautiful."*

"Thanks for the love bite. Let's go home."

~*~

Eliana's heart thundered and her hands shook as she watched the live video feed on her home computer in Alexandria, Virginia. She could scarcely believe her eyes, but there it was, live and in color, proof of the existence of Jinn *and* the power of the werewolves. Furious, she began to type up her report, and cursed her boss.

"Stand down, he said. Stay away from the mine, he said. Stay away from the Carter clan, he said. You *killed* that corporal with your foolhardy scheme, he said."

Despite the wealth of intelligence she'd gathered from Fred Johnson's research, her by-the-book boss had refused to listen to her and had told her to get back to Virginia and prepare to be transferred.

She had obeyed his orders—right *after* she installed a dozen infrared, motion activated surveillance cameras in the woods around the abandoned mine. She attached the video clip to the email and hit the send button with a hard click of her mouse.

"Let's see what you have to say about this, el Jefe."

Epilogue
~*~
New Beginnings

Special Agent Eliana Solomon stood by the abandoned mine in Eden and drummed her fingers on the butt of her Sig Sauer. She rubbed her eyes and wished she hadn't been right. That poor soldier had paid with his life. Generations of women and children of Eden had suffered and paid with their lives, too. The Carters had been particularly hard hit. But now, they had a fresh start. And, thanks to Charlene and Zack's unflinching desire to protect the world from this threat, Eliana knew why the Jinn attacked certain groups in a blood feud of biblical proportions.

She sighed, whispered the prayer for the dead in Hebrew, and waved over the military demolition expert, a huge hulking figure of a man whose size belied his intelligence. "This is a Jinn portal. The people of Eden have been terrorized by these deviants long enough. Fill it with iron, whatever you can find. If you've got anything magnetic, throw that in there, too. Then demolish it."

The large man nodded. "I got no problem with that. I'll see what kind of scrap metals we can find in the area."

She flexed her fist and rubbed the heavy signet ring inscribed with pentacles and Hebrew letters. Last night, she received a call from the Virginia Bureau of Investigation. Girls had gone missing and turned up traumatized, alive, and pregnant. Or found dead, torn to bits. When the doctors at Quantico saw the ultrasounds of the babies, they promptly called the Department of Homeland Security, Science and Technology Directorate, and Special Agent Eliana Solomon, aka, "The Jinn Hunter."

She was going to need some help in the Virginia coal fields, someone who had personal experience with the Jinn. She knew *exactly* who to ask—a tall, dark, and dangerously handsome psychiatrist and Islamic scholar she'd worked with on an extremely difficult case two years ago. But he was the *last* person in the world she ever wanted to see again. Not that she held a grudge, mind you, but didn't she have the right to be pissed at a guy for leaving her for *dead?*

~*~

The orchard exploded in pink with newly opened buds, tables overflowed and bowed under the weight of food, and little tow-haired girls, decked out in their best dresses, played hide-and-seek, their laughter ringing through the trees. Mothers chatted, their excitement palpable. The boys from the bus route poked at their mothers and signed, "Where Charlene?" Trotter made rounds, investigated each partygoer with his gentle nose, and created a ripple of giggles in his wake. He found Joey, sat down at the foot of his wheelchair, and began to snore.

Tired of surveyeing the pack and listening to its happy rumbles, Zack turned to Jethro and demanded, "What's taking her so long?"

The Old One looked up from whittling the wolf head on his new apple wood cane, amusement glinting in his sky blue eyes. "Don't you know women take whatever time they need? You'd better learn to be patient."

"I can't stand this," he growled and fisted his hand with the large signet ring. "Why can't Rebekkah make her move faster?"

The door flew open, framing Rebekkah. Strands of hair fell out in wild angles from her normally impeccable bun. She grabbed Zack's wrist and said, "Get in here. Now!"

Seized with a type of terror he had never experienced before, even when he faced the Jinn, Zack turned to his elder. "Come with me?"

Jethro shook his head. "Sorry. You're on your own, son."

Rebekkah dragged him into the bedroom.

"Charlene?"

His radiant wife sat up in bed, holding not one, but two babies in her arms. She gave Zack a wobbly smile. "Would you like to meet your boys?"

"Are they—?"

Rebekkah's no nonsense voice cut through his fog of fear. "These are the pinkest, healthiest babies I've ever delivered."

Zak touched each child's cheek with a trembling finger. "They're so...perfect." He leaned down and kissed Charlene's forehead. "Thank you. I love you."

Tears slid down her flushed cheeks. "I love you, too. Let's share the good news."

Rebekkah nestled the infants in Zack's arms and placed a metal bracelet around each one's wrist.

Love and pride rose in Zack's chest as he watched his wife dress. He knew she had to be exhausted after the ordeal of birthing twins, yet she put the pack's needs ahead of own. He cuddled the sleeping boys and sniffed their heads. "They have both our scents."

Charlene held out her arms to take a child. "Let's show our family our beautiful babies."

Rebekkah preceded them, opened the screen door, and stood aside. When Zack and Charlene stepped out onto the porch, Jethro stood. Silence fell and all eyes gazed upon the blanket-swathed bundles.

Zack removed the swaddling cloth and lifted the naked baby up over his head: "Behold, I give you Z'ev Jacob." He passed the wriggling infant to Rebekkah, took the second naked squirming one from Charlene, and raised him on high. "And, I give you Joshua Zebadiah."

The now wide-awake blue-eyed babies cried in unison, and their voices merged into an infant-sized howl. Laughter rippled through the crowd, and the pack joined the newest members in a paean of joy for the rebirth of happiness and hope in Eden.

THE END

✶

ABOUT THE AUTHOR

After working in health care delivery for years, Sharon Buchbinder became an association executive, a health care researcher and an academic in higher education. She had it all--a terrific, supportive husband, an amazing son and a wonderful job.

But that itch to write (some call it an obsession) kept beckoning her to "come on back" to writing fiction. Thanks to the kindness of family, friends, critique partners and Maryland Romance writers, she is now published in contemporary, erotic, paranormal and romantic suspense.

When not writing, she can be found attempting to make students and colleagues laugh, herding cats and dogs, deep sea fishing, or dining and having a few laughs with good friends.

Made in the USA
Lexington, KY
08 September 2012